TRADING CLOSE TO LIGHT

TRADING CLOSE TO LIGHT

THE MAGIC BELOW PARIS™ BOOK THREE

C. M. SIMPSON

MICHAEL ANDERLE

TRADING CLOSE TO LIGHT TEAM

Thanks to our Beta Readers

Mary Morris, Nicole Emens, Larry Omans, and John Ashmore

Thanks to our JIT Readers

Jeff Goode
Misty Roa
Dorothy Lloyd
James Caplan
Charles Tillman
Diane L. Smith

Editor

SkyHunter Editing Team

DEDICATION

This is for all those who believed in me enough that, eventually, I had the courage to believe in myself.

Thank you.
—C.M. Simpson

To Family, Friends and
Those Who Love
to Read.
May We All Enjoy Grace
to Live the Life We Are
Called.

— Michael

SHADOW MONSTER AMBUSH

Now you've done it...

Roeglin's voice whispered through Marsh's head, and she resisted the urge to give him the finger.

Not that it was hard to resist. Her mule snorted and stomped as the first shadow monster shrieked their discovery. Marchant needed both hands to control her mount—which was a problem since she also needed her hands to defend herself against the monsters that were now howling through the darkness toward them.

Mordan's blatant disgust as the big kat ran beside her was easy to ignore.

"Ride!" Gustav shouted. "We'll try to outrun them."

"Where to?" Marsh shouted back, but she was already kicking her mule into a gallop, the hoshkat running beside her.

Behind her, the shadow guards followed them, their mules needing no urging.

"Mid-Point!" Gustav shouted back. "We'll hole up in the station."

Mid-Point. They'd been planning to go right past it, with Marsh giving it a quick once-over with her ability to sense life. Roeglin and Gustav were confident someone—or something—would have taken it as a home by now, and Marsh agreed.

The waystation with its protective wall and many rooms and outbuildings would make an ideal lair for cavern creatures. There was probably more than one already living in its halls, and Master Envermet, with his clearing force, was going to deal with it when they came through. Marsh's and Roeglin's team were only supposed to scout it, hopefully keeping the hoshkat in check.

Well, they'd be doing much more than that now, starting by hiding in the gatehouse, followed by hoping they survived long enough for Master Envermet to reach them. There was no way they could defeat the pack coming after them on their own.

Tell me he's coming, Marsh thought, knowing Roeglin would pick it right out of her head.

He's coming, Roeglin said, *but he is a day behind. Even if they ride hard, they won't reach us for another six hours.*

Six hours! It was an eternity, given what they were facing.

And then it got worse.

Hoots and screams came from ahead of them, and Gustav cursed. Mordan snarled in defiance and bounded ahead into the dark.

"Try to go around them!" he called.

"And if we can't?"

"We go through." There was a finality in Gustav's tone that told Marsh they had *better* go through.

They could not afford to stop and fight since it would mean the twenty monsters on their tail would catch up.

All because she'd sneezed.

Don't beat yourself up about it. You couldn't know.

But Gustav had told her to stay away from the purple caps, and then she'd blundered right into a patch of them, and been showered with spores and shroom-dust for her trouble.

They don't usually grow that high up.

Roeglin's mind voice sounded breathless, like he was speaking out loud while riding hard. Except he was only speaking in her mind. How could breathing affect that?

You'd be surprised. Now, concentrate!

Marsh peered at the trail ahead; the howls and shrieks were getting closer. She swept her eyes over the terrain on either side of the trail, noting it was too rough to take the mules over—and that was saying something, given how rough the trail had become in two months of disuse. Ahead of them, she could see both the heat and shadow of the monsters gathering to block their way.

The fiery warmth that was Mordan was working its way around the edge, positioning herself for an attack rather than trying to sneak past. Marsh's heart sank, and then she had an idea of how to clear the path.

"Let me ride ahead," she called, urging her mule to greater speed.

In front of her, Henri and Jakob guided their mounts far enough apart for her to fit between them, and Gustav eased his own beast over. She noted the slight reduction in their pace, and couldn't fault them for not slowing more. Instead, she pushed her mule forward and looped her reins around one wrist. It was hard to keep her balance, and Marsh only hoped she could.

"Don't you dare!"

Roeglin's cry of alarm was accompanied by a hurried snatch at her armor as she went past. Marsh felt the light graze of his fingertips on her arm and then she was through, overtaking Gustav and hoping her mule didn't stumble as she spread her arms wide and called the shadows to her hands.

Feeling them come, and fighting to ignore the faint tug of the reins on her wrist, Marsh brought her hands to her chest, gathering the shadows before her. Beneath her, the mule faltered, confused by the mixed signals she was sending to its mouth.

Marsh dug her heels into its ribs, struggling to concentrate. She needed to focus, to push a wall of shadow before her and use what she had gathered to topple the monsters ahead. As she thought it, she thrust her hands out in front of her, sending the shadows rolling over the creatures and releasing all tension on the reins.

She also lost her balance, wobbling in the saddle and grabbing at the pommel in an attempt to stay on. Still wrapped around her wrist, the reins drew tight, jerking at the mule's mouth. If it hadn't been for the shadow monsters howling behind them or the fact they'd bounded into the middle of the ones Marsh had felled with her wall of shadows, the beast might have stopped.

As it was, the mule pulled back, fighting the bit and jerking Marsh farther out of the saddle as it leapt over the bodies of the creatures in its path. Marsh scrabbled for purchase, then wrapped her hands in its mane, aware that

Gustav and Roeglin were trying to catch up. Aware, too, of the shadow mages and guards galloping in her wake.

If she fell, she wouldn't have time to be torn apart by shadow monsters; she'd be trampled first. Marsh didn't bother trying to control the mule. She just focused on hanging on, glad that Roeglin was quiet. She was also glad that none of the group slowed as their mules raced past the fallen monsters.

The wall of shadow hadn't killed the creatures, only knocked them down. It hadn't even swept them clear of the path, and some of them were starting to stir. Fortunately, her group was farther up the trail and out of their reach when the first one clambered to its feet.

That didn't deter them, though. In fact, it had made them angrier than before. With a scream of outrage, the first monster bounded after them. It was so furious that it left its fellows in its wake, but not for long. Soon the rest of them had regained their feet and were roaring in pursuit.

Mordan had returned to her place beside Marsh's mule, pacing them easily as they followed the trail around a rock-studded curve. More shrieks echoed from the dark behind them and the sound bounced past, piercing the relative silence of the tunnel leading to the surface.

What if there are more of them? Marsh wondered, grateful she'd managed to find her balance again. Now, if only she could get back into the saddle before the mule stumbled and threw her completely from its back. As Marsh pushed against the mule's neck, trying to get back into position, she was startled by the strong forearm that swept across her middle, giving her the boost she needed.

She didn't have the breath for thanks, though. That had

been knocked out of her by the same blow that had put her back in the saddle. Marsh was both grateful and not.

Just get your mount back under control, Roeglin told her. She realized he'd come alongside her, while Gustav had gone past and returned to the lead. *We're almost there.*

As tempting as it was to see how the others were doing, Marsh was too busy. Taking the reins in one hand, she disentangled her wrist. It was a good thing she'd done so much riding when she'd been working for Kearick. She'd have been in a lot more trouble if she hadn't.

You'd have been on your ass on the floor.

Roeglin's comment made her wonder where the shadow mage got the energy to speak.

You almost fell off.

Like she needed to be told!

She hoped the gatehouse was clear, and that their headlong flight didn't take them through it and into the station beyond. That would put them in the middle of a courtyard surrounded by walls and buildings—and any number of unknown enemies.

By the Deeps! For all she knew, the waystation was where all these shadow monsters had been making their home, so they might be heading out of the frying pan into the fire.

"This way!" Gustav shouted, guiding his mule off the trail.

It was barely warning enough, but Marsh and Roeglin looked up in time to follow, and the rest clattered through the turn behind them, the mules bleeding off speed to make it. The animals' instincts for staying with the herd were a boon, particularly as they fought to keep up with their leader.

The turn took them between two tall stands of calla shrooms, momentarily bathing them in pale purple light. Towering outcrops of rock flashed past, and she was just thinking she should be scanning ahead for life forms when a dark shape slammed into the side of her mule. The beast went down kicking and Marsh reached for the shadows, pulling herself from the mule's back into the darkness above it.

Ahead of her, Gustav and Roeglin were trying to pull their mounts to a halt. Behind her, Henri was tugging Gerry out from under his mule, while Jakob, Zeb, and Izmay were struggling to remain in their saddles. Beneath her, a shadow monster tore into the soft underbelly of her mule.

Gouges in her mount's sides and throat showed where the monster had thrust its clawed hands into the mule as it struck. Dammit! She'd *liked* her mule. Fury rolled through Marsh, and she pulled a sword from the shadows. Taking a firm grip on the hilt, she angled the point downward, and then she dropped out of the shadows onto the creature's back, driving the blade into its body as she landed.

It shrieked and twisted, its cries drawing the attention of some of the monsters attacking the rearguard. Marsh yanked her sword out and stepped back, changing her grip so she could sweep the blade down a second time. As she did, Gustav ran past her, Roeglin hard on his heels. Mordan stood her ground, yowling her defiance at the oncoming horde.

Only when Marsh was sure the monster at her feet was

dead did she join them, the kat bounding ahead of her. The two men were engaging the monsters that had come after Marsh when she'd killed the first. Seeing what they faced, she was relieved to note that these monsters did not share the size or the coloring of the one that had taken down her mule, but not so relieved to hear the sound of more hoots and screams coming toward them.

"Move!" Gustav shouted as he felled the monster he was facing and then took down one of those blocking Henri's path.

The man had one arm wrapped around Gerry's waist, even as he parried the clawed strikes of another monster. He'd have been in worse shape if the other monsters hadn't been more interested in the mule than him and the shadow guard, and if Mordan hadn't intervened. For his part, Gerry had pulled a shield from the shadows and was doing his best to help Henri keep their attacker at bay. From the look on his face, the kat had his eternal gratitude.

"Move!"

Roeglin took out the last of his opponents as Marsh reached him, but he didn't join Gustav. Instead, he pulled a dart from the shadows, sending it through the head of another of the monsters. Marsh raced past him as he pulled a second dart. As she did, another of the mules went down and Izmay tumbled away from it, barely avoiding the claws that lashed out toward her. Mordan took the monster down with a well-timed leap and Izmay rolled clear.

Again, two or three of the monsters went after the mule instead of the human. That was new, but Marsh didn't have time to think about it; the horde they'd been escaping was getting closer, and they needed to reach the waystation.

She joined Gustav in clearing a path so the others could reach them, relieved when Izmay gripped Jakob by his forearm, pulling him out of his saddle and shoving him clear. Relieved, also, to see Dan taking down the worst of the threats around them.

Jakob's mule gave a shrill whinny and tried to bolt past the monsters, only to fall before it had gone more than two strides. Jakob drew his sword, coating it in shadow as he turned to face what monsters hadn't gone after the mule. That stopped them from going after Izmay long enough for the shadow guard to help Zeb get free of his own panicked beast.

It didn't take the guards and kat long to reach Marsh and Gustav once they were on the ground and able to defend themselves properly. The fact that many of the shadow monsters went after the mules, also helped, and the eight of them made short work of those that pursued.

They worked their way back to where Roeglin was waiting and then they took to their heels, running down the trail and hoping the waystation wasn't too far off. From the sound of the screeches and howls behind them, the horde they'd fled was gaining ground—and shadow monsters could move a lot faster than humans.

Marsh hoped they didn't run into a second ambush before they reached the station.

SHADOW POISON

Marchant's hopes weren't realized. They faced and fought their way through two more small clusters of shadow monsters before they reached the gatehouse, only to find it closed and barred against them. Glancing up at the walls, Marsh thought she saw faint signs of movement, but she couldn't be sure, and she didn't have time.

"Wait here," she said, sliding into shadow form and turning to look down the length of the wall.

Before Roeglin could ask her what she was doing, Marsh had stepped into the darkness, asking the shadows to find her a door. It took her only seconds to find the threads of darkness connecting her to the answer, and a few seconds more to find the small door in the wall not far from the gatehouse.

Thinking of what the path had looked like in front of the gates, Marsh focused on becoming one with the shadows and stepping through them to shorten the distance in between. Her arrival startled the guards, and only Roeglin's swift warning kept her from being skewered. As it was, Gustav barely managed to turn his blade away in time.

The shadow master rolled his eyes, and Marsh ignored him.

"This way," she said, cutting through Gustav's apology. "There's a gate."

Again, she drew on the shadows to guide her, but this time she didn't seek to become one with them, remaining solidly human. Leading the way through the shrooms and boulders clustered around the base of the waystation's wall, she took them to the gate and was relieved when it opened beneath her hand. The kat brushed past her to investigate the territory behind, and Marsh didn't try to stop her.

None of her companions made any comment, but she knew that more than one of them would be thinking that whoever had taken over the station had made the same mistake as Monsieur Gravine—they'd barred the gate and forgotten the secondary entrance.

Or they left it clear so they could escape if they needed to, Roeglin murmured.

Marsh might have rolled her eyes at his words, except the man had a point. Drawing on the shadows and on a more natural magic, she tried to see if there was anyone waiting inside. It was a relief when the shadows showed the space on the other side of the gate to be empty. It was even more of a relief when her nature magic showed that the dark ahead of them was devoid of anything except Mordan's brightly flaming life force.

Now all they had to do was reach the gatehouse. She led the way along the wall, hoping there was an inner gate as well as an outer one. The Deeps knew her uncle had insisted two gates were safer.

She glanced back to make sure the others were following and muffled a snort when she saw Gustav carefully lowering a locking bar over the small doorway. Someone, at least, had learned from past mistakes, even if they weren't his own.

To her relief, they reached the gatehouse without encountering anyone or anything—and the original builders *had* decided to install an inner gate, which the current occupants had closed. Once they'd quietly opened them and slipped inside, Gustav and Izmay shut it again and lifted the locking bar and dropped it back into place. The sound echoed loudly around them.

It probably echoed loudly in the courtyard beyond too, but that didn't matter. What mattered was that they'd reached safety and could finally rest. Marsh was feeling the effects of the long ride, the battle, and using her magic, but there were more important matters. She looked over at where Henri was helping Gerry settle to the floor.

The redheaded shadow guard was looking pale in the light of Henri's lantern.

"Need a hand?"

Henri looked bleak.

"He got clawed."

Of course, he did. Marsh looked around the gatehouse.

"Anyone else get clawed?"

Her question led to restless shuffling as everyone stopped to check themselves. Zeb gave a soft exclamation of surprise and sank to the ground. His action drew Gustav's attention and the guard captain uttered a quiet oath, reaching down to help the man to his feet and guide him across to sit beside Gerry.

"I thought you shadow mages were made of sterner stuff."

Zeb managed a tired chuckle and pointed an accusing finger at Marsh.

"Didn't notice it until *she* made me look."

"Yeah, she's all kinds of trouble, that one."

Gustav patted him on the shoulder and looked at the others.

"Anyone else?"

Marsh wondered if they could be that lucky, and breathed a soft sigh of relief when the others shook their heads.

"Nope. All good here," Izmay said, and Jakob echoed her.

They'd been luckier than they deserved.

Agreed, Roeglin said, then added, *You'd better get to work.*

Marsh glanced at him, and then at Izmay, who was rummaging in her pack. She shot a look toward Mordan, but the kat had settled along one wall and was cleaning her paws. If she'd been hurt, she'd have been licking the wound, instead. Izmay's voice drew her attention back.

"Lost what I had on the mule, but I've still got these," the dark-haired shadow guard said, pulling out a small bag and looking at Marsh. "You know how to clean a wound?"

Marsh shrugged.

"I can learn."

"I do." Jakob's quiet assertion made them both turn, and they watched as he pulled his own small bag from his pack.

"What?" he asked when he caught their stares. "Plenty of guards get hurt on the caravans. I learned."

Marsh wondered if anyone had suggested he try seeing if he could heal using magic, but he'd already taken a pannikin from his pack and was tipping the contents of his canteen into it. He passed both to Gustav.

"I need hot water," he said. "Those wounds need to be cleaned."

He seemed completely unaware that he'd just given his senior an order, and taken the reins from Izmay without asking. Neither of them argued with him, though. His attention was focused on the two injured.

"Someone want to light a fire? We need to sterilize the wounds." His face was grave as he looked around, his voice somber when he added, "We have to try, anyway."

"I'll help," Marsh told him. "I can draw the poison from the wound."

His eyebrows rose. Izmay's and Gustav's, too.

Zeb gave a half-hearted laugh.

"So we *do* have a chance…"

From the sound of it, he might not have much of one if she didn't hurry, but Marsh hesitated. She looked at Jakob.

"Your call," she said. "Which one needs me more?"

Her words made him blink, and he crossed swiftly to where the two men waited.

"You need to lie down," he told them, helping Zeb do as he asked while Henri assisted Gerry.

Neither of them looked good.

Zeb had three deep grooves on the outside of his thigh, and Marsh wondered how he'd been able to run.

Battle heat, Roeglin told her. *You don't feel a thing until it wears off. That, and the deeper the wound, the more your mind blocks your awareness of it—until it can't.*

Great, Marsh thought, watching as Jakob finished inspecting Gerry and then looked at Izmay.

"You any good with a needle and thread?"

She glared at him.

"I'm not a seamstress."

"I meant for stitching wounds." He sounded exasperated. "I don't give two shits for your skill at mending clothes."

Izmay colored, then nodded, bringing her bag of supplies.

"Never done it before." She slid him a look laced with sly humor. "But if the ability to mend a seam will help…"

"It's better than nothing."

Marsh wondered if he'd meant to be that short, but Jakob was already looking at her. When he saw he had her attention, he pointed to Gerry, and Marsh noticed what she'd missed before: the man's side was soaked with blood.

The shadow guard caught her expression and his lips twitched.

"It's what armor's for," he said, and Marsh realized Henri had cut the armor away so Jakob could inspect the wound.

She crossed to where he was, hoping the shadow monster's claws hadn't gone too deep, but was severely disappointed by what she saw.

"*A la putain.*"

"That's one way to put it," Henri told her. "Do what you can."

From his tone of voice, the man wasn't holding out much hope for the shadow guard's survival. Marsh didn't bother replying, just nodded and knelt beside them. As soon as she was settled, she closed her eyes, laying her hands on either side of the injury and concentrating on the guard's life force.

It was stronger than she'd feared, and Marsh felt a small part of herself relax. If he was still this strong, he might make it until the healers on Master Envermet's team could reach him.

Not if you don't deal with the poison.

Roeglin's voice was an unwelcome distraction in her head and Marsh pushed it aside, finding the dark threads of shadow poison lacing their way through the brighter reds and yellows of a healthy life force. Marsh drew a deep breath and let it out, reaching for the shadows and asking for their help, then linking the shadow of the poison to the shadows outside the wound.

The darkness inside the body was connected to the darkness outside it, right? The shadows in the poison linked to the shadows of the air beyond…and she'd done this before.

For Roeglin.

Don't remind me, the mage protested, but Marsh needed to remember, if only to remind herself it was possible.

Roeglin had been injured by a poison-laced blade. Shadow poison and the dark; she could do this.

Holding firmly to that belief, Marsh focused on pulling the poison from the wound, drawing it back along the shadows and out of the body. When the dark threads no longer stretched tendrils from the wound, and only faded health could be seen, she opened her eyes and looked for somewhere she could put the poison.

When she'd done this before, she'd realized she couldn't

just dismiss it to the shadows, or it would affect anyone who came into contact with it. She'd had to... Roeglin pointed to the discarded fragments of armor and clothing that had been cut away from the injured, and Marsh directed her ball of shadows and shadow monster poison into it. When she was done, she disentangled the shadows from the poison before returning them to the corners of the room, then looked at Jakob.

He was staring at her.

"How... When..."

"Later," she told him. "I'll work on Zeb next."

Roeglin stirred uneasily, and Marsh hoped he wasn't about to suggest she rest first because there wasn't time. Shadow-monster poison acted fast. If she rested, it might be too late.

"I know," Roeglin told her aloud, but his voice was laced with worry. "Just...do what you can. Okay?"

At first, Marsh didn't understand why he was so concerned, and then she went to stand. Izmay caught her before she could fall forward onto Gerry, and Henri helped his fellow guard drag Marsh upright again. Jakob looked on with concern.

"Are you sure you're up to this?"

Marsh looked from him to Zeb, casting a glance at Roeglin that dared him to deny her. The shadow guard was watching her, and from the look on his face, he expected her to have to stop. His expression mingled resignation and understanding, and he closed his eyes when he saw she'd noticed.

"It's okay."

"Yes," Marsh said, glaring at Roeglin and pushing away

from Izmay and Henri, grateful when they kept a hold on her and helped her reach Zeb's side. "Yes, it *is* okay."

Ignoring Mordan's sudden growl of alarm, she placed her hands over the lacerations in Zeb's thigh. This time, she didn't close her eyes but used her life sight to overlay the map of the poison's path on what she could see of his body. The dark veins had already threaded their way to a brighter line of red tracing the way up the inside of his leg; it was spreading fastest along that.

"Well, *merde*," she murmured, and asked the shadows to come once again to her aid.

This time, she had three wound entrances to clear, three different sources from which the poison spread. A dark web of deadliness traced its way out of each wound but converged on the thick red line to become a river. She was going to have to use a different approach.

Taking another deep breath, she went to work. Instead of following the poison along the pathways of the body and drawing it back, she turned to where it pooled in the gouges in Zeb's leg. Gathering the shadows, she sought the shadow in the poison infecting his thigh.

It was harder this way. The dark puddle slid and twisted away from the darkness she called from the corners of the room. Marsh frowned and called more shadow, trying to get the poison to soak through the threads she drew into the wound and willing it to flow out and seek a new home in the mat of shade she'd pulled over the wound.

As she worked, she noticed how the shadow mat overlapped the second gouge, so she spread her concentration to begin drawing the well of poison from that wound as well. When the shadow threads were saturated, she lifted it away and separated poison and shadow, soaking the pile of waste cloth with what she'd taken.

When the shadows were empty, she applied the mat to the wound again, drawing more poison until the wounds were empty and no longer able to feed the river streaming into Zeb's body. After that, she began the more familiar process of pulling the strands of poison from the tracery of veins it had followed.

Balling it in shadow, Marsh moved to place it in the pile. As she did, she felt her concentration falter, saw the ball start to dissipate, and tried separately to regain control as the room wavered and faded. The last thing she heard before she lost consciousness was Roeglin's alarmed shout.

She didn't know if the shadow would stay as a ball, or dissipate and release the shadow monsters' poison to vanish into the air around it.

REUNION

Marchant woke with a pounding headache and a raging thirst. She groaned as she stirred, trying to open eyes that felt like they'd been glued together. The minute she made a sound, someone's hand descended over her mouth and Roeglin's voice whispered through her mind.

Ssshhh.

Marsh lifted a hand that felt like lead and wrapped her fingers around his wrist. She raised her other hand and rubbed the gunge away from her eyes, slowly unsticking her lids. When she could open them, she looked up to see Roeglin crouched above her, his head raised and tilted to one side as though he was listening to something.

Taking a deep breath and then holding it, Marsh turned her head, listening to see what he'd heard. It took her a couple of minutes, but she was able to make out the sound of footsteps outside the door leading into the waystation.

Lots of footsteps. Mordan crouched beside her, tense and ready, her tail lashing.

Marsh moved her head again, and Roeglin lifted his hand as he looked into her face.

I ought to kick your ass.

Why don't you? Marsh thought back. It wasn't like she could stop him.

For some reason, Roeglin ignored that, and there was a moment's silence as they listened to the monsters moving outside. Marsh sat still, her whole body feeling like she'd run a marathon and taken a beating afterward. Her mouth was dry, so she swallowed trying to moisten her throat, but it didn't help, and her breath caught. She managed to stifle the resulting cough, but that only made it worse. She couldn't stop the ones that followed.

Outside the gate, the footsteps stopped. Gustav cursed, softly, and Mordan growled in disgust.

"Well, now they *are* sure," the other shadow guards said.

Marsh looked in their direction and caught both Henri and Jakob give her stares of utter exasperation.

"I told you we had until she woke," Roeglin said. "It's not like you weren't warned."

"Should have knocked her out again," Gustav grumbled, while Jakob raised a brow at the suggestion. Henri just shook his head and turned away.

"Thanks for that," Marsh muttered, and the words caught in her throat, making her cough again.

Roeglin hauled her into a sitting position, leaning her against his chest while he lifted a canteen to her lips.

"We don't have anything else," he murmured after she took the first few sips and discovered water.

Marsh didn't reply. She was too busy trying to piece together what had happened. She'd been pulling the poison out of Zeb's wound…*had* pulled it out, had balled it into shadow, hadn't… She swept the room with a glance, noting Henri, Jakob, and Gustav standing with their swords drawn as they faced the waystation's gate.

She looked farther and saw that Izmay stood facing away from her, her hands outstretched as though she were leaning on the gates without touching them. Gerry and Zeb were sleeping, but their chests rose and fell in a regular rhythm, and some of her fears eased.

"How are you all still alive?"

Gustav snorted, and Roeglin's mouth twisted in a wry smile. It was Henri, however, who answered.

"I dumped a blanket over the top of it," he said. "It caught the poison when the shadows went back to wherever you'd called 'em from. You're welcome."

Marsh stared at him as though he'd slapped her.

He pretty much just did, Roeglin told her, keeping it between them, but before Marsh could respond to that, Henri spoke again, adding insult to injury.

"It was *your* blanket."

Marsh opened her mouth to reply, then closed it again and rested her head back against Roeglin.

Honestly, what was the point?

He lifted the flask in front of her face and shook it.

"More?"

Marsh shook her head. She'd had enough to drink. Now she needed… The internal gates rattled, and she jumped. Roeglin set the flask to one side and wrapped his arms around her chest. Before she could protest, he scrambled to his feet, taking her with him so he could move her into a corner.

"Sorry, Marsh," he said, propping her against a wall, and tucking her feet close to her butt. "We're gonna need the space."

And I'm as useful as a rotting shroom, Marsh thought, but she was grateful when Roeglin didn't confirm it. She leaned against the wall, missing the warmth of his chest as the cold leached out of the stones into her back.

By the Deeps! Why did she feel so…so…so sick!

"You pushed the magic too far," Roeglin said, glancing down at her.

He'd call a shadow-blade to one hand and a shield to the other, and stood with his back to her. Mordan had gotten to her feet and was standing beside him. The gate rattled again, and Izmay grunted.

"Ro…" Izmay began, but something crashed into the outer gate and they all jumped, cursing in surprise. "Never mind."

Exactly why she'd canceled what Marsh knew was a request for the mage's help was obvious. Roeglin had dropped the sword and shield and flung his arms out, mirroring Izmay's position but facing the outer gates. From where she sat, it looked to Marsh like he was leaning on the gates—except he wasn't. He had called the shadows, slamming them against the gates and sealing the timber from view beneath a thick veneer of black.

Marsh tried to help, but her headache flared the minute she tried to touch the darkness surrounding them.

"No magic, Marsh."

As a command, it sounded like it was given from between gritted teeth.

Sure, Ro. Marsh closed her eyes. She'd meant that last to

be said out loud, but her mouth hadn't moved, and all she wanted to do was close her eyes.

"Gustav, can you give the girl a cookie?"

If the emissary thought it was a strange request, he didn't argue.

"Where?" He could only mean one thing.

"Pack."

Again, it sounded like the mage was speaking through gritted teeth. There was another thump against the gates, and they shuddered. Roeglin pushed forward as though resisting the pressure. He glanced at her and grimaced.

Marsh thought it might have been meant to be a smile, but it failed miserably. The gates rattled again, the sound accompanied by what sounded like the frustrated scrabble of claws. Marsh tried to push to her feet, but her legs refused to hold her and she swore.

"And I thought you tried not to say anything stronger than '*merde*', shadow mage?"

Gustav had returned, and he had a bag in one hand. He knelt beside her and held it out.

"Can you get your own cookies or do you need me to feed you?"

Feed her? Oh, by the Deeps, no!

Marsh forced her hand up, trying to ignore the way it trembled as she closed it around the bag. She wanted to say something witty, but the words wouldn't come. Instead, she took the bag, settling it into her lap as soon as she could. Gustav reached over and opened it when she couldn't coordinate her fingers enough to do it for herself, but he drew back when he was done.

He didn't get up, though, even if he kept casting anxious

looks toward the gates. He stayed crouched beside her until he'd watched her fumble one cookie clear and lift it to her mouth. Apparently satisfied that she'd be okay, he stood and moved over beside Roeglin.

"Eat them all," Roeglin said, and Marsh felt his words echo through her head, and the strange sense of compulsion that followed them.

It didn't help that she was already hungry and her body craved the sugar in the pastries. She'd chewed through three big bites and was lifting her second cookie from the bag before she'd registered what he'd done.

I'd be mad at you if I could be bothered, she thought, but she knew she couldn't. She just didn't have the energy. There was another loud bang, and the doors rattled again. Roeglin grunted and pushed back, pulling more shadows from the ceiling and the corners of the room, and thrusting them against the gates.

Marsh wondered just how effective a shadow barricade would be against shadow monsters, her mind drifting as she wolfed down her third—or was it fourth?—cookie. What if the creatures could slide along it and into...

"Not helping, Marsh."

Oh.

Marsh reached into the bag for another cookie, but this time her hand came up empty. She looked down at the bag and realized there really *was* nothing in it. With a sigh, she leaned her head back against the wall.

Why was she so tired? She'd used shadow magic; it was *her* magic, dammit! She should be feeling energized, not... not like this!

Can't. Help. You there. Roeglin told her, his thought

voice punctuated by grunts as more thumps came from the gates. *We'll look into it later. Right now. You need. To. Sleep.*

Sleep? Oh, he wouldn't...

Even as she thought it, Marsh's mind slid toward oblivion.

When she woke up, they were going to talk about... this...

Only, when she *did* wake up, they didn't. They weren't alone, and it wasn't Roeglin who came to her when she stirred. Marsh caught sight of an unfamiliar face and lashed out. Fortunately, the healer was faster, closing a fist around her wrist and arresting her strike before it could connect.

"Son of the Shadow Deeps!" Marsh shouted, twisting to her feet and lashing out with her other hand.

The healer caught that too and then turned her around, pulling her against his chest and wrapping her tightly. Marsh lashed back with her foot, catching him in the shin and drawing an exclamation of pain.

"Shadow Mage Leclerc!"

Envermet's voice rang out, the command buried in its tones breaking through Marsh's panic and outrage. She froze, but the healer didn't let her go. He held her tightly until Master Envermet was standing in front of her.

Instead of scolding her, the shadow-guard captain tilted his head and looked into her eyes, his face a mixture of consternation and compassion.

"How are you feeling?"

"I'm..." Marsh had been about to say that she was all right, but it struck her that she wasn't. Rather than admit it, she changed the subject. "Where are the others? Did they…"

She swallowed against the sudden fear that stole her words, and then she tried again.

"Did…"

Again she stopped, silently cursing her weakness, but the shadow master understood.

"We reached them in time," he said, "but they are sleeping."

Again that head tilt.

"As should you be. Please don't hurt my medics; they're only doing as I asked them."

He went to move away and then stopped.

"How much magic *did* you use?"

As Marsh tried to formulate a reply to that, another voice replied, "She drained herself dry before they broke through. I put her out."

Roeglin sounded like he'd then done his best to use up all of his own reserves as well, and Marsh almost laughed— except he'd *what?*

Master Envermet turned toward Roeglin.

"Why?"

"If you hadn't arrived, she'd have been helpless."

The implications of what he wasn't saying sank in, and Marsh felt her stomach go into freefall. Her head spun and she caught herself starting to sag but straightened up, pushing back a rising tide of nausea.

"Let me go," she said, fighting to keep her voice even. Then, more loudly when the arms around her didn't immediately loosen, "Let me go!"

This time the medic complied and she pushed herself

away from him, reaching out to gain support from the wall.

"I'm going outside," she said, her voice hoarse with emotion even as it defied anyone to say otherwise.

The healer reached out as though to stop her, but Marsh caught it when Master Envermet tapped him on the shoulder and shook his head. It was a relief that no one else tried, even if someone fell into step just behind her not long afterward. Marsh ignored them, heading for the first door she could find. It took her another four steps to realize she was no longer in the gatehouse, and she stopped, waiting as another wave of dizziness passed.

Where in all the Deeps was Mordan?

The person accompanying her stopped also, but they did not touch her—and they did not speak, for which Marsh was grateful. When she resumed her journey to the door and through it, they came with her, but they neither spoke nor reached out to her. Marsh did her best to ignore them, just moved slowly out into the courtyard beyond, wondering what had happened to the kat.

When she saw the courtyard, she stopped to take in the troops in the space. One squad of twenty was doing sword drill, except that each and every one of them was calling shadows to coat their blades, finishing their kata, and releasing the shadows before repeating the process. Two more squads were practicing group maneuvers with physical swords and shields, while another cluster of men and women sat around outdoor tables, relaxing as they ate.

A familiar brown and grey form was sitting on a rooftop, overseeing it all. She turned her head as Marsh appeared, and although joy leapt along the link between them, the kat didn't move. She was content. Her pride was safe—her attention returned to the soldiers—and the hunters were improving their technique. They were in good company.

The sight was enough to make Marsh pause. She might not know the faces of the folk in front of her, but she knew the uniforms; the insignia of the Four-Caverns Protectors gleamed dull copper, silver, or gold on the chest of every tunic or corselet she could see. Marsh moved to one side of the infirmary door, preparing to lean against the front of the building she'd woken up in. That changed when she saw the rough bench drawn up against it.

Without a word to her silent companion, she dropped onto it and buried her face in her hands. Tremors ran through her body as the full meaning of Roeglin's words slammed home. He'd put her out so she wouldn't… He…

She ended up on her knees throwing up.

What the shadow monsters did with their prey when they caught it…

Her stomach lurched again. When it was finished, Marsh stayed on her knees, her eyes closed as she tried to steady her breathing.

Well, that had been less than elegant, she thought as a familiar voice spoke.

"You done?"

Just what exactly did Brigitte mean "was she done?" Of course, she wasn't done. She might never be done.

"You're not going to be much use to the children in that condition."

There was sympathy for you. No concern for her, just

for the children, like the little brats needed any. *They were…*

Wait…

They were *here?*

Outrage sparked through Marsh and she pushed herself to her feet, turning on the journeyman in anger.

"Do you mean the children are *here?*"

Brigitte flashed her a quick smile and then fixed her with a stern stare.

"When you're finished feeling sorry for yourself, Master Ilias says you need to eat—and Tamlin and Aisha are waiting at the table."

Marsh was mortified. What if they'd seen her? She'd been a mess; not at all what a guardian should be. Brigitte read her face and tucked her arm through Marsh's.

"I made them sit inside for a reason," she said. "They didn't see a—"

"Marsh!" Aisha's clear voice rang across the courtyard, and Marsh had to laugh at the expression on Brigitte's face.

"You were saying?" she teased, although her voice sounded cracked along the edges. "Come on, before the little brat… Never mind."

She sighed as Aisha scampered between two formations of soldiers, Scruffknuckle and the hoshkit bounding alongside her. It was hard to say which of them caused more devastation as soldiers tried to avoid stepping on or skewering them…or as they barreled under upraised feet and took people's legs out from under them.

Then Tamlin ran through, the second kit at his heels.

"Sorry!" the boy yelled, apologizing as he went. "Sorry. Sorry. Sorry! Oops.

That last was punctuated by a resounding crash and the clatter of metal as the boy and two soldiers hit the cobbles in a shower of armored flesh and dropped shields and swords, the kit dodging out of the way before it was skewered. Tamlin lost no time in pulling himself free and running for the edge of the practice ground, cries of outrage in his wake.

"Petitfeu!"

"You!"

"Boy!"

"Deeps damn it, child!"

"Hey!"

"Leclerc!"

Marsh didn't know whether to laugh or cry, and it was certainly too late to hide. Instead, she just watched the kids come, not sure whether to scold them or beg forgiveness for their interruption.

"I'd beg forgiveness," Roeglin said from the doorway.

He sounded tired, but Marsh heard the smile in his voice.

"No. *I'll* beg for forgiveness." Master Envermet didn't sound like he knew *how* to smile. "You need to get them corralled before they do any more damage."

"I'll see to it," Roeglin told him as the children arrived.

Aisha hit with the force of a small boulder and Marsh ended up back on the bench, dragging Brigitte down with her. Aisha scrambled into her lap and Scruffknuckle put both paws on her shoulder, the young hund washing her face with undiminished enthusiasm as his tail blurred with joy. Tamlin stood to one side, the kits sitting solemnly at his feet. When Scruffknuckle finally stopped licking her and contented himself with hopping up on the bench beside her, Marsh looked at the boy.

"You staying out of trouble?" she asked by way of greeting, and he shrugged, looking at the courtyard, which was slowly coming back to order.

His mouth quirked.

"What do you think?" he asked, gesturing at the rapidly diminishing chaos. "And we haven't even had breakfast, yet."

Aisha sat up and looked behind them.

"Oh. Oops."

Brigitte groaned.

"You *had* to ask."

Marsh watched as Master Envermet moved from one squad commander to another, speaking with each one as he went and looking chagrined as he did. More than one smiled at his apology and shook their heads, as they glanced at the children. Marsh blushed.

"Come on," Roeglin urged. "Mess hall is that way."

Mess hall. It took Marsh a moment to realize he meant the dining hall, and her stomach rumbled.

Aisha slipped off her lap and slid her hand into Marsh's.

"Come on! They have pancakes."

Pancakes? Marsh wondered where they'd got those from. Tamlin caught her look and answered her question.

"The raiders hadn't been here long enough to eat everything in the pantry, and whoever ran the place had just stocked up before they were taken."

Now that she thought about it, Marsh remembered passing a caravan going in the opposite direction when she'd made her last trip from Kerrenin's Ledge. That seemed like a very long time ago.

"Different world," Roeglin agreed. "Are you coming? Do you need a hand?"

His words caught Aisha's attention, and the little girl frowned. She looked up at Marsh.

"You hurt?"

"Too much magic," Roeglin told her like he was helping, and Marsh rolled her eyes.

"I'm fine!"

It was too late. Aisha gave her a shocked look, then put both hands on Marsh's stomach and shoved her back onto the bench.

"Magic hurt?"

Marsh shook her head, even though she felt like she'd been run over by an entire pack train.

"I'm fine, kiddo," she said, trying to stand up. Aisha did not believe her and pushed her back before she could get to her feet.

"Are not!"

Marsh glared at her and Aisha glared right back, her blue eyes blazing.

"Not nice to lie."

Roeglin started to snicker.

"Hear that, Marsh?" he teased. "It's not nice to lie."

Marsh rolled her eyes.

"Fine! I'm *fine*. I just need to rest and eat and..." Marsh stopped mid-sentence as Aisha shifted her hands so they touched bare skin.

"Wait..." she began, but the little girl's eyes shifted from blue to a brilliant shining green and Marsh felt energy rush through her, pushing aside the fatigue and aches.

The surge lasted for less than a heartbeat, then Aisha's eyes returned to their natural shade...until she turned to Roeglin.

"You, too?" she asked, advancing on the mage.

Roeglin shifted back two hasty steps, almost falling over, and it was Marsh's turn to laugh.

"Remember, Ro, it's not nice to lie…"

"Aysh, I…" It was too late; the child reached out and took him by the hand, her eyes flaring briefly green before she let him go.

"See?" she asked, looking up at him, her eyes their natural shining blue. "All better."

Roeglin stared at her, astounded.

"Yes. All better," he said, casting a surprised look over her head at Marsh. "Right, Marsh?"

It didn't take Marsh long to agree.

"Yes." She looked at the child. "Thank you, Aysh."

"Master Leger." The shadow captain had returned.

Marsh stood as she and Roeglin turned to face him. Master Envermet wasted no time coming to the point. He glanced at Aisha and then back at the shadow mages.

"Master Ilias needs her. He's used all the magic he dares."

It wasn't a question, and he wasn't asking permission, but Marsh and Roeglin understood. They weren't the only ones recovering from the battle.

"Was anyone else clawed?"

Master Envermet turned to her.

"After you've eaten," he said, his tone showing he'd tolerate no argument.

"Do they have time?"

He hesitated and Marsh caught his eye, daring him to tell her a lie.

"I'll check," he said, and Brigitte sighed.

"Tams and I will go find food."

"And kaffee," Roeglin told her.

"And chocolate," Marsh added.

Tamlin sighed, and Marsh turned toward him. Instead of trying to reach him with words, she crossed to his side and wrapped her arms around him in a hug. He tensed briefly, then returned it.

"I missed you too," Marsh told him as she stepped back.

He nodded like he didn't trust his voice and turned away. After he'd taken a few steps, he stopped and looked over his shoulder.

"Don't fall over while I'm gone," he said and led Brigitte back across the courtyard.

4

HEALING MISCHIEF

It didn't take them long to find Master Ilias. He smiled when he saw Aisha and frowned at the sight of Marsh and Roeglin on her heels.

"What are *you* doing here?" he asked, and Aisha rebuked him.

"Rude!"

He reached out and ruffled the child's hair, keeping his gaze fixed on Marsh and demanding an answer.

"You've got people who've been shadow-clawed."

His face clouded but he didn't deny it.

"I do."

"Which one is in the worst shape?"

He started to turn and then stopped.

"You're in no condition to…" He let his words trail off as Marsh glanced down at Aisha, their eyes meeting in a look of complete understanding. Both of them had caught the flicker of Ilias's eyes toward one corner of the room.

They moved as one, Scruffknuckle getting under the medic's feet as the man turned to follow. His soft "oof" as he stumbled was enough to have them hasten their steps, Aisha taking Marsh's hand.

"Dis one," she said, stopping beside a blanket carefully spread on the floor.

The woman lying on it had seen more than one battle, but the one just gone through looked like it would be her last. Marsh caught Aisha's eye.

"We got this?" she asked, and the little girl nodded, dropping to her knees beside the injured soldier.

"Got it," she said as Marsh knelt beside her.

When she saw how far the poison had spread, Marsh muttered a silent prayer to the Deeps and then drew the shadows into the wound, hoping Roeglin had remembered to bring something for her to wrap the poison in after she pulled it out.

At one point, the poison threatened to evade the shadows' grasp, and Marsh remembered what Ilias had said about the poison not being part of the shadows. The thought almost made the stuff slip from her grasp, but she reminded herself that even if it *wasn't* related to the shadows, it could still be drawn into them. After that, her grip firmed, and she pulled both shadow and poison from the wound, relieved to find a pile of rags waiting. Burying the first ball of shadows and poison in the cloth, Marsh tried pulling the shadows free and leaving the poison behind instead of dismissing the shadows entirely.

It worked, and she used them to remove the rest of it. As she pulled the last of it, she realized Aisha had been working right alongside her, and the child's healing magic was changing the color of the life force infusing the damaged parts of the soldier's body. Once the poison was gone, those parts brightened and glowed more strongly.

When she was done, Marsh touched Aisha on the shoulder and watched the green fade from the child's eyes. The little girl glared at her.

"Not done," she declared, and Master Ilias cleared his throat.

"Medic Calaidon can take over here. There are others who need your help."

Aisha hesitated, looking from the master medic to the woman standing beside him. When she spoke, it was to her and not her master. She waved a hand at the soldier.

"Can fix?" she asked, and the woman nodded, her eyes wide with awe.

"Can fix," she replied, sounding stunned.

"No lie?" the child prodded, as though lying adults were part of her everyday life.

The medic looked shocked.

"No. No lie."

"Good," Aisha told her, then looked at Ilias. "Who next?"

To Marsh's surprise, the medic pointed at her.

"Marsh," he said. "She's looking pale."

Marsh frowned; she wasn't *feeling* pale. She glanced down at Aisha as the child glanced up.

"Marsh fine. Next."

Marsh heard a snort and turned to see Roeglin hiding a smile with his hand. Aisha kept her eyes firmly fixed on Ilias. The medic sighed.

"This way."

The next wound wasn't as bad, and Marsh found she didn't get as tired working next to Aisha, even though the child leaned on her during much of the process. They were straightening up from the fourth patient when Marsh noticed Aisha wrapping her hand in the fur of Scruffknuckle's neck while the girl reached for her hand.

As their palms touched, she felt a soft rush of energy and came to an abrupt halt.

"You healing me, Aysh?"

The child kept walking, trying to tow Marsh toward the next patient.

"Uh-uh."

"Aysh…" Marsh growled, and the child stopped with a heartfelt sigh. "Well?"

Aisha turned and gave her a wide-eyed look of innocence.

"Yes, Marsh?"

"Did you just heal me?"

Aisha's eyes widened farther, gleaming a more intense blue than before.

"Nooooo…"

Tamlin started snickering, and Roeglin swiftly followed. Even Ilias managed a chuckle.

"Busted, Aysh," Tamlin said, then added, "and I think Scruffknuckle needs a rest."

Alarm spread across Aisha's features, and she turned to the pup.

"Scruffy! You 'kay?"

The krypthund gave a snort wuff and licked her nose. Aisha looked down at him, scowling.

"No, you not. Go sleep."

The puppy whined, and Aisha stamped her foot.

"Sleep! Now!"

Marsh caught herself wondering where she'd learned *that* tone of voice.

Have you listened to yourself at bedtime? Roeglin asked, keeping the comment between them.

I'm not that bad, Marsh thought, startled by the finality in the child's tones.

Roeglin gave a short bark of laughter.

Wanna bet?

Whatever Marsh might have said in reply to that was lost when Aisha turned to Master Ilias.

"Have to wait," she said. "I need Scruffy."

She looked up, her hand tightening on Marsh's.

"Marsh needs Scruffy."

Marsh frowned.

"What does she mean?"

Tamlin groaned.

"The Rock Wizards taught her how healing magic worked," he said. "They showed her that she could draw energy from the life around her when she needed it."

He gave his sister a stern look.

"They taught her not to take too much, and that the creatures who lend her their strength need to replenish their own strength over time." He paused, then added, "Sometimes she forgets to check."

"The rock mages know healing?" Marsh asked, surprised since none of the ones she'd traveled with had known how.

"No," Aisha said, scowling, but it was clear she was lying again.

Master Ilias sighed.

"Thank you," he told them, his eyes darting to another

of the forms lying on a blanket. "Perhaps you can come back later?"

"I can do another couple before I fall over," Marsh said, sliding a sly look at Tamlin.

It was true. The boy and Brigitte had come back with food, and she'd eaten between patients, feeling her strength slowly return.

"I don't want you falling over," Roeglin said as Captain Envermet returned and added his own vote.

"We need your group to move out in the morning, so don't overdo it."

Marsh turned away from the pair of them.

"How many will you lose if I don't?"

The medic didn't reply straight away but looked over his shoulder at Roeglin. Marsh cleared her throat and tapped him on the chest with her forefinger.

"How. Many?"

"I…" Again his eyes darted past her.

Marsh turned, looking down at one of the soldiers, who was watching the exchange, his face carefully blank. She turned back to Ilias, Roeglin, and Envermet.

"We're not going until I can't help anyone else."

Envermet turned his head, looking at two men waiting by the door.

"Ceres, Valglin, remove the shadow mistress from the infirmary," he said. Marsh realized he'd come prepared to do exactly that.

"I don't think so," she said, and stretched out a hand, pulling shadows from the edges of the room and dropping them over Envermet's head.

She'd forgotten he was a shadow mage too. Even as the

shadows flowed over him, she felt them twist and turn in her hand as the shadow captain wrenched some of them from her control.

"I got dis," Aisha said, watching her struggle.

Before Marsh fully understood what the child intended, Aisha had crouched and laid her hand on the stone floor, her eyes going as black as pitch.

"Aisha! No!"

Tamlin's cry coincided with Master Envermet's shout of surprise, and the guards on the other side of the room started running. It took Marsh several heartbeats to realize what the child was doing, but when she did, she reached down and grabbed her, lifting her from the floor, pulling her to her chest, and spinning in a circle.

"Stop!" she said in case the distraction wasn't enough. "Please, stop!"

When she'd come full circle, she halted, relieved to see that the stone stretching up to encase the shadow captain had stopped at mid-thigh. Aisha was completely unrepentant.

"Not done yet," she said and wriggled out of Marsh's arms as a large form leapt through the door, knocking the two guards to the floor as it bounded over to Marsh.

Marsh groaned, but the hoshkat's sudden arrival was accompanied by her appearance in her head. Concern washed over her as Mordan landed before her and turned to interpose herself between Marsh and the rest of the room. The big kat's soft snarl stroked the air around them.

Once she was in position, the kat flicked her ears toward Marsh, a sense of confusion following.

Where was the threat?

The guards picked themselves up from the floor and looked at Envermet. He held up his hand and glared at Marsh.

"I think someone's mentioned the examples you set?"

Marsh didn't dignify that with an answer. Of course, someone had. He was standing right beside the shadow captain, and Monsieur Gravine had spoken of it as well. To her. No one had said a word to Aisha about following those examples.

She's five, Roeglin muttered inside her head, but he didn't move, and Marsh knew why.

With Mordanlenoowar standing guard, not even Roeglin would dare to intervene. The kat tilted her head to eye the shadow mage, and Roeglin raised his hands and backed up a step. Ilias did the same when the beast turned her head toward him.

You are in so much shit that I may never be able to dig you out. Roeglin told her. *Master Envermet is furious!*

Marsh ignored him and turned to Aisha.

"We are in a *lot* of trouble," she said, then pointed at the injured soldier. "Help me fix him?"

"Yes. Dan help, too."

Oh, Dan would, would she?

The big kat backed up slowly so Aisha could lay her hand on her haunches.

Marsh raised her eyebrows. Well, apparently she would.

"We need to do this fast," she said, but Master Envermet interrupted, his voice full of sarcastic grace.

"Oh, no. By all means, take your time. I'm not going anywhere." He gestured at the stone encasing his legs. "I'll be right here when you're done."

Beyond him, Brigitte bit her lip, until Marsh wasn't sure if the journeyman was stifling a smile or worried about the frustration in the captain's tones.

Big trouble, Roeglin repeated, and Marsh resisted the urge to stick out her tongue.

As though she'd heard him, Aisha shifted to look toward him and held up one hand, carefully folding down her fingers with all the concentration of a five-year-old doing something new and trying to get it right. When she was done, she held up her perfectly arranged middle digit, accompanying it with a perfectly tailored glare.

"Not. Done," she told him, firmly, wagging it back and forth in a gesture Marsh didn't remember teaching her, and then she turned back to the soldier.

Marsh went to kneel beside the child. The soldier was staring at the pair of them, his gaze one of apprehension mingled with faint hope.

"Thank you," he said, but Marsh was already focusing on what she needed to do to ensure his survival.

This time, she was aware of Aisha's small hand covering her own as she worked.

"Dan has lots of healing," the child said.

As if to confirm it, the kat sent a sense of concern for the welfare of her pride. She was happy to do what was needed to ensure the health of all of its members. When they were ready, the hunt could continue.

This time, when Marsh drew the poison from the wound, Tamlin was waiting with a cloth to contain it. Marsh looked up at Ilias.

"Where next?"

He didn't argue, just pointed, and Marsh and Aisha

continued to the next patient. They didn't stop until Ilias looked around the room and shrugged.

"I think that's everyone," the medic said.

He paused, casting a nervous glance toward where Envermet and Roeglin were standing in the middle of the room.

"Thank you."

Marsh gave him a small smile.

"We're sorry for the fuss," she began, but Mordanlenoowar gave a curious growl and turned her head to survey the patients around them.

As Marsh watched her, the big kat lowered her head and drew a series of gentle, snuffing breaths before pacing purposefully to one of the soldiers lying on the floor. Again, she gave a sound of curiosity and nudged the soldier's arm.

Marsh stared, receiving the kat's thought that this one too smelled of darkness.

"Truly?"

The hoshkat lifted her lips in a silent hiss, and the man before her drew a sharp breath. Marsh crossed to him, Aisha hurrying in her wake. His gaze flicked from the kat to her to the child, and back to the kat again. Marsh's voice drew his attention back.

"You got clawed?"

Again, he looked up at Mordan, and, again she raised her lips in a silent snarl. He looked quickly at Marsh.

"Bit."

Behind her, Ilias gasped.

Being bitten was worse?

Marsh didn't stop to ask, she just searched for what

he'd been hiding from the medics. A chunk had been taken out of his hand and the wound was flaring red, its edges starting to blacken and flake. Marsh guessed it had been missed in the midst of the other injuries that had already started to heal—and that the man had then hidden it so as to keep the healers from worrying about something they could do nothing to heal. He cast a guilty look at Ilias.

As well he might, Marsh thought, but the soldier was trying to explain.

"Some circled back. One got past."

Ilias looked horrified, and Roeglin's eyes sheeted momentarily in white.

Oh.

His eyes cleared and he pointed at three other men.

"Have the kat check them as well. See if there are others carrying injuries they haven't admitted to yet."

One of the men shifted uneasily on his blanket.

"Start with that one." He looked at Marsh. "You know your eyes shift between green and black when you do this, don't you?"

Marsh shrugged.

How in all the Deeps was she supposed to know that? She wasn't exactly looking in a mirror.

"And watch out. The venom works differently."

Marsh nodded and took the man's wrist in her hands. She was aware of Mordan settling down beside them and Aisha twining her fingers in the kat's thick, soft fur. A frown marred the child's small face as she studied the injury, and then she looked at Marsh.

"No touch," she said, and Marsh was wondering how the child knew when Aisha added, "Not yet."

"Sure, whatever you say, kiddo." Marsh sat back and looked at the soldier, seeing how the colors of his life force faded and crisped around threads of black that were slowly snaking their way up the veins in his forearm. This time there was more than just the ebon webbing. As Marsh studied him, she saw a faint patina of darkness creeping over his skin.

The venom had spread farther than just the crisp blackness already visible on his hand. The life force sheathing his skin had started to fade all the way up his forearm, and a lichen-like discoloration was visible past the wrist she'd grabbed. So much for not touching.

Well, it was too late for regrets. Roeglin could groan all he liked, but she couldn't change the past. What was done was done.

Idiot.

"Use your outside voice," Marsh murmured, gathering shadows and smoothing them over the soldier's skin.

"Idiot."

"*Oui*, thanks for that."

She figured the venom was a bit like lichen, so it should soak up shadow the same way lichen soaked up water. Once it did that, she should be able to coax it off the skin and onto—she looked around—onto a cloth or a... She thought about it.

"I need a shroom," she said out loud. "A brown nose, or something with the same kind of flesh."

"Yes," Aisha said, and her small voice hissed with effort.

She glanced up at Marsh.

"Show me how."

It made Marsh wish she'd had time to pursue Roeglin's

idea that she might have some kind of mental magic, but she thought he might be mistaken.

"Ro?"

"I'll link you. Aisha, watch Marsh. Can you see?"

"Uh huh. Oh. No need shadow!"

That last came out as a squeak of delight, and Marsh waited, hoping the child would explain. When she didn't, Marsh continued to soak the venom with shadow. She hoped Tamlin would hurry, and heard running footsteps.

"Got it."

"Put it beside his arm."

As soon as Tamlin had done as she'd asked, Marsh focused on moving the shadow-soaked venom from the soldier's skin to the shroom, but it didn't move. The shadow came out of it and moved to settle over the mushroom's flesh, but the venom stayed exactly where it was. Marsh stared at it in consternation.

"No. Like dis." Marsh watched as the lively green of Aisha's power swept over the man's skin, burning the lichen-like growth marking his flesh in a swift burst of heat and light. The man gave a short, sharp gasp of pain, then relaxed.

"You killed him," Tamlin said, and Aisha stuck out her tongue.

"Did not." She looked up at Marsh. "All done."

All done, huh? Marsh had her doubts about that, but when she looked, she saw that Aisha was right. She *was* all done. Not a smidgen of venom remained to mar the man's wound, and there wasn't any sign of the tracery of black that had been running through his veins.

She remembered the flare of heat and studied the bright

threads of life running beneath the soldier's skin. They *seemed* okay, and the man's life-force looked a bit brighter than it had been before.

"Dis one," Aisha said, and Marsh realized the girl had already gone to crouch beside the next man.

Before she could do or say anything to stop her, the child had touched the man on the head. Her eyes flared bright emerald, and he gave a short, sharp cry before losing consciousness. Aisha looked down at him as though studying the effects of what she'd done, and then she glanced at the kat.

"*Cherche*, Mordan."

The instruction was delivered in a tone that expected immediate obedience, and Marsh felt her eyes widen. The hoshkat tilted her head toward Marsh before focusing on the girl. As Marsh watched, the kat got slowly to its feet, gave a luxurious stretch, and bared her ivory fangs in a long yawn. Aisha hopped from one foot to the other, her small face anxious as the kat sat and made a show of licking her foreleg.

It took the child a few minutes, but she finally got the message.

"*S'il plait*, Dan? Pretty *s'il plait?*"

The kat stopped grooming and regarded the child with her azure gaze.

"Please *cherche*."

With a soft growl, Mordan got to her feet and wandered through the wounded, occasionally stopping to sniff at one or another. After a single round, she came back and looked at Marsh. Apparently, the pride was clean. No more darkness tainted their wounds.

Marsh breathed a sigh of relief and looked down at Aisha.

"Mordan says no one else."

The little girl sagged and walked over to lean on the kat.

"Good kitty," she said, stroking Mordan's fur. "Good, good, kitty."

Across the room, Master Envermet cleared his throat.

Marsh lifted her head at the sound, stretching out her hand for Aisha to take. She glanced toward Master Envermet and led the little girl closer.

"Aisha, do you have something you'd like to say to Master Envermet?" she asked, and the only warning she had of impending trouble was the slight frown that creased the child's brow.

By then it was far too late.

Aisha let go of her hand and stalked up to the shadow captain, stopping in front of him long enough to tap his stone-covered thigh.

"You are a very bad man," she told him. "No stop helping. Is rude."

She stamped her foot and looked at Marsh.

"Dere," she declared, and she walked out of the infirmary, her small head held high.

A snort came from one of the neighboring blankets, followed by a muffled laugh and then a groan from another. The sound shook Marsh out of her drop-jawed disbelief, and she closed her mouth.

"Aysh..." she began as the little girl vanished into the courtyard, but Aisha showed no sign of hearing her...or stopping if she had. "Aisha!"

Tamlin started to sputter, and Roeglin made a sound

suspiciously like a choked-down snort. Marsh hurried to the door.

"Aisha Liliana Danet!"

Behind her, Tamlin started to snigger, and Roeglin unsuccessfully tried to muffle a chuckle.

"Aisha!" Marsh shouted, catching sight of the little rat walking toward the first formation of soldiers, but the child paid her no heed and kept walking. The soldiers faltered in their first round of katas but then continued.

Marsh quickened her pace, only to freeze as Master Envermet's voice rolled out of the infirmary and over the parade ground.

"Apprentice Danet! Report!"

Marsh was relieved when Aisha paused and devastated when the child started moving again—in the opposite direction. Master Envermet's voice rumbled past a second time, and Marsh wished she could have stepped out of its way. The sound was like a breeze blowing over her skin.

"Apprentice Danet! This is your second warning!"

The soldiers in the formation started laughing. Marsh wondered what they knew that she didn't.

"Three!"

And the soldiers snapped into three perfectly straight lines.

"Cookie..." the multi-voiced whisper echoed around the courtyard, and Aisha's footsteps faltered.

Marsh looked around, wondering where the whisper had come from.

Aisha looked over her shoulder.

"Two..."

The men started chanting.

"Coo-kie! Coo-kie! Coo-kie!"

To Marsh's utter surprise, Aisha gave a shriek of frustration and bolted back across the courtyard.

"I coming! I coming! I coming!"

As soon as she'd disappeared back into the infirmary, the soldiers started laughing—right up until their commanders barked out orders to resume their katas. Marsh looked from the men back to the infirmary, and then around the courtyard.

She jumped as Master Envermet's voice reached out again.

"Shadow Master Leclerc, return!"

This time, the men did not stop performing their katas, and after a moment's consideration, Marsh turned around and followed Aisha's path back to the infirmary. To her surprise, Aisha was standing in front of the Shadow Captain, and the stone had returned to the floor. He looked from the child's upturned face to the door as Marsh entered.

"Come here, Shadow Master."

Marsh stifled a sigh and went. Master Envermet apparently had a point to make, and they were right at the center of it. His voice was almost pleasant when he spoke, although Roeglin's completely blank face did not bode well.

Marsh's fears proved well-founded.

"I believe you and Apprentice Danet have volunteered to assist in clearing the stables and latrines this evening," he said, his voice deceptively mild.

Marsh heard Aisha draw a breath and nudged the child before she could speak. Master Envermet caught the movement, and his eyebrow twitched.

"I also believe," he continued, "that you both needed to study the local fungi. I have a team gathering edibles and clearing the ground around the walls tomorrow morning. You will join them."

"Ceres and Valglin will escort you."

The two guards Mordan had knocked to the floor were waiting near the door. Marsh stifled a groan, then said the only thing she could think of.

"Yes, Master Envermet."

It was a relief to hear Aisha's voice echo the words.

5

GOODBYES

"No crying," Marsh said, sternly waving a scrubbing brush at Aisha. "You did it."

"You did too!" the little girl howled, and Marsh's heart went out to her.

Truth was, Aisha probably *wouldn't* have done it if Marsh hadn't shown her the way—just like the time she'd snuck out of Monsieur Gravine's fortress to follow the Protectors sent to rescue Marsh—and that had been just over a fortnight ago. Marsh had snuck out first, and it had been her fault she'd needed rescuing in the first place. Marsh sighed. *Oui…*

She was supposed to be the adult. Time she stepped up and adulted.

"You want a hug?" she asked, and, just like that, the child was in her lap, winding her arms around Marsh's neck and sobbing into her shoulder.

Marsh set the scrubbing brush aside.

"You need a bath," she said.

"Do not."

"Uh huh." Marsh got up and walked to where a communal tub had been set up in one corner.

The water was lukewarm and just a bit murky, but she got Aisha into it and soon had her scrubbed down and wrapped in a towel that was cleaner than what she'd been wearing.

"Let's get you to Brigitte," she said. "I'll finish up here."

"You be up all night," Aisha protested and Marsh shrugged, letting the smallest of smiles touch her lips.

"It's my fault," she said. "I set a bad example, and you copied me."

"Did not."

"Did too."

"Did not."

"Uh huh…did so too."

"I not have to copy."

Aisha's face was solemn, and Marsh ruffled her hair.

"True, but you're littler than me. I get to do the most scrubbing."

"Do…" Aisha's argument was swallowed by a huge yawn. "Not," she finished as Marsh reached the dining hall.

On her way out of the latrines, she'd realized she didn't know where they were supposed to sleep. Nudging the door open, she crossed to the food service area.

"Do you know where I can find Journeyman Petitfeu?" she asked the woman behind the counter.

"Kitchen."

The woman gestured over her shoulder, then screwed up her face at the sight of Aisha in Marsh's arms.

"You can't take *that* through there."

Marsh raised her eyebrows and smiled sweetly.

"If you don't fetch the journeyman," she said, "I'm going to leave *this* sleeping on your serving counter."

"You would—" The woman shut her mouth abruptly as Marsh stepped up to the counter, shifting Aisha in her arms.

Judging by the child's dead weight, she'd fallen asleep on the way across the courtyard. Marsh started smirking as the woman scuttled through the door to the kitchens, returning shortly afterward with Brigitte in tow.

"Marsh!"

"I'm sorry, Journeyman, but I've got to get back to scrubbing. Do you mind?"

Brigitte bustled around the counter to take the sleeping child in her arms.

"Of course, I will. You'd better go before…" She sighed, her eyes turning to someone who'd just come into the dining hall behind Marsh. "Never mind."

Marsh sighed as well and turned, knowing exactly who Brigitte had seen waiting behind her. There were days when she hated being right; whole weeks, even. Her heart sank as she saw Master Envermet.

"I was just returning," she said.

His face was stern.

"I did not give you permission to leave. Do you like missing meals?"

"No, Master."

"That's too bad. Don't bother reporting for breakfast."

"No, Master."

"The apprentice too," he added, and Marsh bristled.

"The *child*," she snarled, "is not missing a meal on my behalf. I decided it was her quitting time, and I decided it was her bath time, *and* her bedtime, *and* I brought her here for the journeyman to put to bed. Those were not her choices but *mine*."

"Nevertheless—"

"Nevertheless, nothing!" Marsh snapped. "She's learned her lesson, and you're going to let her be."

Beside her, Brigitte gasped, but Master Envermet merely quirked an eyebrow, and his mouth twitched in what might have been amusement.

"I think I will be the judge of that."

"Not tonight, you won't, and not tomorrow, either. She is my responsibility, and I say she has had enough."

"She is under *my* command, and *I* disagree."

"I contest your right."

Marsh didn't understand why Brigitte was moving away from her, but the woman was no longer at her side. Marsh heard footsteps—*two* sets of footsteps—heading for the kitchen door.

"You are also under my command," the shadow captain reminded her in the mild tones he used when he was particularly angry, "and you're already under disciplinary measures."

"I'll skip her meal for her," Marsh said.

Roeglin stepped into the hall behind the shadow captain and came to an abrupt halt, his eyes drawn to the ceiling above them.

"Master Leclerc," he said, acknowledging Marsh's presence even as his face paled and he swallowed hard. He looked at the captain. "Master Envermet, may I speak with you?"

"When I've finished here," Envermet replied, but

Roeglin darted across the hall, slid his arm through the captain's, and wheeled him around.

"You're done," Roeglin assured him. "Come with me, and I'll explain."

"Master Leger!" The captain was outraged, but Roeglin towed him to the door and shoved him out into the courtyard before he could protest further.

He looked back at Marsh.

"Take three deep breaths, then clean up that mess on the ceiling," he instructed before pulling the door firmly closed.

Marsh stared at the closed door.

What mess on the ceiling?

She looked up and took several hasty steps back.

Shadows rolled and crackled in an inky mass over her head, and when she moved away from the cloud, it followed. Across the room from her, the door cracked open and the darkness struck out. The door was pulled shut seconds before shards of dark lightning slammed into it. They lodged there momentarily before sizzling back to the ceiling and sliding back to join the cloud.

Marsh backed up a bit farther.

"I said *three*. *Deep*. Breaths, Leclerc!"

And there he was, shouting at her again. If the man wanted her to calm down, he needed to try something different.

Uh huh. How about I kick your ass?

Yeah, you and what shadow army? Marsh thought and watched as more lightning lanced out from the rolling mass over her head. This time the door exploded.

"Shadow's Deep, shadow mage! There are folks out here want to eat sometime before mid-cycle!"

What was it with men and their food?

I heard that.

Yeah, and you resemble that remark, Marsh thought, but she didn't say it out loud.

Hey!

If the boot fits...

Roeglin sighed in her head.

You want to tell the shadows that you really are okay and they don't need to protect you? You know, before someone decides the stew's good enough to risk their life for?

And here she'd thought supper was long over.

Roeglin's reply was succinct.

Changing of the guard.

Well, Shadows Deep and damnation. *That* made things awkward. Okay...

Marsh spread her arms, letting out a long breath before taking another and pulling her hands in close to her chest as though drawing both air and shadow to herself. This time, when she let her breath out, she kept her arms furled against her chest.

The next time she took a breath in, she lifted her hands toward the ceiling like a cup.

"I am safe," she said, pushing aside the idea that Master Envermet was going to have her hide for exploding the door.

"No, he won't!" Roeglin called from behind the safety of the wall. "He promises."

"Promises what?" Envermet might not know what

Roeglin was saying on his behalf, but he was smart enough to know it *was* on his behalf.

Marsh let Roeglin answer for her.

"Not to have her hide."

"Oh, no, I won't have her hide." Master Envermet paused as though searching for a suitable alternative. What he came up with wasn't much better. "I'm just going to make her sorry she was ever born."

There was a soft grunt, as though the shadow captain had just copped an elbow to the ribs, and Marsh felt laughter bubble out of her at the thought of the look on Roeglin's face.

Whatever makes you happy, he muttered. Out loud he asked, "Are they gone yet?"

Marsh opened her eyes and looked at the ceiling. The shadow still hung above her, but it was less restless, and the lightning didn't flicker as often in its depths.

"All safe," she told it, giving Roeglin's question the attention it deserved, "and I have tasks to complete. Thank you for your protection."

She waited, watching the cloud and wondering how she had managed to call so much so fast. She also wondered how she'd managed to get lightning to come when she couldn't call enough energy to light a glow, and she wasn't under any threat.

Maybe you need to think of the light as lightning? Roeglin suggested, then added, *Is it gone yet?*

Marsh looked up, but the cloud was still there. It was no longer a seething mass, but more a sheet of rolling dark.

As she was wondering exactly what she'd have to do to

get it to go away, another voice interrupted, "Are you done yet? Cos we're starving out here!"

Marsh rolled her eyes. Trust Henri to whine the loudest.

"You wanna come through the door and see?"

"You mean the one that's not on its hinges anymore?" He filled the empty doorframe. "Why don't you give it your best shot?"

Marsh laughed, scattering the shadows with a wave of her fingers as she stalked over to tap the big guard on the chest with her forefinger.

"Couldn't skewer you with lightning, Henri. Lennie would have my hide, and I'm partial to it being attached."

"Shouldn't piss the captain off so bad, then," he retorted, pushing her hand back to her chest before stepping around her and heading for the eatery.

Marsh figured the man might have a point, but Master Envermet was standing right next to the open doorway, and she wasn't going to give him the satisfaction of hearing her say so. Instead, she kept walking, heading back to the latrines and the scrubbing brush she'd discarded to give Aisha a hug.

She finished late and was up early, remembering her punishment from the night before and skipping breakfast to help muck out the mules, clean the latrines, and join the foraging team. She was swinging a shadow scythe with brutal efficiency when Roeglin tapped her on the shoulder. It was no surprise to see Captain Envermet at his side.

Marsh turned, releasing the scythe to the darkness.

"We leave in an hour," Roeglin told her. "You need to get ready."

Marsh glanced past him at the shadow captain.

"You're released from duty," he said, and moved on to speak to the forage team's leader.

Marsh fell into step beside Roeglin.

"So, how much shit am I still in?" she asked, and he glanced around to make sure no one was nearby.

"Nowhere near as much as you should be. Captain had to make a point to keep discipline. You were dumb enough to force his hand."

Marsh thought about that and shrugged. Man had a point. She *had* kinda earned the captain's wrath. It was a thought that Roeglin didn't let go past without comment.

"Yuh think?"

Marsh decided not to dignify that with an answer.

"So, what's for lunch?"

"Nothing. You're skipping a meal for Aysh, remember?"

Marsh groaned. *Now* she remembered.

"Forgot. I'll go saddle the mules."

Roeglin shook his head.

"No mules to spare. We're walking the rest of the way. Your pack's waiting by the gates."

"Thought you said I had an hour to prepare?"

"Do you need it?"

Marsh thought about that. There really wasn't any point in taking a bath; she'd be covered in sweat inside a mile.

"Not really."

"See? We can get an early start out the gate. Shadow Captain *will* be pleased."

The shadow captain snorted as he hurried past, and Marsh smirked.

"It will take more than that to keep *him* happy."

If Master Envermet heard her, he didn't react, his pace not slowing as he passed into the waystation. Marsh thought about that for another five steps, then remembered something else.

"I need to say goodbye to the children."

They were approaching the gates as she spoke, and she started as Tamlin stepped out of the shelter of the gatehouse.

"Glad to hear you say that," he said, turning to his sister. "You owe me a cookie."

He held out a hand, and Aisha shot Marsh a dark look as she handed over his prize. Marsh watched them open-mouthed. She glanced at Aisha.

"You bet that I'd leave without saying goodbye?"

The child nodded, her blue eyes dark with sadness.

"Since when have I ever?"

Aisha sidled closer to Brigitte.

"Up," she said, patting the journeyman's hip.

"Nuh-uh," Brigitte told her. "You go say goodbye to Marsh, first. And say sorry, since you were mean."

The child sighed as though Brigitte was asking the impossible, but she came over and looked up at Marsh, her expression unreadable. In the end, Marsh broke the silence that stretched between them.

"I'm sorry, too. I gotta go, kiddo. You be good for Tamlin and Brigitte, okay?"

"'Kay."

They stood there staring at each other until Marsh could think of only one thing that might break the tension.

"You want another hug?"

Aisha raised her arms, nodding solemnly, and Marsh lifted her from the ground, hugging her tight. When they drew apart, Marsh looked into the child's eyes.

"You think I should hug Tamlin too?"

Again Aisha gave her a solemn nod, and Marsh raised her eyebrows before replying in a mock whisper, "But he's a boy. D'you think he'll mind?"

"Deeps, no," Tamlin said, wrapping his arms around her waist. "*He* doesn't mind, but he doesn't want to see his guardian get her tail kicked again, and he hates goodbyes, so can we kinda get this over and done with?"

Marsh had pulled him to her side, but now she drew back.

"Wow, boy. You sure know how to make a guardian feel wanted!"

She watched him blush and waited until he'd started to stutter an apology before she let him off the hook.

"Kidding, child. Take care of your sister, and do as Brigitte says. Okay?"

"Sure thing, Marsh," he said and turned back to the gate. He'd almost reached Brigitte's side when he added, "We won't do anything *you* wouldn't do."

"Hey!"

Roeglin grabbed her arm before she could go after him. "Little rat's pulling your chain," Roeglin told her, "and we need to go."

On hearing his words, Brigitte came over and took Aisha out of Marsh's arms, disentangling the child's hands when she clung more tightly.

"See you in Kerrenin's Ledge," she said, giving Marsh a

brief hug. "Don't go digging up any more shadow monsters. That last lot was more than enough."

"No chance of that." Master Envermet had returned. "That last battle drew in pretty much everything that was left."

He caught Marsh and Roeglin's looks of disbelief and shrugged.

"I had the scouts check. Looks like you drew every single creature within howling distance, which means halfway to Kerrenin's."

"So, there *is* a chance of us running into more of them, then," Marsh said, thinking his guestimate left a lot of ground uncovered.

Envermet shrugged.

"They don't like being that close to the surface. You *might* run into another raiding band, but the number of raiders we killed here means it's unlikely. This was a pretty major outpost, and with the tunnels sealed, they'll have trouble taking it back." His lips thinned. "We're going to make sure of that."

"Were there any survivors?" Marsh asked. Judging by the expression on Envermet's face, it was a question he'd been hoping she wouldn't ask.

A sudden shuffle of feet by the waystation's gates signaled that Brigitte was taking her leave with the children. Marsh had time for one quick wave goodbye, then they were gone. Master Envermet watched them go and caught Roeglin's eye.

"This way," he said, and looked over at where the shadow guards and ex-caravan guards were standing clustered in one spot. "Wait here; this won't take long."

Marsh's stomach gave an uneasy flip and swallowed against a vague feeling of nausea. She had a feeling the next few moments were going to be—

Difficult, Roeglin finished for her. *They're going to be difficult, but you'd have had to deal with it sooner or later. It might as well be now.*

And *there* was something she hadn't wanted to know.

"Fine," she murmured. "Let's get it done."

"Getting it done" was a fair description.

A large pit had been dug at the back of the waystation, and a small contingent of shadow guards and Protectors were stacking bodies in it.

"We killed the survivors," Master Envermet told her.

Ignoring her look of horrified disbelief, Master Envermet rounded the next corner. As he did, a bolt of darkness shot out of the shadows, followed by a shape in the dark leather armor both raiders and Protectors wore, but without the colored rings adorning the Protectors' chests.

If Roeglin had been moving a step faster or Master Envermet slower, one of them would have died. As it was, Master Envermet barely got a hastily-called shadow shield between him and his assailant. Shadows hissed as the raider's blade slid against the shield, and then the man was past and swinging at Marsh.

She took a step back, pulling her own blade from the shadows and sweeping a foot across the raider's ankles. He went to his knees, and Marsh hefted a boot into his gut. He grunted but scrambled to his feet, coming around to face her while stepping clear of the shadow captain.

"You look too tasty to be running with the likes of these," he taunted, and Marsh flashed him a grin.

"You'd be surprised what I had to do to get these scaredy-boys this far up the tunnel."

He gave a bark of laughter, and Marsh realized she'd used the wrong words, something he confirmed.

"Girl like you? I bet I wouldn't be surprised at anything you did, or just how far any man would go to get it."

It was almost enough to make her try to take off his head, but Marsh wanted something else.

"What are you still doing here?" she asked. "Not ready to run home to Mama?"

He sneered.

"Girlie, *none* of us want to run home to *her*. If we do, we die, but not before she kills our families, burns our homes, and murders anything else she thinks we have a fondness for. She's less a mama than a right mother, and for all the wrong reasons."

He lunged forward. Marsh parried his blade and decided to try something else.

"Why not join us and help us make a house call? We could solve all your parental problems."

He gave a bitter laugh.

"You're a bit slow, sweetie. My wife and kids get to live even if I don't. If I take you back that's not guaranteed."

He lunged again, and Marsh didn't hesitate. She parried, stepped, and countered with a strike that gutted him in one fell swoop. As he fell, she brought her blade around and down and took him in the neck. He dropped lifeless at her feet.

"Damn," she said and turned to the shadow captain. "Is this tour done?"

Envermet nodded.

"We took no prisoners."

Roeglin cleared his throat, and the captain rolled his eyes.

"Fine. There were wounded, and we killed them. We don't have the manpower to guard them and hold the waystation, and we can't afford to let them roam."

Marsh looked down at the body of the man at her feet and nudged him with the toe of her boot. The waste of it crashed through her.

"He was protecting his family," she said, sadness welling up inside her. "That's probably all that the rest of them were doing too. How many were there?"

Master Envermet's voice was solemn as he replied.

"We've counted two hundred and fifty-three."

He looked down at their attacker.

"Two hundred and fifty-four."

The number struck Marsh hard. They'd been husbands, fathers, sons... She looked past the shadow captain to where his men had resumed burying their foes. Dashing away sudden tears, she turned to Envermet.

"I'm sorry, Captain. This is stupid."

To her surprise, he reached out and laid a hand on her shoulder. His face held an indefinable sadness as he looked into her eyes.

"Marchant Leclerc," he said, "it is *never* wrong to mourn the loss of a life or the lost potential for that life to have been used for other, better things—and even the best of men will betray their values to keep their families safe. We can only try to make it so they don't have to. Yes?"

He shook her, and Marsh nodded.

"Good," he said, straightening. "Now, go make that happen. You too, Master Leger. *Try* to keep her out of trouble."

The last comment came out in tones touched by pain and Marsh rolled her eyes, schooling her expression to obedience and clearing her throat when she caught him looking at her.

"Yes, Shadow Captain Envermet."

He regarded her for a few heartbeats longer and then turned back to his men.

"Come on," Roeglin said. "We've got a lot of ground to cover today."

He was right, but his comment left Marsh wondering why it felt like they'd already walked for miles.

ARRIVAL AT KERRENIN'S LEDGE

Marchant felt a sense of relief as the path beneath her feet took on a definite upward tilt.

"Almost there," she said, more for her own benefit than for that of those around her.

Most of them would know the path already, especially Henri and Jakob. The Deeps knew how many times those two had made the journey between Kerrenin's Ledge and Ruins Hall.

"Just shift your ass," Roeglin said. "It's blocking the road."

Marsh caught sight of a cluster of brown noses and shoved him toward them, attempting to snake a boot around his ankles as she did so. He grabbed her wrists, dodged her boot, and spun her around himself and toward the knee-high toadstools, instead. Marsh caught herself in a few short strides and turned back up the trail.

They'd taken five days, where the mules would have taken only one, but they'd detoured several times to check on farmsteads or prospector camps on the way. Everything had been abandoned, and they'd overnighted in empty bunkhouses or on deserted cottage floors. It had been better than camping cold along a trail where the cavern creatures had returned to make their homes.

From what Marsh could divine as she scouted, the raiders had kept only a light presence at this level, as though they wished to avoid chance meetings with the folk of the Ledge. Master Envermet had been right—they hadn't encountered a single group of shadow monsters since leaving the waystation. Mid-Point, indeed!

She smiled. The climb ahead was going to be tough, but their journey would end in just a few short hours. It was the reason that the climb into Kerrenin's Ledge had always been the worst and best part of any trip with a merchant caravan. On the one hand, it was Hell on mules and men. On the other, there was hot food, soft beds and warm water at its end. It was no wonder her uncle's waystation, Hawks-Ledge, did so well

He had plumbing…and water-pressure—and he kept a good stock of soaps and towels, selling the services for a good price. He also didn't differentiate between traders, guards or townsfolk. Anyone's coin was good—or trade, if it was something he needed. It was the same for the dining hall.

Her uncle…

Marsh's heart gave a happy skip blended with appre-hension. He hadn't heard from her since she'd left. All he'd have heard was that the road to Ruins Hall was closed, and that shadow monsters roamed the trail. All he'd have had was the hope that she'd made it through before the trail closed—accompanied by the fear that she hadn't.

That was only if *he* was still safe.

Up until that moment, the thought that her uncle was anywhere except safely tucked away in his waystation at Kerrenin's Ledge hadn't crossed her mind. She hastened her steps and then had to pull back as the effort left her breathless. Roeglin wasn't impressed.

Is this a private panic party, or can anyone join in?

Marsh turned her head.

"My uncle..." She paused, not sure how to go on. "I don't even know if he's still there."

He gave her a brief grin.

"That's okay, Marsh. We don't even know if Kerrenin's Ledge is still there—or who runs it if it is. These are just two of the things we have to find out."

His grin had faded almost as fast as it had come.

"We'll head to the station, first." He made a show of sniffing at his underarm and screwed up his face. "This waystation, it *does* have hot water, right?"

"Yeah." Marsh felt some of the tension ease from around her heart. "Hot, running water, and soft beds."

"And food?" Henri asked, his voice almost plaintive. "Real food?"

"And beer," Marsh tossed over her shoulder, and the guards groaned.

"Beer."

"Cold?"

"Except where it needs to be warm."

"Oh, yeah."

Their footsteps firmed, even if their pace stayed the same.

Marsh listened to them following and figured they

must be the smallest caravan to have made the journey from Ruins Hall to the Ledge. Deeps! They were the *only* caravan to have made the journey since raiders had extinguished the glows protecting the paths—and released bands of shadow monsters to roam the road.

The monsters didn't roam it anymore.

Marchant's smile grew wider.

There weren't any left. They'd killed them all—and the teams working behind them had taken out any they'd missed, and then replenished the glows. When she made the return journey, the trail would be the brightest path between the two caverns—and the safest...which meant they brought good news to Kerrenin's Ledge. They could tell the traders it was safe to go back into the deeps.

Of course, they'd have been able to tell them that sooner, if they hadn't lost the mules to the third successive wave of the monsters. And they'd have been a lot faster if they hadn't needed to take refuge at Mid-Point. With shadow monsters trying to break through the outer gates, and shadow raiders trying to get to them from the inside, they'd been in dire straits.

Actually, if the shadow raiders hadn't had to fight the shadow monsters, as well, and, if Master Envermet hadn't caught up with us, we'd have been shadow chow.

Roeglin's voice drifted through her head, and Marsh glanced around.

Roeglin was right. If Master Envermet hadn't caught up with them, they *would* have been monster chow.

"We were lucky," she agreed, speaking aloud so the rest of their companions could join in since it was too easy to get lost in a private conversation. She was about to add more when she caught the first whiff of the surface. It was a blend of warm earth and stone, threaded through with the smell of leaves and grass. Behind her, the guards and mages accompanying them drew deep lungfuls of the air.

"I am never getting tired of that smell," Henri declared, joy and longing lacing his voice.

It surprised Marsh. She would never have picked him as someone who was fond of the surface, given how long he had spent taking caravans beneath. If he missed the surface so much, why…

*That's a story for another time…*Roeglin told her, *but she fell for his brother, and now his brother is gone, and his head is in turmoil.*

Well, that explained Henri's uncertain temper, Marsh thought.

Indeed.

They fell into silence, each of them surveying the tunnel around them, noting which shadows moved, and which did not, and working their way closer to the Ledge. They reached it just as the setting sun bathed its cavern in red and gold light. Even the brightening luminescence of the calla shrooms took on the colors of the sunset, shedding their usual shades of purple and lavender, for blood-tinged reds with hints of gold. The brown noses clustered at the base of their trunks took on shades of caramel and burnt copper, and the other shrooms joined in the festival of color.

The fungi weren't alone, though. Traceries of leaves draped the walls where vines clung to pockets of soil in the rock, and trees cast long shadows from the edges of the tunnel mouth, which was a two-hour walk from the town proper. Only at the end of the day, was the angle right for the sun to stretch its fingers from tunnel entrance to the cavern walls.

Marsh looked past the shrooms clustered around the path ahead of them, seeking the rise of the Kerrenin's Ledge walls. It wasn't until they rounded another curve in the road, descending into a stream-carved gully and climbing to the top of the rise on the other side, that she caught her first glimpse.

There was open space past where the trail wove between a small forest of stalagmites. It was almost shocking after the close feeling of the fungi forest, and Marsh slowed her pace. The rich reds and golds of the sunset had dulled to pink, and then faded through a soft purple light to the grey of twilight. Looking around, Marsh felt her spirits lift at the sight of the shadows growing thicker between the calla and rock formations.

Roeglin came alongside her, and they looked toward the torchlit outline of the gates set in the Kerrenin's Ledge walls.

"That's new," he said, and Marsh had to agree; there had never *been* any gates blocking the archway through the town walls, not in all her years of living there.

Still, she shrugged away his concerns.

"I guess the monsters changed their minds about having an open-door policy."

Gustav stepped away from the other guards. The emissary had spent most of the journey keeping watch at the rear, with Izmay and Zeb. Now he came to stand beside Roeglin and Marsh.

"You think they'll let us in after nightfall?"

Roeglin gave him a startled look.

"Any reason why they wouldn't?"

"Unfriendly things come out in the dark?"

Marsh took his point.

"You're saying we need to hurry."

"Yup."

"Okay."

She looked back at the others.

"We're gonna try to make the gates before they decide they want to keep them closed for the night. You coming?"

Not waiting for their reply, Marsh stepped into the open space before the walls and headed straight for the gate. If she was lucky, there'd be guards on the walls who could see them—and if she was *very* lucky, they'd give the group half a chance to introduce themselves. As she approached, something nagged at the back of her mind, something about their welcome not being assured—and there being a very good reason for it.

She mulled over the thought as she led the others along the glow-less trail. When they reached the gates, she stopped, but the gates remained closed. Marsh studied them.

When last she'd passed through this way, the gates hadn't existed, and the walls had arched over an empty space. She stopped before them, noticing the thick iron bands reinforcing it, and the multitude of nicks and scratches marring its surface. After a long moment, she raised her hand and knocked, but the thick wood absorbed the sound, and she sighed.

Gustav came alongside her.

"May I?"

Marsh gestured toward it.

"Be my guest."

Before she knew what he was doing, Gustav had pulled his sword, reversing it so he could strike the gate with its pommel. This time the sound boomed out, echoing beyond the gate and into the city beyond…or, at least, a small portion of it. Gustav leaned on the wood, resting the pommel of his sword against it so that the blade stuck out above his head.

The hurried scuff of footsteps followed as the echoes died away, and Gustav stepped away from the gate, making sure he was standing in clear view of the walls as he sheathed his sword. Marsh and the others moved back with him, and it was only when they all stood in the circle of light thrown by the torches that they heard the metallic clank and grind of locking bars being lifted.

"Wait," Gustav cautioned, as silence descended and the gates slowly ground open.

It took Marsh a few minutes to see why. Three men worked to push each half-open, and then they ran to the other side and threw themselves against it to stop it from opening fully. And they were not alone.

Beyond them, blocking the entrance were two rows of armored soldiers.

"Looks like the Ledge has got a head start on the founder's idea," Marsh murmured, and Gustav nodded.

"Good," he said. "At least we know they're prepared to defend themselves."

"I know those men," Henri said. "They used to be guards."

"They still *are* guards," Izmay argued, as though she didn't get the point Henri was trying to make.

Sometimes Marsh wished the woman would give the man a break—and then she wondered what the ex-caravan guard had done to deserve the stirring he got.

"*Caravan* guards!" Henri clarified, his voice thick with disgust, just as the front row marched forward.

"*City* guards," their leader corrected. "State your business."

Marsh drew herself to her full height, aware of Gustav and Roeglin doing the same beside her. She'd been about to speak when Roeglin stepped in.

"We are emissaries from Monsieur Gravine, the Founder of Ruins Hall. He seeks an alliance with Kerrenin's Ledge."

The guards' leader stepped forward and tapped the joining circles on Gustav's chest.

"And these? What do they signify?"

"I am Captain Moldrane of the Ruins Deep Protectors, and Monsieur Gravine's formal representative. The four circles represent the four caverns, and our sworn duty to assist in their protection. More than that, we need to discuss with your rulers."

The man studied his armor, the circles, and the weapons that he carried. He then moved on to inspect Marsh and Roeglin, and the men and woman behind them.

"And these?"

"Helped ensure we reached you."

The man snorted, his gray eyes flashing.

"It would take more than these to protect you from what lurks down in *those* tunnels."

"Another matter we will discuss with your council," Gustav broke in, smoothly.

He glanced back at the darkened trail and the now pitch-black forest.

"May we come in, Captain…"

The man's lip curled in an expression of distaste…or possibly it was disgust that he was not the rank Gustav thought he was.

"*Sergeant* Thierry."

"Sergeant," Gustav said, correcting himself.

He made a point of looking around, once more.

"We might have cleared the shadow monsters from the trail, and the raiders holed up in Mid-Point, but the night is still dangerous." He gestured toward the gateway. "With your permission."

The sergeant snapped him a quick glance, and then surveyed the trail and forest behind them.

"You will come with us," he said.

"Agreed," Gustav told him, and the sergeant rejoined his waiting troops and led the way through the gate.

7

DELAYED MEETINGS

Much to Marchant's relief, Sergeant Thierry and his men did not want to put them in cells overnight. Instead, with the gates once more firmly closed and barred behind them, they were taken to a small stone building serving as an office just on the other side of the wall.

Here, their details were recorded, and they were asked to go through to a small waiting room.

"Captain Brodeur will want to speak with you," he said.

He did not add how long the captain would take to see them, and Marsh decided she wouldn't ask unless they were there for a prolonged period of time. In the end, she didn't have to. The good captain arrived scant moments later.

"Good evening," he said, wasting no time coming to the point. "I hear you want to speak with the council. On what matters?"

Gustav regarded him coolly, and then stood and offered his hand.

"I am Captain Gustav Moldrane."

When Brodeur had dutifully taken and shaken his hand, Gustav turned and indicated Marsh and Roeglin. "These are Shadow Masters Leger and Leclerc. We are here to speak to the council regarding an alliance between the Ruins Deep and Kerrenin's Ledge communities, as well as our mutual security."

Brodeur regarded them, caution vying with hope in the dark blue depths of his eyes. He ran a hand through his tousled, dark hair.

"Is that all?" he asked, scanning all of them. "Surely the shadow mages aren't mercenaries for hire. What is their stake in all this?"

"That is a matter we'll be discussing with the council," Gustav told him, smoothly.

Brodeur frowned.

"I'm afraid it isn't. It is my duty to assess the security risks to the town and report to the council. I will need to advise them."

Gustav nodded but refused to back down.

"Then I expect to see you at the meeting," he said, "because these matters are not open for discussion outside of it. Monsieur Gravine insists.

That was news to Marsh, but she kept her surprise from her face, regarding the Captain calmly, when he looked from Gustav to Roeglin to her and then back. After holding Gustav's stare for several long heartbeats, he stepped back from the table.

"I have sent a runner," he said, "but it takes time for the council to convene."

He didn't quite stop the disapproving twist of his lips as he said it, and Marsh figured the council's tardiness at convening must have been a thorn in his side for some time. She tried to keep that realization from her face and stayed silent. The time for speaking would arrive soon enough, and even these small glimpses at the political landscape were of value.

When none of them spoke, Brodeur continued.

"Where were you planning on staying?"

Gustav looked over at Marsh, and she looked up at Brodeur.

"We were going to stay at the local waystation," she said. "Could you direct us?"

The captain's face broke into a smile.

"Leclerc?" he asked. "You think I don't' recognize the name?"

He looked her over carefully.

"Your uncle's been up here every day for weeks, asking if we've had news from Ruins Hall. I think you know very well where your waystation is."

Marsh blushed at being found out, and she shrugged.

"I didn't mean to deceive you," she told him. "I just couldn't be sure it was still there…or that my uncle…" Her voice caught, and a brief hint of sympathy flashed over Brodeur's features.

"I don't know what you might have seen in the depths," he told them, "and I'd like to discuss that with you, if I may?"

His eyes caught Gustav's nod, and he relaxed a little as he hurried to explain.

"We've fended off several raids, hence the gates you came through, but we've lost none of the townsfolk." His eyes took on a worried look. "I don't know how the farms deeper have fared…"

"The farmers are gone," Marsh told him, regretting the bluntness of her words when she saw him flinch. "I'm sorry. That is something else we'll be discussing with the council. I trust you'll be there?"

He nodded, his face looking more drawn than before.

"I asked to take men out," he began, his skin paling. "I…"

His words faltered to a stop, his failure to go against his orders looking like it had affected him more deeply than it should. It didn't take Marsh long to figure out why.

"I'm sorry. Who did you lose?"

Her quiet question caught him off-guard, and he shook his head.

"Not me," he said, "but I promised I'd try…"

He chose a point on the wall opposite, and stared at it, his throat working as he pulled his emotions under control. After a moment, he blinked and looked back at them. Marsh had an idea of how he felt. She'd let people down, too—a whole cavern's worth—when she'd followed the shadows to Leon's Deep, instead of those the raiders had taken from it.

Of course, if she'd followed the raiders, she and the children wouldn't have been able to fight them, as they were doing now. They'd have been bundled up with everyone else the raiders had taken and vanished into Depths. Turning toward Leon's had been the best choice to make, even if she didn't feel it.

It was. Now, pay attention. Roeglin's gentle reminder pulled her from her memories in time to hear Gustav's reply.

"The shadow mages will be going after those that have been taken," he said, and Marsh stared at him.

He caught her look and the one Roeglin shot him and shrugged.

"Some things just have to be said," he explained. "The captain needed to know."

Brodeur moved toward the door, casting Gustav a solemn look.

"I did. Thank you." He paused before he left the room, fixing Marsh with an almost friendly look. "The waystation's where you left it, Leclerc—and your uncle will be happy to see you. I won't spoil the surprise by sending someone ahead to warn him."

He stepped out and then stepped back in again.

"But I *will* send a runner to the station as soon as I have an appointment for you. Did you have any other errands you needed to run?"

Gustav shook his head.

"Beyond finding a place to stay and repairing our equipment, this is our primary task. We've no plans to leave until it is completed."

The captain hesitated and took another step into the room.

"You do have the means to support yourselves?" he asked, looking uncomfortable with the question, but Gustav put his fears at rest.

He unhooked a small pouch at his belt and sat it on the table, the rattle of stones inside it easy to hear. Opening the drawstrings, he removed three of the gems and set them on the table. Brodeur's eyes widened, and he turned back to the door.

"That is good to know," he said. "Thank you."

He vanished around the door, and Sergeant Thierry appeared shortly afterward.

"You can go," he said. "We'll send someone to Hawks Ledge as soon as your appointment is available."

He accompanied them to the door and waved them in the general direction of the station, and then he returned to the gatehouse.

"I wonder how many men they have in their guard force," Gustav murmured, glancing after the man.

Marsh shrugged, adding it to the list of questions they should ask the council. Butterflies fluttered through her gut, their wingbeats turning from discomfort to mild nausea as they drew closer to where Hawks Ledge was situated.

"You okay?" Roeglin asked, and Marsh nodded.

"Just fine."

He tutted.

"Aisha would be disappointed," he told her. "It's not nice to lie."

"Why don't you get the Deeps out of my head, before I *kick* you out of it?"

Roeglin opened his mouth to reply, but Gustav clapped him on the shoulder and shoved him toward the tall, narrow door in the waystation's walls.

"We need to check out the beer," he said, following after. "Marsh will catch us up when she's ready."

As if his words were a signal, Izmay, Gerry, Zeb, Henri, and Jakob followed, leaving Marsh standing on her own on the wooden walkway outside her childhood home. She looked up at the stylized pair of hawks painted above the entrance, took in the broad set of gates the caravans used when they arrived and stared at the door as it closed behind them.

She stood there long after the others' footsteps had faded, but couldn't' bring herself to go inside. Nerves and nausea rolled through her, and she took a step back. At first, she intended to just lean on the wall and stare at the street for a bit, but she knew she didn't have long. Her uncle would be sure to ask where his latest visitors had come from—and, once he discovered they'd traveled from Ruins Hall, he'd ask after her…and then he'd come looking.

Marsh turned away from the door.

She wasn't ready for this. She needed a minute. She wondered if Roeglin was keeping tabs on her mind, or if Gustav was distracting the mage enough to give her some privacy. The thought made her pause, but when the mage made no comment, she figured it was the latter, and she had a bit more time.

Which reminded her…Marsh looked up and down the street and spotted the turn-off for Kearick's. It hadn't gone anywhere, but she was feeling just a little off-center, so it took her a moment to recognize it. As soon as she did, she stepped off the walkway, and trotted across the street, then down a block to the corner.

As she went, Marsh remembered that the trader had sent a seeker after her…with orders to kill her while retrieving the commission she'd been carrying—for an agent of the shadow raiders. Kearick had had all the time he was going to get!

She wondered if he already knew she'd arrived. Now that she was doing something other than facing the thought of meeting her uncle, the memories of working for Kearick were returning. Her boss had always seemed to be well-informed. Was his network still intact, or had it changed with the raiders' attacks?

Marsh glanced up and down the street, both glad for and wary of the glows lighting her way. While they'd reveal anyone waiting in the shadows, they'd show her progress, too, and she had no desire to be an easy target. It didn't take her long to reach the Emporium, and she was surprised to find it closed.

Just after sunset was far too early.

Taking another look up and down the street, Marsh walked over to the entrance and tried the door.

Nope. That is well and truly locked, she thought and tried to peer through the front window. She couldn't see anything in the unlit depths beyond and sighed. She was left with only one option.

Marsh turned and walked back out to the street. A few more steps took her to a narrow alleyway running along the Emporium's side. She took a moment to scan it for life, and then to tweak the shadows to ensure no one was waiting. When the shadows came back empty, she moved quickly from the walkway and into the dark, hurrying to the small set of steps leading up to the landing and side door halfway down the Emporium's side.

That, too, was locked—but it didn't matter; Marsh had a key...of sorts.

Drawing a slender needle of shadow from the dark, she made short work of the lock and slipped inside. When she'd closed the door behind her, Marsh looked around— just in time to see a blade slicing toward her. She leapt forward and felt the impact as the edge lodged in her pack, but she didn't stop moving, stepping back lightly, and pulling a sword from the shadows cloaking the shop's dark interior.

To her surprise, there was no one in the direction the attack had come from. Calling a shield to her arm, Marsh made another turn, carefully surveying the inside of the shop. Still no one, not even when she blended the shadows with her ability to seek out the glow of an existing life force. Once she was sure she was clear, Marsh shrugged off her pack and pulled the blade out of its side.

It was more a spear than a sword, with a short shaft and a broad-bladed head. Studying it, Marsh realized it could be thrown.

"Or launched," she murmured, suddenly understanding why Kearick had always warned her against letting herself in when he didn't expect her. "Kearick, you are such a misbegotten son of the Deep."

It made her look for the nearest glow, taking the cover from the stone so that she could better see what she was doing. Kearick might not be here—and he might not have left anyone behind to guard the Emporium, but he hadn't left it undefended. It made her wonder what he had to hide. Knowing the man, he either planned to return, which meant he had something to return *for*, or he was sending someone to collect what he'd left behind.

She wondered which of his seekers would try to kill her next.

I don't know about seekers, Roeglin sounded furious, *but I might give it a shot!*

Marsh shoved him to one side and decided Kearick's office might be the best place to start.

Don't you da— but Marsh shoved him, again, pushing him out of her mind, as she glared at an innocent bedroll stacked on the shelf beside her.

"Sons of the Deep!" Roeglin cursed, lifting his hand to his head.

Gustav gave him a startled look, and sighed, setting the rich, dark, shroom brew on the counter before him.

"What's she done, this time?"

Roeglin shook his head, indicating the man behind the counter. Introducing himself as Per, Marsh's uncle was a bit taller than most, but his face carried features Roeglin recognized in Marsh: dark grey eyes, narrow build, skin touched by the color of stone…and hair shaded copper and bronze, pulled back into a braid. He finished serving the other small group of customers clustered at the opposite end of the bar and returned.

"Have you traveled far?" he asked, and Roeglin let Gustav answered, trusting the emissary's instincts for people.

"We've spent a week on the road."

Per gave him a quick smile and a shrug that said he'd caught the evasiveness in Gustav's reply, and that it didn't bother him.

"Well, let me know if there's anything you need. A meal, perhaps?"

Roeglin gave him a grateful look and pushed back his chair.

"We'll come back for that. Can you tell me where we can find Kearick's?"

Per frowned, as though the question troubled him, but he answered, nonetheless.

"Sure. Take a right when you're facing the street, and then the first left, but…"

Roeglin didn't wait to hear any more but sprinted for the door.

The others followed him, leaving the station owner momentarily speechless.

"We'll need rooms!" Gustav threw over his shoulder. "We'll be back, soon!"

"Wait!" Per called. "You need…"

He fell silent as Gustav hit the door, heading out across the courtyard toward the street. Frowning, Per debated whether or not to send for the Guards, but then his eye fell on the half-empty glasses lined up along the bar, and the pack Gustav had left on the seat behind him, and he decided to take a chance that they'd be coming back, after all.

As Per reached over to put the pack behind the bar, one of the men's voices drifted back to him.

"Is Marsh in trouble, again?"

Marsh? Per's heart gave a skip of hope; he only knew of one person others called Marsh—and she'd disappeared in the Depths…where the shadow mages came from. Thinking on it, there had been at least one shadow mage in that group. He recalled the dark uniforms worn by the guards. Maybe more…

"Daniel! Take over the bar!"

His son was busy in the kitchens, and he'd complain, but Per knew the boy would manage. Finding Marsh was all that mattered. Per left his cleaning rag on the counter and hurried for the door. If he was quick enough, he could catch them in the street. Ignoring the strange looks from the merchants at the end of the bar, he left.

"Wait!"

But the strangers did not wait, and Per caught sight of them just as they turned down the road leading to Kearick's. Per ran after them.

"Wait!"

It did him no good. They didn't stop until they'd reached the Emporium, and discovered, for themselves, that it was closed. Their leader turned toward him, as he approached.

"How do we get in?"

8

UNDER ARREST

As Marsh stacked documents on Kearick's desk, she heard the sound of wood splintering at the front of the shop.

"What *now?*" she murmured, laying the next lot of papers on the desk and moving to the office door.

"Marsh!"

She recognized that bellow. Marsh released the sword she'd drawn from the shadows, and sighed.

"Here."

She hadn't meant to sound so tired and resentful, and she didn't wait for them to reach her. She turned back to the records box she'd found hidden behind a cabinet in the office, and dragged it across the floor and over to the desk. She was stacking papers back into it when Gustav arrived at the office door.

"You okay, girl?"

"Fine," Marsh told him and was surprised by a shout of joy.

"I'd recognize those sulky tones, anywhere."

The sound of the voice made her freeze, and she shot Gustav a look of pure mortification. The emissary returned her look with an expression that said he wasn't sorry. He shrugged, looking over his shoulder before stepping farther into the office. The move left the doorway clear for the man that came through, and Marsh froze.

Her uncle didn't stop—and he seemed oblivious to her shock.

"Marchant Marie Leclerc!" he exclaimed, and was on her, engulfing her in a hug, before she could react. "I have missed you!"

His words gave Marsh enough impetus to wrap her arms around him and hug him tight.

"Uncle…"

"You're okay," he said. "Thank the Deeps you're okay. I thought…"

His voice faltered.

"I thought the worst."

"I'm sorry."

"Don't be. It's not like you could have sent a message." He drew back, releasing his hug, but sliding his hands to her shoulders and not letting go. "How *did* you get here, anyway? The road is closed."

Whenever her uncle mentioned roads, he was only ever speaking of trade routes, and Marsh knew what he was asking.

"It's not going to be closed for much longer."

"And Kearick?" he asked, letting go of her and gesturing around the office. "What made *him* the first thing you had to see when you came to town?"

Marsh's face hardened, and her uncle stilled. It made

her realize he'd never seen her with that look, before. She ignored his reaction. If she spent more time at the Ledge, he would probably see it again. It would be best if he got used to it sooner, rather than later.

"Kearick's working for the raiders," she said, "and I'm going to stop him."

She watched as some of the joy went out of his expression, and he studied her face.

"You're serious," he said, after a long moment.

"Yeah, she's serious," Roeglin growled, "but she still needs her ass kicked."

He gestured around the office.

"You never think you should ask for permission before you go breaking into the local businesses? I mean, how are you going to explain *this* to the Guard?"

His words were punctuated by the crunch of footsteps over broken boards, and he sighed and rolled his eyes, waving one hand toward the Emporium proper in a 'See?' kind of way. He raised the other hand and held them both at shoulder height as he stepped very carefully out of the doorway and out of sight.

Marsh heard a thump followed by a soft grunt.

"Stay there. The rest of you, come out."

Marsh scowled. Well, she'd be damned if they weren't making all kinds of friends, tonight! She watched as Gustav moved through the door, next, lifting his hands away from his sword as he came in line with the door.

"There are two more," he said.

"Armed?"

"One like me."

"The other?"

"A civilian. Unarmed. Assisting us in our investigations."

"Assisting you? We'll look into that back at headquarters. Next!"

"I'll go," Marsh said when her uncle went to move toward the door. "It was my idea, anyway."

"Your idea?" said the Guard leader, when she appeared at the door, and then he looked at her more closely. "Don't you *work* for Kearick?"

Marsh regarded him with a stony expression.

"I *used* to work for Kearick—and then he sent an assassin after me when I didn't make a delivery after being attacked by shadow monsters on the road. Now, I'm trying to see what his *other* links to the shadow raiders are."

As a way of putting the joffra in the hen-house, it worked as though she'd released an entire pack.

"You're under arrest."

"Figured."

Marsh let them take her sword and dagger, noting that they'd already taken the weapons from Gustav and Roeglin. As they used a rope to bind her hands, she wondered what had happened to Henri, Jakob and the rest —and then she noticed that her uncle hadn't come through the office door, which only made her wonder why.

One of the guards stepped over and looked into the office.

"I thought you said there was a civilian…" he said, and Gustav didn't try to hide his surprise.

"Did I?"

The man tying Marsh's hands gave the bindings one final jerk and looked over at him.

"You know you did," he snarled, but Gustav gave him a confused look.

"Are you sure?"

The guardsman turned to Roeglin.

"You!"

Roeglin jumped.

"Was there anyone else in the office?"

Roeglin frowned, and then shook his head.

"Marsh rifling through documents found in a hidden compartment, Gustav and me telling her she should have asked for permission. No…no, that seems to be about all of us."

All of them? Marsh frowned. What had happened to everyone else?

Not sure, Roeglin said, but they're not here, and these guys aren't looking for them, so they might have got away clean. We'll catch up with them, later.

The guard leader gave them all an exasperated look and then went to check the office for himself. He returned empty-handed and looking slightly baffled, but made no farther comment.

"Bring them," he ordered the three other men, who had arrived with him.

Roeglin and Gustav pushed off the wall, and let themselves be manhandled into a line with Marsh at the back.

Personally, I'd be putting you at the front, where I could keep a better eye on you, Roeglin said. Troublemaker.

They ended up hands free but without their weapons in the same meeting room they'd met Captain Brodeur in before. This time he wasn't impressed.

"What am I supposed to do with you?" he asked. "You

broke down a door and rifled through a merchant's private records—a *respected* merchant's private records."

"Did you secure the records?" Marsh asked. "Because they're all we've got to take us to whoever his contacts were."

Brodeur sighed.

"No. By the time the Guard got back, the chest you claimed to have pulled from the wall was gone. We have no way of telling who took it, or where they are, now."

He paused.

"Your companions were found drinking at the Hawks Ledge Bar…and the station master swears they were there all night. You don't have anything to say about that, do you?"

Marsh shrugged and kicked back so that she was balancing her chair on two legs. Gustav and Roeglin exchanged looks and slouched in their seats. Brodeur surveyed them with a look of disgust, and then he tried a different tack.

"You want to tell me why you think Kearick was working with the shadow raiders?" he asked.

"Okay," Marsh said, but Roeglin interrupted.

"Why don't I just pull the memories from your head so he can judge for himself?"

Marsh closed her mouth on what she'd been about to say. She looked over at the guardsman.

"What do you think, Captain? Is memory acceptable?"

From the look on his face, he hadn't even known it was possible.

"Captain?" Roeglin pushed.

The man blinked.

"You can do that?"

"Yes," Roeglin replied, and his eyes flashed white, "just as I can see that you're worried for your sister and her daughter."

Captain Brodeur froze, and then a look of complete sadness swept over his face, and he cleared his throat.

"How…How do you know that?"

"Because I am a mind mage, as well as a master of shadows."

He pulled a ball of darkness from the corners of the room to prove his point, and then let it go.

"What do you think?" he pressed, then added, pointing at Marsh. "Are her memories acceptable?"

The captain hesitated, and then he pursed his lips and nodded.

"Show me."

Roeglin pushed back his chair and walked to an open space in front of the tables.

"Marsh?"

Marsh followed him into the space and then closed her eyes.

"Go ahead." She didn't need to see Mikel searching her room again, or the scorn in his eyes as he explained why Ruins Hall was going to fall and that the monastery was next.

It was bad enough hearing his words repeated in Roeglin's voice. Marsh listened as the battle in her room was played out, and then as her conversation with Mikel was relived. When he was done, Roeglin squeezed her shoulder.

"You can open your eyes now," he told her, before returning to his seat.

Marsh returned to her own chair, avoiding the captain's gaze. He, for his part, remained silent as she returned, and then he stayed quiet for a little longer. When he did speak, it was to ask one question.

"Can you do that again?"

Roeglin sighed and looked over at Marsh.

"I can, but only once more tonight. Why?"

"Because I want to show my sergeants, and…someone else."

Someone else, hey? And he didn't want to name them. Marsh was curious, but she managed to keep her tongue.

"Wait here."

Like they had an option, but Roeglin disagreed.

"We could insist on being released, given the captain knows we're telling the truth," he said, and Brodeur gave him a short, bleak smile.

"And I could tell my men I didn't believe a word you said, and that your magic was a way of deceiving the mind into believing something that wasn't real."

"Ouch," Gustav muttered.

Roeglin stared, dumbfounded, his eyes going momentarily white as he looked into the captain's mind.

"You really would."

He looked shocked. Brodeur's smile broadened, and Roeglin sighed.

"Fine. We'll wait."

Marsh wasn't sure when she'd ever seen him looking so disillusioned.

I thought we could trust him.

Studying Brodeur's face, Marsh thought they still could, but she decided to push the man, anyway.

"How do we know you won't do that, anyway?" she asked, and he turned a regretful look toward her.

"I do what I must to ensure our security," he said, "and I have others who need to see what I have seen." His face hardened, and he added, "and what you did from the time you entered the Emporium."

Marsh stilled.

"You're sure?"

The captain turned away, and his next words did not give her the answer she was looking for.

"You will wait here."

This time, when he turned to leave, none of them said a word. Gustav slid further down in his chair and closed his eyes. Roeglin leaned forward and rested his chin on his hands, staring at the wall. Marsh watched his eyes sheen white and knew he was exploring the other minds in the headquarters. She wanted to ask him if he had the energy to do that but decided not to disturb him. Closing her own eyes, she followed Gustav's example and tried to catch some sleep while she could.

The sound of the meeting room door opening woke her from a light sleep sometime later, and she was half out of her seat, reaching for a sword that wasn't there as she turned to face the newcomers before her eyes were fully opened. Her sudden rush of movement made Captain Brodeur pause at the door.

"We're sorry to startle you, shadow mage," he said, sounding anything but, and Marsh felt her skin heat from throat to hairline.

"Not at all, Captain," she managed before resuming her seat and looking to Gustav and Roeglin.

The fact they were still sitting and watching her with amusement didn't make her feel the slightest bit better, and she had to resist the urge to flip them off.

Let's just say we're both glad you don't have a sword and didn't think to call one, Roeglin said, but his eyes were studying the people slowly filing into the room.

Marsh decided he didn't need an answer and turned to see who Captain Brodeur had wanted badly enough to see her memories, that he'd risked their trust. The senior members of the Guard were easy enough to pick out; they were the ones wearing the dark blue and grey cloth of the Guard's uniform, the bronze triple 'V' of their rank easy to see on their shoulders and hearts. The two strangers who followed them were of more interest.

The first wore a rich copper cloak over a simply cut tunic and trousers. Her boots were sturdy but expensive, their leather gleaming with care, and her gloves more suited to a falconer than a woman of wealth. Her dark hair was drawn back in a French plait, and her dark eyes seemed to absorb the light from the lanterns on the wall, as they swept over Marsh and her companions.

Marsh tried to meet them, but the woman did not stop. She made her way across the room and drew out a seat opposite the door. The man that followed took two steps into the room, and his gaze rested on Marsh. Before she had time to react, he'd done a quick about-face and left, the sound of his running footsteps almost drowned out by Gustav's roar of fury, and Roeglin's shout of alarm.

"Stop him!"

Marsh was moving before the captain or any of his sergeants had time to respond. She'd reached the door before the first of them thought to push back his chair. Shouting erupted behind her in a confusion of orders and conflicting demands.

"Sit down!"

"Come back!"

"After him!"

"Don't move!"

"Stay where you are!"

"Don't let him get away!"

She ignored them all, putting everything she had into trying to catch the figure fleeing down the corridor. The man was racing toward the main entrance, the leather soles of his boots slamming against the stone floor. Marsh didn't bother calling after him. If she'd done what he'd done, she wouldn't have stopped either.

The last time she'd seen him, she'd been wearing a collar and lead, and he'd walked past her joking with another guard that she hadn't suspected a thing. Shortly after that, they'd brought Mordanlenoowar in, bound to two poles, but thankfully still alive.

Dan! she called, as the raider-in-disguise reached the door and made it into the night before her—and then she realized she'd forgotten the kat when they'd arrived. A roar came from beyond the gates, and the raider hesitated; it seemed he remembered Mordanlenoowar, as well.

Marsh did not pause. She kept running, closing the distance between them, until he made up his mind and took to his heels, once more. This time, she angled away from the gates leading out to the road to Ruins Hall. The door slammed behind her, and a myriad of boot steps chased her across the road.

"You! Stop!" came the order, but Marsh ignored it.

She was gaining on the man. He put on a burst of speed, and then slid to an abrupt halt, as a guard patrol rounded a corner in the street in front of him. Marsh heard his bitter bark of laughter as he turned.

"Should have known you'd be the death of me."

Death wasn't what Marsh had planned for him, not yet, but she wasn't about to tell him that.

"Give it up," she said. "You've done enough."

He sneered at her, stalking forward and pulling his sword as he came.

"Little girl, I've not done nearly enough." He came within strike range and lunged. "You're still alive, for a start."

Behind her, the boot steps rattled to a stop, but Marsh didn't look back. She took two hurried steps back, and dodged to one side, pulling her own blade from the dark.

Getting slow.

Marsh didn't have time for Roeglin's comments. She'd been so busy staring, she'd let her opponent get too close—and she could kick herself for that, later. Right now, she was going to try and bring him down.

Kill him, Roeglin argued, *and watch his sword. I don't think you can pull shadow poison out of yourself, can you?*

It was an interesting question and almost made Marsh miss the next strike.

Pay attention!

As if she needed to hear it!

You're overdue for a training session.

"Kinda busy right now, Ro. You wanna scold me later?"

"Name's not Ro, girlie, and I've more than a scolding in mind."

Marsh parried that strike, calling the shadows to her arm in time to catch the next one on her shield. Turning, she pushed the blade aside and brought her own forward in a hard, sweeping blow that caught her opponent across the chest.

"Shadow's Bitch!"

"Not. Polite," Marsh snapped back, following that strike with two more, only one of which he blocked.

The second one hit just below the sternum and sank deep. Tired of the battle, and knowing he wouldn't answer any questions, Marsh directed the shadows in her blade to scatter in shards, turning away from him empty handed as he screamed and dropped.

A gasp of horror from the patrol behind her made her turn, and she was in time to see pieces of shadow free themselves from his chest and stomach.

"Go in peace," she told them, willing them back to the dark, "and thank you for your protection."

She waited as the shadow faded, knowing it drifted back to the cavern ceiling and the deeper patches of darkness that dwelt between the buildings. When it was gone, she headed toward the gate, stopping only when one of the sergeants laid his hand on her arm. She looked down at it, and then lifted her gaze to his face.

"You want to remove that," she said, and it wasn't a suggestion. From outside the walls, came the screech of an angry kat. "I need to deal with her."

The man lifted his hand away.

"It's been stalking the walls since dusk," he said, and Marsh nodded.

"I know."

She didn't bother to explain but hurried toward the walls. When she reached the gatehouse, it didn't take her long to work out that she was going to need some help.

Hold on, Mordan. I am coming.

"Someone help me with the gates."

Every single one of the sergeants moved forward, pushing the gates apart, and then slowing them so they didn't open too wide. Left to walk through the narrow space, Marsh hoped no one followed.

When she'd gone several paces forward, she stopped.

"Mordanlenoowar!" she called, reaching out to find the kat's life force in the cavern beyond "Come!"

Behind her, she was aware of the soft murmurs of uncertainty that rippled through the men behind her. Their voices were accompanied by the nervous shuffle of feet, and Marsh hoped none of them had thought they'd need a crossbow.

You're good, Roeglin reassured her, *but you might want to hurry.*

Okay, then.

"Dan! Where are you, girl?"

Hopefully, the knuckleheads by the gate would understand she was calling the kat. Marsh scanned the calla and vegetation that surrounded them. Her eyes traced their way over a cluster of rocks that she couldn't see past, and she scanned her surroundings, again.

There really wasn't anything else the kat could be hiding behind. Marsh started walking toward it, searching the shadows nearby for what might lie in the outcrop's shadow. One thread connected her to an image of Mordan waiting cautiously in the dark, just out of reach of the torches at the gates.

"Dan?" Marsh asked, approaching slowly, and sending thoughts of concern and calm. "Are you all right?"

Relief washed over her, the kat coming into her mind and rubbing itself along the inside of her head in an unprecedented display of joy and affection.

"Are you hurt?"

Again Marsh sent thoughts of concern for the kat's well-being.

The kat stood, stretched and shook itself from nose to tail, shaking out each leg and paw separately. She was fine, but the humans by the gate did not understand that she was a friend, and she would need her pride around her if she was to pass through the human herd safely.

Marsh knelt and wrapped her arms around the kat's neck, picturing them walking side by side through two ranks of Guards lined up at the gates.

It almost happened that way.

Marsh and Mordan emerged from the shadows, and the men at the gates reached for their swords. Mordan stopped, and looked up at Marsh, sending a thread of uncertainty through their link.

Would the humans trust Marsh enough to not attack?

"I will protect you," Marsh told the kat, reinforcing her words with the idea that she would cover Mordan with shadows strong enough to stop arrows and swords.

The big animal bunted her head against Marsh's thigh, and together, they stepped forward once again. Unease swept through the waiting sergeants, and Marsh stopped in front of the gates.

"This," she declared, "is Mordanlenoowar. I have promised her safe passage in the town, as well as my assistance in retrieving her cubs from the shadow raiders. You will not harm her."

"Will she harm us?"

"Not unless someone tries to hurt her—and if someone does that, you'd better hope the kat gets to you before I do."

So saying, Marsh rested her hand between the hoshkat's shoulder blades and walked forward. As they approached the gates, some of the men and women nearest them tensed, and others shuffled back, but not a single one of them reached for their weapons. Even so, Marsh didn't relax until they'd made it back to the meeting room at the Guards' headquarters.

"I'm sorry I took so long," she said, walking in with Mordan at her side. "I had to fetch a friend."

The lady in the copper cloak shifted in her seat, leaning forward to get a better look at Mordanlenoowar, and then looked up at Marsh.

"I hear you have proof that Kearick was involved with the raiders," she said, continuing before Marsh could do more than nod. "I take it you also have proof as to why Asher had to die…"

"He was one of the guards on the slave caravan I was taken by," Marsh told her, and watched the woman's eyes widen in surprise, and then it was her turn to continue before the woman could interrupt. "Roeglin can show you that memory as well if you like."

She watched the woman while she waited and saw it

when she decided she had to see the memory, rather than just accept Marsh's word for it.

"Yes, please."

Marsh didn't bother returning to her seat, she just moved to the open space Roeglin had chosen before and waited for the shadow mage to join her. She was glad when Mordanlenoowar settled beside her, sitting so that Marsh could keep her hand on the kat's head. Together they watched as the sergeants filed back into the room. They were still observing the others as Roeglin arrived beside them.

"Let's get this done."

Once again, she chose not to watch the replay of Mikel's betrayal. This time, she found she wished she could block Roeglin's voice from her ears, but she couldn't, and had to endure hearing Mikel's hateful promise in Roeglin's tones. When he revealed the memory of Gravine as a guard, the kat had apparently had enough.

No sooner had he repeated the man's words, than Mordan had brought her paw down on the images of mist and shadow, scattering both with the impact. Laughter spluttered through the audience, and Roeglin sighed.

"Was that satisfactory?" he asked, "Or do I need to play that last memory, again."

This time, Mordan hissed, drawing more laughter from their audience.

"No," the copper-haired woman told him, her face and voice serious. "I have seen enough."

She turned to the captain.

"I'd like to see the documents from Kearick's office, just as soon as they can be retrieved."

As she said it, her eyes slid toward Roeglin and Marsh, and then back to Brodeur.

"And I'd like to speak with the shadow mages and their entourage, at their earliest convenience. I will send word with an appointment."

So saying, she rose to her feet and glided gracefully from the room. As if her departure was a signal, the sergeants also stood, and Captain Brodeur dismissed them, before turning to Gustav.

"You're free to go," he said. "We will send for you, tomorrow."

9

HOMECOMING

The journey back to the waystation seemed to take longer than before, and Marsh guessed that it was because it was late, and they were walking slower.

"And we're tired," Roeglin told her, his voice laced with exhaustion.

"And we haven't had dinner, yet," Gustav added. "Do you think your uncle will have saved us some?"

Marsh's stomach rumbled.

"By the Deeps, I hope so."

They kept going, too tired to speak, and too tired to do more than glance down the street that led to Kearick's Emporium. When they arrived at the waystation, Per was waiting for them. He hesitated when he saw the hoshkat, and then walked up and wrapped Marsh in his arms. The kat snarled, and he froze, turning his head to look at the beast.

"Would you like a hug, kat?"

Alarm surged through Marsh as he released her, and knelt in front of Mordan.

Don't hurt him! she begged, too afraid to move in case she startle the kat into doing something they would both regret. *He is pride!*

By then, Per had placed a hand on the kat's neck and looked into her eyes. Marsh watched in amazement as his grey eyes changed to green. After a minute, Mordan bunted him with her forehead, and he straightened, running his hand through her fur as he got to his feet.

"Mordan," he said, and then caught the look on Marsh's face, and smiled.

"I'm not stupid, girl. I asked her permission, first. She likes you, something about you being pride." He frowned and looked over at Gustav and Roeglin. "Along with these two."

The kat grumbled softly to herself, and moved to the door, nudging it with her nose.

"And me, apparently," Per added, "and, since this is my home, I am responsible for the food."

Mordan's tail lashed from side to side, and Marsh felt the depth of her hunger. Per, too, it seemed, for he laughed, pushing past her to open the door and lead them back to the building that served as both bar and mess hall.

The fact he could speak with animals stunned her, but the kat needed feeding, and there was no time to learn more. Marsh looked around the room. It was good to see the rest of their friends sitting around a table in the corner, even if they recoiled when they approached.

"What?" Marsh asked, puzzled by their reaction.

Izmay was the first to reply, and she did so while holding one hand in front of her face and waving the other before her.

"No offense," she said, "but the three of you stink like you've been traveling and haven't had a bath in days."

Marsh looked at Zeb, and he leaned back from her.

"Don't look at me," he said. "I didn't say anything."

"But you *do* stink," Gerry added.

"It's enough to put a man off his food," Henri chimed in, Jakob nodding sagely alongside.

Marsh looked at Roeglin and Gustav.

"I think they're telling us we need a bath," she said, and Mordan gave a series of sneezes.

Marsh stared at her in disbelief.

"Not you, too!"

The big kat blinked, swishing her tail slowly from side to side, and Gustav sighed.

"Let's go," he said. "I'm not saying they're right, but we'll never hear the end of it if we don't."

"Anything to shut them up," Roeglin added, managing to sound put upon, as well as tired.

Jakob was quick to pick up what he'd said.

"Anything?"

"No!" came as a chorus from the three of them, but they turned away from the table and followed Per's finger when he pointed to the back of the dining room.

Marsh had only meant to take a short bath, just enough to wash the dirt off her skin, but the minute she slid into the hot, soapy water that plan went out the window. She might have felt guilty about that, except she heard twin groans of pleasure from the adjoining cubicles, and knew neither Gustav nor Roeglin were in a hurry.

Hurry? By the Deeps, no. I could lie here forever.

Roeglin's reply made her smile, and Marsh sat still for

many long minutes before she could make herself move enough to thoroughly wash her hair and skin, and then she sank back against the side of the tub, slipping low enough for the water to lap around her chin. It might have been an hour or a half-hour before Per woke her; she didn't know, and she didn't care. At least the water was still lukewarm.

"Dinner's getting cold, and Henri's threatening to eat the table," Per said. "Much as I'm tempted to let him, the carpenter takes weeks to make a new one, and with the station so busy…"

Marsh laughed.

"Busy? You telling me you're getting a flood of caravans from Dimanche and the surface?"

Per laughed, but his smile quickly died away.

"No, girl. The caravans have been less over the season, and that's not because the roads to Ariella's and Ruins Hall have been cut. I've seen fewer surface traders this season than any other, and just when they'd started to come regularly. There's something else wrong. Are you going to fix that too?"

"Only if you don't let Gustav and Roeglin drown in their tubs."

Per got up and moved away.

"I'll try not to."

He indicated a gown hanging by the door.

"This was one of your favorites," he said. "That is, when we could get you to wear a dress."

Marsh followed the direction of his pointing finger and smiled.

"It'll do nicely," she said, eyeing the simple garment of dark-blue wool. "Thank you."

He nodded and left her to get out of the water and change, pulling a curtain across the cubicle doorway as he did. Marsh was relieved to find a towel sitting on a simple wooden stool beside the tub—and a spiky hairbrush as well. By the time she was ready, the boys were dressed and waiting.

"Took you long enough," Roeglin managed after one stunned look at her.

Marsh smirked and indicated the dress.

"These things take a long time to get into."

The look that crossed his face said the wait was worth it, and Gustav sputtered with half-suppressed laughter.

"What?" Marsh demanded, but the emissary waved her away and hooked his hand under Roeglin's arm, turning the shadow mage around and guiding him back out to where their meals were waiting.

Zeb whistled when he saw them, his eyes stopping when he caught sight of Marsh.

"Why, thank you," Gustav said, striking a pose with Roeglin and taking the attention off her.

Marsh felt her face flush red and regretted not demanding her usual uniform of trousers and a tunic, but Izmay patted the seat beside her, and she hurried over to join her.

"You don't have another one of those floating about, do you?" the guard asked.

She looked down at her own fresh uniform.

"It would be nice to get out of this for a bit."

"Keep it fresh, too," Gustav said, overhearing her as he joined them. "We'll buy clothes tomorrow."

"Before or after the council decides to meet with us?"

Gustav didn't hesitate.

"First thing. We need to dress to impress."

"What, our uniforms aren't enough?"

"Your armor needs repair, and your clothes won't be laundered in time to be presentable. I'm sure Per can recommend somewhere."

"I can do one better," Per said, bringing over a pitcher of beer and refilling their glasses. "I'll have the tailor come here."

He glanced over at where Mordan was stretched out in front of the fire chewing on a haunch of mouton.

"Be better for the kat."

Mordan raised her head, a strip of meat hanging from the side of her mouth. Marsh laughed, and the kat gave a disgruntled rumble and returned to her meal, but not before letting Marsh know she approved of their newest pride member.

He hunts well.

The thought brought a smile to Marsh's lips, but only for the time it took her to raise the first spoonful of thick meat stew to her mouth. After that, all thoughts of conversation vanished. She might have been embarrassed all over again if everyone else at the table hadn't been equally silent and focused on their food.

Per oversaw their meal with the speed and efficiency of an experienced waiter, keeping their glasses full and bringing a course of hastily fried potatoes mixed with bacon and topped with something green that gave the dish a little bite. This was met with murmurs of appreciation, contented crunching, and very little else.

It was the dessert that brought on groans of pure

delight. Smooth, creamy, and with just a hint of citrus, it was the perfect end to the meal.

"Thank you, Per," Marsh said as Gustav pulled out his bag of gems.

Before he could open the drawstring, however, Per folded his hand over the top of Gustav's fingers.

"Your trade's no good here," he said and looked sternly around the table. "And that goes for the rest of you. No one at this table has anything I want beyond what you have already given."

He indicated Marsh.

"My daughter/niece's safe return. Thank you."

Marsh felt her eyes fill with tears and ducked her head, but her uncle hadn't finished with them.

"Your rooms are upstairs. I will wake you when the tailor arrives in the morning. If you will follow Daniel, he will guide you."

Marsh waited as the others rose from their seats and followed Daniel from the room. She hadn't known he'd been there, and now she wondered why he hadn't come to greet her. She was about to ask when she realized she wasn't alone. Roeglin and Gustav were waiting right beside her, and they seemed to have read her mind.

"You never did say how you got out of Kearick's office," Gustav said as Roeglin's eyes sheeted white.

Per smiled, his gray eyes alight with laughter.

"Your Henri came in through a passage beneath the desk. Seems he'd done enough guard work for Kearick that he was moved up as a reserve for the man's protection detail."

Which begged the question of why Henri had been

guarding a caravan that took him to Ruins Hall, but her uncle had the answer to that too.

"His brother asked him to keep an eye on Lennie because they'd be on two different caravans and Lennie had a tendency of putting herself in danger. Jorj couldn't get a swap between the caravans. No one wanted to take the later trip. Something about two caravans making good beds and baths scarce in Ruins Hall, and first in, best dressed. That kind of thing. The caravan captains wouldn't let Lennie trade with anyone on Jorj's caravan, either. Something about distractions. Kearick was furious but couldn't give him enough of a reason to stay, so Henri went."

"Kearick knew," Marsh said.

Per nodded.

"Yes. Anyway, lucky for me, because Henri got me out of the office before young Dunkel stuck his head through the door, and we had the trapdoor closed and blocked before a proper search was done. We were back and at the bar before the captain thought to send anyone to check."

"What about your other guests?" Marsh asked. "Won't they know?"

"They were in the baths by then, enjoying the complimentary glass of wine that went with them." He looked over his shoulder at where his son was returning down the stairs. "Daniel's idea."

Daniel flushed, nodded, and went into the kitchen. Marsh frowned.

"Have I done something to offend him?"

Per cocked his head.

"You didn't come straight home," he said. "Dan's a bit cross about that."

"I'll go speak with him," Marsh said, but Per laid a hand on her arm.

"Best give the boy a bit of time to cool down," he said. She looked at him.

The boy didn't seem all that upset. Pots rattled in the kitchen, followed by a muffled curse, and Marsh hurried toward the sound. She opened the kitchen door in time for a pot to come flying through it.

"Deeps-cursed, ungrateful..." Daniel spat when he looked up and saw her standing in the doorway.

Marsh stepped through and closed the kitchen door behind her, smiling sweetly.

"You were saying, Daniel dear?"

He'd already blushed a brilliant red, and now he went a shade darker, picking up another saucepan.

"You didn't come home!" he snarled, brandishing it in her direction.

Marsh made a show of looking around and then moved toward him, trailing her hand along the kitchen counter as she went.

"Oh, I don't know, kiddo. This looks pretty much like home to me, and I *am* here, aren't I?"

"Smart ass!" he shouted and threw the pot.

Marsh ducked and charged at him, wrapping her arms around his waist and knocking him off his feet.

"I'm sorry, okay?" she said when she'd managed to pin him on his back and had trapped his fists against his chest. "I'm sorry. I'm sorry. I'm sorry. I'm ungrateful and forgetful and Deeps-cursed, and whatever else you want to call me, but I'm sorry I was away for so long, and I'm sorry you thought I was dead, and I'm sorry I didn't come straight home when I arrived, and I'm sorry you're hurting and upset. I'm sorry, okay?"

She wound her arms around his shoulders, pulling him close but keeping his hands pinned tightly between them.

"I'm really, really sorry, and I'll try not to do it again. Okay, Dan? Okay?"

He made a sound that might have meant "yes" and Marsh sat up, moving her hands so his remained trapped and looking down into his face.

"I didn't mean for you to be angry."

He scowled at her, his gray-blue eyes dark with anger and distress, his copper curls tousled. Marsh kept her eyes on his and waited. She'd been dealing with Daniel all her life. He loved her but had a lot of trouble showing it. Come to think of it, he had a lot of trouble showing anyone how he felt, even when he liked them a lot.

And he had no way of telling someone when he was angry. He usually just hid it away while he found a quiet space to throw things in until he felt better. She wondered if Per knew and then realized that neither Gustav nor Roeglin had come barreling through the kitchen door to save her. Per knew, then—and he was trusting her to fix it, now that she'd refused to leave well enough alone.

Idiot.

Not what she needed to hear from Roeglin, but Daniel finally spoke and Marsh ignored the shadow mage in her head.

"Did you like dinner?" her cousin asked and Marsh smiled, remembering the glorious meal she'd just had.

"It was perfect," she told him. She waited for him to tell her he'd done something horrible to hers, but he didn't.

He just smiled, his face lighting up with joy.

"I made it for you."

A lump formed in Marsh's throat, and her nose prickled. She stood up, letting go of Daniel's hands so she could dab at her eyes.

"Thanks, Dan."

He scrambled to his feet, dusting his hands on his trousers.

"Is the kat yours?" he asked, his voice as eager as a child's.

Marsh shook her head, and he looked disappointed.

"She's her own beast. I made her a promise, so she's sticking around until I keep it. You want to come meet her?"

His smile formed a full-blown grin, and he nodded so hard Marsh thought his head would fall off.

"Come on, then," she said, nudging Mordan through the link that had formed between them. "I'll take you to meet her."

The kat grumbled sleepily in her head, and Marsh told her she had another member of her pride to meet. Marsh opened the kitchen door just in time to hear Mordan's long-suffering sigh from across the room.

"She's sleepy," Marsh explained when Daniel gave her a look that asked what the sigh was all about, and he stopped.

"I can meet her in the morning," he said, but Mordan raised her head, yawned to show all her teeth, and looked at him.

"She's waiting. See?" Marsh said and took Daniel's hand.

"This is Gustav," she said as she passed the emissary and ex-bodyguard, "and that's Roeglin. They're *supposed* to keep me safe when we travel."

"Hey!"

"What the…"

Marsh snickered and led Daniel over to meet Mordan. When he was kneeling beside the kat and happily running his hands through her thick fur, she returned to Per. Before she could say anything, however, she yawned so hard it felt like her face was going to crack in half. Daniel was at her side in an instant.

"I'll show you to your room," he said and looked sternly at Roeglin and Gustav. "You, too."

It was more a command than an offer, and Marsh stifled a smile.

Daniel had always had trouble with his people skills. She turned to her uncle.

"Good night, Papa."

"Welcome home, girl."

WAITING

The next morning Marsh woke with a start, flinging the cover aside and calling a sword from the shadows before she was out of bed. She was on her feet and facing the door before she registered she was alone, that her bedroom door was still closed, and that the sound that had woken her came from downstairs in the dining room.

Laughter, the clash of dishes, and the rattle of pots and pans.

Releasing the sword back to the shadows, Marsh set about getting dressed. It was *her* room, after all, and she'd left at least one change of clothes hanging in her closet. They weren't anything fancy, but they'd do for breakfast.

It was a good thing her uncle had called for the tailor since she'd never owned anything suitable for a council meeting. The shadow mages probably did, but there'd been no time to return to the monastery and retrieve it. They were on their own, and had been ever since they set out to restore the trails between the monastery and Ruins Hall.

Marchant sighed and took a closer look at the clothes, wondering if any would fit Izmay. Grabbing a spare set, she stepped out into the hallway to find out. Mordan watched her from a blanket folded in one corner of the room, and then got to her feet and followed.

Izmay was still in her room when Marsh knocked, the big kat on her heels.

"They're better than anything I've got now," Izmay told her, taking the clothes and pulling Marsh into the room and closing the door behind them.

Marsh waited while the shadow guard changed and watched as Izmay tucked the trousers into her boots to hide their lack of length. The shirt, which was loose on Marsh, fitted Izmay with a snugness Marsh found enviable.

"Not bad," the shadow guard said, turning this way and that in front of the mirror to inspect herself. "Thanks, Marsh."

"Anytime." Marsh looked toward the door and sighed. "We'd better get moving or they'll send someone to wake us."

Izmay looked at Mordan and the kat gave an obliging yawn, showing all her fangs.

"Yeah," the shadow mage said. "I doubt that."

"It's never stopped them before," Marsh told her, refraining from adding that Izmay should know since she was usually the instigator.

As if to prove her point, a series of very loud knocks came from down the hall. Izmay flashed Marsh a grin.

"Go stand over there," she whispered, shooing Marsh into a corner where she couldn't be seen from the doorway.

Catching an idea of what the guard wanted to do, Marsh obliged, pulling Mordan into the corner with her.

Shortly afterward a knock came at the door.

"What?" Izmay snapped, sounding irritated.

"You're needed downstairs. Marsh too, if she's there."

"Why would Marsh be here?" Izmay demanded, managing to sound outraged.

"Uh, you mean she isn't?"

"You mean you've lost her again? Wasn't it your turn to keep an eye out for her, Zeb? Master Ro is going to be very upset."

"No. Master *Ro* is going to be very upset if you two ladies don't get your tails downstairs and stop holding up the tailor," snapped Roeglin from outside the door. "I *do* have a link with her, you know."

Miscreant echoed through Marsh's head and she rolled her eyes.

Izmay caught her look and mirrored it, then pulled the door open and walked out into the hall. Marsh followed on her heels, flashing Zeb a quick grin and Roeglin a glare.

Yeah, save it for someone who cares. He led the way down the hall. "The tailor is waiting."

All Marsh could think was that the tailor must be awfully keen, given the hour.

Per gave him the impression he had a lot to do. Thanks for finding Izmay something to wear in the meantime.

Marsh was about to tell him it was okay when she realized he wasn't wearing his usual robes.

"Are those Daniel's?" she asked since his shirt looked familiar.

"Gabe's," he replied. "Daniel's didn't fit."

Well, that made sense. Daniel was broader than Gabe. She just hadn't known Gabe had left any of his wardrobe behind when he'd left.

He left enough.

They hit the bottom of the stairs to see the tailor step back from Gustav and make some notes in a leather-bound ledger.

"Next," he said, looking around the room.

His eyes came to rest on Roeglin, Zeb, Izmay, and Marsh, and he focused on Zeb.

"Ah, good. Zebediah, is it?"

Marsh watched Zeb's ears redden.

"Zebedee. Just call me Zeb."

"Very well, Zeb. You're next, followed by you, sir. Uh…"

"Roeglin."

"Excellent." The tailor flipped a page and wrote at the top.

Marsh figured he'd dedicated a page apiece to them and followed Izmay over to the kitchen door.

"It's coming," Daniel shouted. "Now get out of my kitchen."

As a greeting, it wasn't bad. Marsh went before he started slinging saucepans for emphasis. The Deeps knew the boy already had the art of making a threatening gesture with a ladle down pat.

"That bad, huh?" Izmay asked as Marsh retreated.

The kitchen door opened in her wake and a young woman walked through, a pot of kaffee in one hand and a pitcher of hot chocolate in the other.

"Your table's over there," she told them, waving the

kaffee pot at where she wanted them to sit. "Cups are coming."

Marsh didn't have to be told twice. The scent of the chocolate caught her and she turned to follow it, studying the waitress as she did so. The woman was slightly taller than she was, but she had long red hair that would hang to her waist when it wasn't caught back in a plait and her eyes were the color of the brews she carried.

Once she was settled, hot chocolate in hand, Marsh studied the tailor. The man hadn't come alone. As Roeglin had said, he was under the impression he had a lot to do—and judging by the rolls of cloth and leather taking up one table and the men and woman already cutting and sewing at two others, he wasn't far off.

She watched as the tailor expertly measured Zeb and then consulted with a man and woman who'd been standing by while he'd worked.

"Same as for the older gentleman, I think," he said, tearing the page with Zeb's measurements from the book and handing it to the woman.

"May I suggest the green instead of the blue?" she asked, then added. "The eyes, you know."

The tailor stilled and then nodded.

"You are correct, Letitia. Make it so." He turned back to where Roeglin was waiting, smiling quietly as though he hadn't seen the woman hold out her hand and make a distinctive "pay-up" gesture.

Her male colleague shot the tailor a glance but he paid, and the pair of them pulled bolts of cloth from the pile, consulting Zeb's measurements as they chose a table to work at. In the meantime, the tailor completed Roeglin's measurements and looked around the room.

"You," he said, his eyes falling on Marsh.

She took a hasty swallow of chocolate and set her cup down. As she crossed over to him, the tailor glanced at Gustav.

"Gown or trousers?" he asked, and Marsh caught the look of sheer mischief in the emissary's eyes.

"Both," he said, "but the women need to match the men regardless."

"Dancing?" the tailor wanted to know.

"Not to start with," Gustav told him, and Marsh breathed a sigh of relief. "And both have to be able to carry their weapons."

Marsh felt the tailor's hands still, and then the man sighed as though Gustav had just told him to do something uncivilized.

"Very well, sir."

The way he said it Gustav's request was anything but well, and Marsh gave the man points for not arguing. At least he respected what his clients wanted. The measuring went swiftly and painlessly, but the man asked them not to go too far since the fitting was a much more important part of the process.

Roeglin offered him and his people kaffee, and he directed refreshments be set aside on a table well away from where they worked.

"Now, if you don't mind..." he said. "We have much to do."

As though the measuring didn't count.

Marsh kept that thought firmly behind her teeth and

focused on the hot shroom pastries Daniel had sent to their tables. Per came to join them as soon as the tailor had settled to work with his staff.

"So," he said, looking at Roeglin and Gustav, "what are your plans for the day?"

"Plans?" Roeglin asked, and gestured toward the tailor. "We try and get suitably dressed for a council meeting."

He looked around the table.

"We're going to need an armorer too. I noticed we need some repairs."

Marsh snorted.

Repairs? Some of them needed replacement!

Unfortunately, there's no one I can ask to step into your shoes, Roeglin retorted, deliberately misreading what needed replacing. *Seems none of them have that big a sense of adventure.*

Thanks, Ro.

"What happens if we have a meeting today?"

Roeglin pointed to a table where almost-completed garments were being worked on.

"They're making some quick alterations for that."

Marsh realized that, unlike the garments being made, *these* garments weren't almost-completed but ready-made and being adjusted to fit. Every now and then, one of the seamstresses and tailors would stop work and cross to another table to glance at the page of measurements their colleagues were working from.

Roeglin turned his attention back to Per.

"Why?" he asked.

"Because we have some paperwork for you to go over that might help in your investigations."

Roeglin raised his eyebrows and glanced at the tailors. "From the office?"

Marsh straightened in her chair. There was only one office he could be referring to, and that was Kearick's.

"Where?" Roeglin wanted to know.

"Upstairs." Per gestured toward the tailors. "They won't need us just yet, and I've told Monsieur Calais which room to come to. He assures me it is an acceptable arrangement."

Oh, he did, did he?

She didn't say it out loud, just waited for her uncle to explain, which he very shortly did.

"Henri helped me."

He stood as he spoke and lifted the tray of pastries from the table. Gustav followed his example, taking the pitcher of hot kaffee and his mug. Roeglin lifted the chocolate, and together they headed for the stairs.

"We'll be upstairs, Dominique," Per called, catching the tailor's eye.

Dominique paused in pinning the cloth of a pair of trousers and looked in his direction. When his eyes had roved over all of them, the tailor waved and nodded and went back to work. A few short moments later, and they were settled around a table in what looked like a meeting room set in one corner of the waystation's second floor.

Marsh frowned, looking around at the chamber—and Per smiled.

"A while back we had a surface caravan that wanted somewhere 'private' to discuss business with its clients… and a way for those clients to attend the meeting without being seen coming and going.

He crossed the room and lifted a lever hidden in the wall.

"Here it is."

Marsh watched as a panel of stone slid aside to reveal a set of stairs leading down.

"Comes out in a change room downstairs," Per explained, "or the ladies powder room, depending on who needs it. I had to borrow a rock mage, and it took me a while to find one that wanted something I could actually find for them. Fortunately, hot baths haven't gone out of fashion in the Deeps."

When they'd all come in and settled themselves around the table, he closed the door and joined them.

"Before we begin," he said, "you should know that Kearick left a couple of weeks ago. Took six heavily laden mules and headed for Dimanche, with a short detour through Downslopes in the hopes of meeting someone there. Didn't say who, but I got the impression he wasn't fussed. Sort of like it was a chance meeting."

A couple of weeks…

"Did he plan on waiting to see who showed?" Marsh asked.

A couple of weeks would put his departure just after they'd left Ruins Hall, almost a week after Madame Monetti's assassination. Marsh wondered if Kearick was really running from them…or if there was someone else he was more afraid of. Of course, he could always be running *to* someone…

"That's interesting timing." Roeglin's voice brought her attention back to the table. "I wonder what triggered it."

Per shrugged, but the shadow mage wasn't finished. He

leaned back in his chair and regarded the station master with curious eyes.

"How *did* you get the boxes out of Kearick's office?"

Per cast a glance at Henri and the big guard blushed.

"That was me," he said, continuing when Roeglin signaled for him to say more. "I worked for Kearick. He wanted me as a spare bodyguard, so he ran me through a trial run and then assigned me to one of his teams. Only problem was that when Jorj wanted me to look after Lennie on that last run. Kearick was furious. Threatened me with all sorts of mayhem, so I said I'd quit. He came round, said I could do this one final run, but I was to tell Jorj no more."

He paused, and Roeglin looked puzzled, like he hadn't heard the story from Per already. If Marsh hadn't known any better, she would have said he was testing Henri's loyalty. It made her wonder what the caravan guard had done to make Roeglin feel he had to.

You can never be too careful, the mage told her where no one else could hear it. Out loud, he said, "I still don't understand how you got the boxes out before the guards came back."

"Kearick had a secret passage built. Came up under his desk. We just went in through that, same as when I snuck Per out before the guards came looking. We waited until they'd left and went back for the boxes before they could hunt us down at the bar."

He cast a quick glance over at Izmay and Zeb.

"Helped that this lot called the shadows to hide us and muffle the sound. Didn't know you could do that. Sneaky bastards, the lot of you."

Marsh smiled.

Henri had every right to call them sneaky; he'd fallen afoul of their dirty tricks often enough during training. Hiding themselves in shadow shouldn't have surprised Henri, but the muffling of sound was new. Marsh wanted to ask more about it, but Henri's next words caught her by surprise.

"Might get you to show me how. See if I can do a bit of what Jakob does when he calls the shadows to his sword. Fight we're heading into, those tricks might just save a man's life."

Might… Man had a point.

Those tricks would go a darn sight further than 'maybe' saving a man's life; they'd go pretty much to being the only thing that made a difference between his life and death. Marsh couldn't blame Henri for hoping he had the ability to do the same things the shadow mages did.

Roeglin glanced over at Gerry. From what Marsh could work out, the redheaded shadow mage was the senior of the three guards.

"Gerry, when this meeting's over, check him out and help him see what he can do."

Marsh noticed that Roeglin said nothing about there being some people who just weren't able to wield the magic, just said it like Henri was going to manage it for sure. She studied his face and noticed not a smidgen of doubt—which was a good thing, given just a smidgen was all it would take to prevent Henri from finding out what magic he might have.

"We got the files out the same way," Per added. "I told the others what you'd found, and we thought the town guard might return for them. We didn't want them disappearing, so we borrowed them for a while."

He gestured at several neatly stacked piles in front of him.

"It's interesting reading, but most of the names I've come across left town around the same time as Kearick."

Kearick, who'd sent the seeker to retrieve his goods and kill her. Kearick, who'd somehow heard of Madame Monetti's fall and their plans to unlock the route between Kerrenin's Ledge and Ruins Hall.

Not necessarily, Roeglin said, but he didn't expand on it.

Marsh frowned.

"Did any of them leave before him?"

Per indicated the piles.

"I've put them in groups according to the time they left. This one's Kearick's"

Per had found five names, only one of which had left before Kearick. By the time Monsieur Calais knocked at the door for the first fitting, they'd found fifteen names, and by mid-afternoon, they had twenty.

Jakob was outraged.

"But I knew him. He was a decent sort of man."

"Don't forget the raiders take family and hold them hostage." Marsh indicated the piles. "There's a good chance some of these might have relatives among the missing."

She turned to Per.

"Are there abandoned farms or mining claims close to town?"

His face darkened, and he nodded.

"Like your parents," he told her.

"Anyone still living outside the walls?"

He nodded.

"Mika's Outlet. It's a small settlement. The Deeps know why they think they can hold off the raiders if they choose to come for them, but they do."

"Maybe they don't need to hold them off," Izmay said, and they all looked at her.

She caught the expressions on their faces and shrugged.

"All I'm saying is that there are other ways to stop someone from attacking you, and it doesn't have to be strength. They might be cooperating with them."

"As much as I hate to admit it," Roeglin said, "I agree. We'll visit the community, but we'll go carefully."

"We also need to know who these people associated with," Gustav added.

He tapped the nearest pile.

"People like these…they have a lot of connections. Not all of them will have gone away."

He was about to say more when Daniel knocked at the door.

"Messenger's here," he told them, and he could only mean the messenger from the council.

"That took them a lot less time than I'd expected," Per replied, pushing away from the table at the same time as Gustav. "Shall we?"

11

ATTACKS WITHOUT AND WITHIN

"The Kerrenin's Ledge Council requests your attendance tomorrow two hours before mid-meal," the messenger said.

She waited, not taking her eyes from Gustav and Roeglin. When they did not immediately respond, she spoke again.

"The council requires your confirmation in reply."

"Two hours before mid-meal may not allow enough time for the matter to be considered," Gustav told her. "Tell the council of our concerns, and that we will meet with them as required."

"Attendance confirmed, but there are concerns that the time allowed is not sufficient," the messenger replied.

"My exact wording," Gustav insisted, and there was a hint of iron in his words.

"Two hours before mid-meal may not allow enough time for the matter to be considered. Tell the council of our concerns, and that we will meet with them as required."

"Thank you."

The messenger turned about and strode across the dining room, the sound of her boots shifting from a swift walk to a trot the second she was out the door. Gustav and Roeglin stared at the door for a moment longer and then Gustav looked at the tailor.

"Will you be ready by then?" he asked, and Dominique nodded.

"I could also have your new outfit completed," he said. "If you would rather wear that…"

Gustav shook his head.

"No, thank you." His lips twitched into a small, grim smile. "I'd like to unveil the new outfits all at the same time. The impact…"

He let the words trail off and made a gesture with his hand that said the tailor understood. Dominique's face lit up.

"That would be the best," he said and went back to his work.

Gustav interrupted him.

"Have you and your people eaten?"

From the puzzled look on the man's face, the thought hadn't crossed his mind, although Marsh noted Gustav's question had caught the hopeful attention of several of the men and women working around the table.

"I will send something," Per told him. "That is, if you don't mind."

Marsh saw anxiety flit through the expressions of the observing tailors and seamstresses, but Dominique nodded.

"Please."

"I'll provide beds for any who wish to overnight here rather than returning home." He paused, catching the tailor's eye. "I take it you'll be working late…"

"Of course."

Marsh watched money change hands at the other tables —quietly and secretively. Apparently, there were some members on the tailor's team who didn't know their master's work habits. When Dominique's attention shifted back to his work, Gustav cleared his throat.

It was hard not to laugh at the man's look of consternation, but Gustav didn't waste any of his time.

"Could I commission traveling clothes for my team?" he asked. "We'll be here for at least a week, and their clothes were ruined on the journey."

That was an understatement.

Marsh shuddered when she thought of the state her clothing was in. Blood from both shadow monsters and raiders stained the cloth, alongside patches of ichor and dirt—and the skirmishes they'd had clearing the road or defending their campsites had all left their marks. Marsh didn't think there was any part of her clothes that didn't have some kind of nick or tear.

"Do you require an armorer?"

Gustav studied him as though searching for some kind of deception.

"Why do you ask?"

The tailor smiled.

"If your traveling clothes are in the condition you say, then the armor is most likely in need of repair—and I have an armorer whose work I'd recommend."

Gustav held his gaze a little longer and then dipped his chin.

"If you could."

"Piet!"

The youngest of the tailors set his work aside and crossed to his boss. The similarity of their features was obvious, and Marsh wondered what it would have been like growing up with and working for her parents at Downslopes. Loss seeped through her and she pushed the thought away, listening as Dominique gave Piet his orders.

"Tell the smith to come see Per at Hawks Ledge for some work."

Well, at least the man had the manners to go through her uncle. It was his station, after all. She watched as Piet left, his blond hair bobbing in the glows' light. The tailor turned back to Gustav.

"Is there anything else?"

Gustav shook his head.

"No. Enjoy your meal."

As he spoke, Daniel and the red-haired server returned to the dining room carrying trays of pies and pastries. Instead of taking them to where the tailors and seam-stresses were working, they set them on a separate table and returned to the kitchen. They were back moments later with cutlery and crockery and set about laying places so everyone could eat.

When Gustav turned to go back up the stairs, Daniel glanced in his direction.

"I'm only serving lunch once," he said, his tone brusque.

Marsh noticed Per color but he held his tongue. Gustav

returned Daniel's glance, his lips thinning in mild annoy-
ance—and then he smiled.

"Good. Then you can serve it upstairs so we can eat
while we work." He turned and headed up to the second
floor, not giving the cook time to respond.

As if on cue, Henri and the other guards followed, and
Roeglin looked at Marsh.

"You coming?" he asked, but what he added was more
for Daniel's benefit than hers. "Gustav gets tetchy when his
work is interrupted."

"Coming," Marsh confirmed, but Per hesitated.

"I need to help prepare for the evening meal," he said.
"I'll have other customers arriving soon."

The tailor opened his mouth, but Per was ready.

"I'll keep your space clear," he told Dominique. "There's
not as many as there used to be."

Marsh remembered the small group of merchants that
had been present when they'd arrived the day before, and it
struck her that he was right. Before she'd left for Ruins
Hall, the Hawks Ledge restaurant and bar had been busy
every night.

"People don't like going out after dark," Per explained.
"That and the lack of trade means things are tight for a lot
of folks."

He gestured at the tailors.

"You're doing a lot of good here."

As he spoke, the door opened, and the merchants she
remembered from the previous night came through. Their
leader, a solidly built man with sandy hair, looked around
the dining room, his eyes widening when he saw the tables

laden with cloth and partially-finished garments. When he found Per, though, he came straight over.

"Stationmaster," he said, "I trust you are open for business."

It was less a question and more a demand for service, but Per greeted the man with a wide smile.

"We are always open for business where you are concerned, Master Gage. Let me show you to a table."

Marsh and Roeglin headed for the stairs, not wanting to keep Gustav waiting, but they had just reached the bottom of the steps when a bell began to toll. That was new. Marsh stopped and looked at her uncle.

He was standing, his head lifted as he listened to the bell and the cacophony of lighter chimes that followed it.

"There are raiders attacking the Deeps wall." He paused, looking at Marsh. "That's the wall facing the route leading to Ruins Hall."

A third set of chimes joined the first two, these harsher and more like the clanging of the bells worn by moutons when they were released into a cavern to graze. Per's face turned grave as the tailors set their meals on the tables and headed for the door.

"They're calling everyone to assist," he said, and then looked at the trader even as he hurried over to the bar. "I'm sorry, Master Gage, but the city needs us."

The trader snorted as though claiming the Ledge was a city was beyond belief. Per ignored him but waved a hand toward the food that had been set out for the tailors.

"If you're hungry, you can share the tailors' lunch...or I'm sure your assistance would be appreciated on the wall."

That caught the trader's attention.

"Appreciated?" he asked, and Per nodded, pulling a sword belt and sword from beneath the counter and strapping it to his waist.

"Oh, yes," he said, reaching back under the counter to take out a sturdy crossbow. Marsh realized his belt had a quiver of bolts hanging opposite his blade.

"Dani—" but Marsh's cousin shoved open the kitchen doors and hurried across the dining hall.

"Fires are banked, and I've pulled everything out of the oven and off the stove," he said, and his mouth twisted with dismay. "We should charge the raiders for every meal they've almost ruined."

"Almost?" The trader sounded hopeful.

"Almost," Daniel confirmed, not stopping on his way through. "If we push them back fast enough, lunch will be fine."

He was followed by the serving girl and three others that Marsh hadn't met yet, although she vaguely recognized their faces from her trip into the kitchen the evening before. She almost didn't recognize them now.

In the time it had taken Per to explain the bells and make the traders understand they were leaving, the staff had ditched their aprons and donned simple leather tunics and sword belts, and each one carried a solid timber staff. They moved after Daniel like he knew where he was going—and they'd go with him even if he didn't.

Per followed.

"You're welcome to join us," he told Marsh, but he didn't wait for her reply.

Marsh didn't bother asking Roeglin if she could go; she

just followed her uncle. Roeglin hesitated, his eyes sheeting white, and then he followed her.

"The others are…" he began, but the clatter of boots on the stairs behind them told her exactly what the others were doing.

None of them said anything when the traders joined them.

"Can't leave our trading partners in the lurch," Gage said, hitching his belt. Marsh noticed he was a good head taller than most cavern folk, and that his skin had the tanned quality she associated with those who lived on the surface. She'd have to ask him what that was like when this was over.

The streets were busier when they reached the board-walk, with groups of people moving in semi-disciplined squads of a half-dozen or more—and every single one of them was armed. It was hard for Marsh not to stop and stare. This wasn't the Ledge she remembered.

It didn't take her long to spot Per and Daniel moving in the general direction everyone else was taking—toward the Deeps wall—but as she watched, a second set of chimes rang out, and her uncle and cousin paused. The chimes came a second time, and they turned about and started running in the opposite direction to which they'd been traveling—the one leading to the surface.

"Now I *am* glad I joined you," the merchant said. "Nice as this place is, there's no way I want to be stuck here with no way out and nowhere to trade."

Marsh understood where he was coming from. Being stuck in Kerrenin's Ledge might not have been so bad if she'd loved the life she had at the waystation, but the constant flow of folks and stories through her childhood had made her want to see what lay in the world beyond… and then she'd met her first seeker and seen what he'd discovered in the ruins scattered through the Deep, and she'd known what she wanted to do.

Now, though? Now she just wanted peace so everyone could live safely. Adventure and discovery could come later.

They waited until Per and Daniel had caught them.

"This way," Per shouted, and they fell in with the catering staff and the tailors, the traders joining them.

Marsh noticed that Dominique scanned the squads around them, looking nervous.

"Anything we can help with?" she asked, and he started.

"I'm sorry. It's Piet." He waved his hand helplessly, and Marsh understood.

"Is it his first battle?"

Dominique shook his head.

"No, but the boy gets excited, and sometimes I need to…" He paused, looking embarrassed, and Roeglin swore.

"We'll find him," he said, grabbing Marsh by the arm. "Which armorer did you send him to?"

"I…there is only one."

They left him in the street looking after them, but Marsh had no time to worry about him. Roeglin was already asking questions.

"You know the way?"

Marsh shrugged his hand from her arm and caught it in her own.

"Follow me!"

They raced through the streets, Marsh taking every

short cut she could remember from a youth of running errands for her uncle. It didn't take them long to reach the smithy. To their surprise, Piet was still there, but he was flat out on the floor, blood oozing from a cut on his head while sounds of battle came from the room beyond.

"He's lucky he isn't dead," Roeglin muttered, glancing down at the boy.

Marsh wanted to know how he knew, but then she caught the faint rise and fall of the boy's chest and relaxed. Leaving Piet on the floor, she followed Roeglin toward the room beyond the shop entry.

"I. Told. Ye. NO!" was punctuated by the clang of metal striking metal, and Marsh remembered the blacksmith was a woman. "And. I. Meant. No."

More clashes followed, which sounded suspiciously like someone had just cleared a workbench of all its tools. Someone grunted with pain, and then someone cried out. Not the smith, to Marsh's relief.

Scan ahead, Roeglin ordered, and Marsh tried to sense how many lives occupied the room beyond.

There were four of them—one faced off against three others. Marsh widened the scan to include the ceiling and asked the shadows to show her who might be hidden. It was no surprise to find a fifth attacker hiding in the rafters, and a sixth stepping back toward the door.

He thinks he heard something, Roeglin told her and pulled a dart from the shadows. *Let me confirm that for him.*

The intruder reached the door, pivoting to scan the shop's interior. He didn't have time to shout an alarm; Roeglin's dart took him in the throat. The shadow mage followed by stepping up to the door before anyone on the other side had time to react. He'd drawn and cast two more darts by the time he'd stepped through, and Marsh heard a heavy thump as something or someone hit the floor.

She wasn't worried, though; Roeglin would have been reading her mind while she scanned. He'd know of the two intruders hiding in the room.

Three, came almost as a gasp, and Marsh swore.

How could she have missed one?

Shadow mage.

Son of the misbegotten Deep!

Marsh wasted no time.

I suppose you got your idiotic ass skewered, you half-bred mind-walking asshole.

"Thanks. Thanks a lot," Roeglin wheezed. Marsh heard startled laughter behind the pain and was glad she'd distracted him from it.

She hadn't distracted him enough for him to forget to send an image of the room to her mind as she charged forward, and she ducked the swing of the mage's blade as she came through the door, stamping down hard and pivoting as she pulled buckler and blade from the dark. The enemy mage's second strike hit the shield and bounced off, and Marsh put all the momentum of her turn into her strike.

She was lucky the mage hadn't known she was aware of where he was, or he'd have been more prepared. As it was, she reached the end of her turn as he dropped to his knees, in time to see Roeglin's dart slam into his side, finishing what she'd started. It took her mere heartbeats to turn back, looking for her next opponent—and she was almost too slow.

These were raiders, and more than one of them had an affinity for the dark. Whatever they'd wanted with the blacksmith, they'd wanted it badly enough to send more than mere cannon fodder. Movement flashed in the corner of her eye and she brought the shield up with barely enough time to turn the next blow, shuffling back just enough that the second, shorter, blade tore through fabric and not flesh.

"Son of the Deep!"

"Take him!" the man facing her shouted, and another raider slid from the shadow and ran toward her.

"No!" but the blacksmith's flurry of blows could not get her past the raider standing in her path.

Marsh tried to keep an eye on both the raider she was fighting and the man rapidly closing the distance between them.

I got this. Although from the sound of it, Roeglin was having trouble getting anything.

"Hang in there," Marsh muttered, parrying a series of fierce strikes as the second raider charged past her.

The rapid tattoo of his feet striking the floor stopped with a startled shout, followed by a series of heavy blows and then a shortened scream. Roeglin's harsh breathing sounded in the semi-silence that followed, but Marsh had to stay focused on the man before her. He was fast, his form blending with the shadows and making it hard to see exactly where he was but giving Marsh an idea.

The man was using real blades, and she knew just how effective those were against shadows. Concentrating on keeping him at bay, she slid into the shadows, letting her body become one with them while remaining separate.

"Clever girl," her opponent muttered, and Marsh decided she was sick of looking at his face.

After all, if she was one with the shadows, there was no reason she couldn't be standing behind him and driving her sword through his back. As fast as thought, she was, hearing her opponent's startled shout as she vanished from in front of him. It was followed by a cry of pain as she missed her first strike, slicing across his back instead of driving her blade into his chest.

She danced back a step, dropping out of the shadows as she recovered her strike and thrust forward, plunging her blade into him as he came around to face her. His gaze dropped to the sword in his chest and he fell back, his weapons clattering to the floor.

"That just leaves you," the blacksmith said.

"Ye're not good enough."

"Wanna bet?" Marsh looked across in time to see the woman slash her sword across the man's throat and then drive a dagger up and into his chest.

"Not laughing now, are ye?" she asked, kicking him to dislodge him from the blade.

She kicked the corpse as it fell, but it did not respond, so she stepped around it and ran for the door.

"My son," she said as she passed. "They're going to use him against me."

Her son? Well, no wonder she'd been fighting like a kat. Speaking of which, where was Mordan?

She'd lost track of the kat when they'd returned to the dining room to answer the messenger's summons, and now Marsh wondered where the monster had gone. The question was answered by the hubbub that erupted up the stairs on the other side of the shop.

"No, Ma. No! It's okay. She's friendly."

"Get out of the way, boy, and get away from her."

"No. She kept me safe."

Marsh bolted up the stairs, coming to a skidding halt when the blacksmith turned to face her, sword in hand. The woman's face relaxed when she saw who it was.

"You!" She gestured toward the room. "Wanna help me deal with this?"

A low growl rumbled out of the room.

"Hoshkat?" Marsh asked, and the smith nodded. "Blue eyes, probably sitting on the bed?"

"Got it in one." The woman's face took on a look of curiosity. "Ye know it?"

"She's mine. I'm sorry. I didn't realize she'd followed me."

"Good thing she did," the boy standing in front of Mordan said. "They sent two after me, while the rest tried to get my ma to go work for them. Said the town would be less likely to fight if they had no armor, and that they'd pay better than the town could afford."

He looked anxiously past her to his mother.

"You told them no, right?"

"That's what the disagreement was about," she said.

"Did we get 'em all?" the boy asked, and by "we," Marsh guessed he meant her and his mother, which reminded her...

"I need to check on my partner," she said. "I think he's hurt."

Roeglin was bleeding from a gash in his side that might

have been worse if the blade hadn't bounced off the hilt of his sword.

"So, there's something to be said for the whole shadow weapons thing," Marsh told him, taking him into the shop proper so she could see the wound. "It's a good thing we've got a meeting tomorrow. Gustav would have been upset when we told him you couldn't travel."

"Who says I'm going to the meeting?" Roeglin challenged, but the smith interrupted before Marsh could reply.

"That needs stitching. Wait one."

The boy had followed his mother into the room. Now he looked under Marsh's arm and then hurried away.

"I'll go put some water on."

"You're from the monastery, aren't ye?" the smith asked, and Roeglin nodded.

Marsh noticed that his face was pale and his skin filmed with sweat.

"Every time, Ro. Every single time," she muttered, but the blacksmith was talking.

"Heard of ye. Never thought to see ye. Didn't think ye'd show yerselves after what the shadow mages are doing in these caverns."

"Not us," Roeglin said. "We fight them when we find them."

He gasped as she probed at the wound.

"Lucky," she said. "No poison on the blade, an' the cut's clean. A couple of weeks' rest and you'll be causing yer girl more grief than ever."

Marsh's eyes widened. His girl? She caught Roeglin's look, and they both blushed.

"Huh. Not his girl, then? Well, I wouldn't wait too long. His kind don't grow on trees."

That's one way of putting it, Marsh thought.

Hey! was quickly followed by, "Ouch!"

"Stop yer gripin', boy."

Marsh saw that the smith had threaded a needle and taken the first stitch. She paused when her son returned carrying a pan of hot water and some clean cloths. The woman turned to Marsh.

"Keep him steady," she directed and went to work.

After another yelp of protest, Roeglin settled, breathing hard as the wound was cleaned and hissing with pain as the smith began stitching. He'd closed his eyes by the time she'd finished, but Marsh could feel fine tremors running through him every time the needle touched.

"There. Done," the woman said and poked Roeglin in the ribs above the wound. "Ye can open yer eyes again, ye big girl."

"Hey!" Marsh protested. "*We* don't make that much of a fuss."

Roeglin managed a chuckle at that.

"Oh, no," he mocked. "The fuss *you* make is on a far grander scale."

The boy interrupted them.

"How d'you think they're going with the attack?"

The woman cocked her head.

"Well, they haven't sounded the all-clear yet, but I'm guessing things will settle down soon."

The boy blinked and turned a wide-eyed stare to his mother.

"Why?"

"Because the raiders didn't get what they came for—and the attacks were a distraction while they tried."

"Oh." Her son was silent for a moment, chewing his bottom lip as he thought over what she'd said, then, "Will they come again?"

Marsh could see from the look on the woman's face that she wanted to say no, that this would be the last time the shadow raiders tried for them, but she could also see that the smith didn't want to lie to her son. In the end, the woman chose the truth.

"They may, Sam. They don't want us here lookin' after the town."

He looked troubled, his coal-brown eyes taking on a darker hue. The smith laid a hand on his arm.

"Don't let it bother ye, boy. They'll come, and we'll make 'em sorry all over again. Isn't that right, shadow mage?"

Roeglin cleared his throat.

"We can give you shelter at the monastery if you need it," he told her, but she shook her head.

"That would be giving them what they wanted, and I don't aim to do that. Why should their lives be any easier than the rest of us?"

It was a good point.

"What about him?"

Again the smith's son interrupted them, pointing at Piet's still form.

"Piet!"

The blacksmith hurried over to the youth, then returned for a damp cloth and her sewing kit.

"Looks like whoever hit him was in a hurry." She caught

Marsh's look as she headed back to kneel beside the boy. "He'd be dead if they weren't. I'd say Master Dominique is a very lucky man."

She bathed the wound as she talked, then carefully stitched the edges together.

"Well," she said when she was done. "He'll be pleased with that, even if his father won't. Boys always like a good scar."

Boys did, did they? Marsh thought, wondering how Roeglin felt about his.

Oh, just fine, Marsh. Always wanted something else to itch and ache at awkward moments. Yeah, thanks a lot. Thanks for asking.

His mind voice sounded tired and irritable, and like he was trying for funny but failing. When she looked over at him, his eyes were still closed and his body was tense, as though he really didn't want to move it.

"I should check in with Gustav," Marsh said, but she didn't want to leave him.

His lips quirked in a failed attempt at a smile.

"He says to stay put. The raiders can't breach the wall, and the battle's almost over."

He shivered, and Marsh looked at the blacksmith.

"You got a blanket I can borrow?" she asked, and the woman glanced at her son.

"Bring two," she told him and he scampered off at a run, the hoshkat padding in his wake.

The smith had stacked the bodies against one wall of the forge just as the all-clear was rung. Piet had come around by the time Gustav, Dominique, and the rest of the guards arrived to see what had gone on.

12

BLACKSMITH'S DEFENSE

Gustav arrived with the Protectors in tow—and he was none too pleased to find Roeglin had injured himself again.

"Of all the careless, clumsy—"

"I didn't do it on purpose…" Roeglin began, trying to defend himself, and the blacksmith agreed.

"No, he didn't. He felled the first one with a dart ta clear the door, and t'other stepped out of the corner like he'd only just stepped into it. Lined the boy up before I could warn him. The Deeps only know how he missed."

Gustav turned his attention from Roeglin to the smith.

"I'm sorry, ma'am—" he began, but she cut him off with a wave of her hand.

"I'm no ma'am, lad. I work for a living. Always have, always will. What's yer name?"

"Gustav, ma…er… What *do* I call you?"

Marsh hadn't seen Gustav blush so deeply before or be that lost for words, but he was doing both now.

"Greta, or Master Greta, if you prefer."

Marsh remembered how her friends had arrived at a run to see how Roeglin was faring.

Honestly, I could do without the fuss, he told her, Gustav was still staring at the smith.

"What?" she demanded. "You're looking at me like you've never seen a rearick before."

Gustav shook his head as though trying to clear it.

"I've seen plenty," he said. "Just never expected to see one here."

Greta stilled.

"Plenty, you say."

Gustav gestured toward Roeglin.

"You've a good hand with battle wounds. Not usually what I'd expect from a smith."

Greta's face reddened.

"We all have our pasts—and some of us don't care to remember."

"No," Gustav agreed, and Marsh noticed he was rubbing his left forearm with his right. "Some of us don't."

Marsh remembered he'd been chosen for the role of teaching the Protector trainees combat tactics because he'd had experience. She wondered where. Looking at the pair eyeing each other, she started to wonder if they'd even fought on the same side and what the war had been over. Whatever it had been about, it had left its mark.

After a couple of seconds of silent staring, Greta and Gustav turned to Roeglin. He glanced nervously at Marsh, and she gave him a feral grin.

"I can't save you," she said, and both blacksmith and emissary shot her a glare.

Marsh shrugged.

"Just callin' it how it is," she said, and they turned back to the mage.

"Take a couple of weeks before he's any good for traveling," Gustav said, examining the wound again.

He straightened, turning away to run one hand through his short-cropped hair. What he might have said next was lost when Piet groaned. Both turned to him, but Dominique was already at his side.

"Hey, son. How are you doing?"

Piet's eyes fluttered open and slowly focused on his father.

"Pa?" but he stiffened with alarm, his gaze shifting beyond his father to search the room as he struggled to get up.

"Easy, son. Shadow mages took care of them. Greta's all right, too." Dominique placed his hand on the boy's chest pushing him back down. "Just lie there for a bit. Let Greta take a look at you."

Marsh flicked her gaze around the room as the boy subsided, and Greta and Gustav closed in to look at the wound. Marsh didn't relax until she'd searched the corners for the glow of a life force and asked the shadows to reveal anyone who might be hidden. Only when she was sure the raiders were truly gone did she start to settle.

Over to one side, Roeglin stirred.

"Can't stay in bed," he said. "We've got a meeting to get to."

Marsh glanced at Gustav, but the emissary was talking to Dominique.

"You want us to help you get him home?" he asked, but the tailor shook his head.

"We need to get back to work; make sure you look your best when you face the council."

"Boy needs at least a day of rest," Greta told Dominique. "No needlework, no running errands, and nothing in between, either."

The tailor frowned, clearly reluctant to leave his son alone.

"He can stay upstairs at the station," Gustav told him. "That way you can keep an eye on him."

"And I'll come over and check up on him," Greta added.

She frowned.

"What *did* you send him over for anyway?"

"These fine folks need armor repaired or replaced."

"They do, do they?" Greta glanced over at Marsh. "Way they fight, I'm not surprised."

Marsh's eyes widened but the blacksmith kept on, her gaze drifting to Roeglin.

"What happened to his? You have to cut it off him when he got hurt the last time?"

"That's what happened to mine," Marsh said before Roeglin could respond.

The smith snorted.

"Figures."

"Hey!" Gustav held up his hand and Marsh shuddered to silence.

"Do you have time?" he asked. "It was a hard journey, and we cleaned the raiders out of Mid-Point and the shadow monsters off the trade route, but it wasn't without damage."

The smith turned to survey the group, running a practiced eye over those still wearing armor and then measuring Marsh and Roeglin with a glance.

"I've got the leather, but it'll take a couple of weeks."

Gustav shrugged.

"We need the gear."

He eyed one of the shields hanging on the wall and indicated a set of thigh coverings on display in the window.

"And it'll be worth the wait."

The smith blushed.

"I'm sorry it will take so long. If you have anyone who can…" She let the words hang, and Marsh was surprised to see Gustav color.

He cleared his throat.

"I can do a little," he said. "I'm no armorer, mind you."

Greta's gaze sharpened.

"Can ye do basic repairs?"

"Aye."

"Then you'll do, and any of yer men up to the same. I'll check for quality, and I'll cut the price for the help."

"Piet will help too," Dominique broke in. He colored when the pair turned toward him. "It will do the boy good to understand how armor is made…and how it sits. I'll trade the experience for his help."

Greta smiled.

"That's a good offer, tailor, but he won't be up to stitching for a few days at best. I'll let him watch if he can get down here."

"I'll bring him," Gustav told them. "Do the boy good to walk a bit."

Greta was about to comment on that when they heard

footsteps outside the door. Light and fast and on their own, Marsh was sure she knew who it might be before the messenger arrived. It was a different girl this time, and she scanned the group before her gaze settled on Gustav.

Once she'd found him, she acknowledged the smith with a brief nod before moving to stand before the emissary.

"The Kerrenin's Ledge Council greets you and apologizes for the short notice. The latest attack has lent urgency to your request. Your presence is now required at first light at the council chambers. An escort will be sent a half-turn beforehand. Please be ready to leave on their arrival. Confirm."

The way she rattled it off told Marsh the message had been delivered exactly as given.

Gustav stared at the girl, his gray eyes dark with thought. She waited, blue eyes unblinking as she watched his face. When he spoke, Marsh swore she could see the girl's mind filing each word and nuance as he spoke.

"Ruins Hall Emissary to Kerrenin's Ledge Council: Confirmed. Please accept our assistance in today's defense as an example of the further assistance an alliance will provide. We appreciate your hospitality." His gaze shifted and he caught the messenger's eye. "Repeat!"

The messenger obliged, her voice mimicking Gustav's every tone and nuance with accuracy.

"Very good," he said when she'd finished. "Is there anything else?"

The girl blinked and then shook her head.

"No. Thank you. I will convey your reply now."

She did not wait for a response but turned and trotted

for the door. The sound of more footsteps came before she could reach it and the doorway darkened with a familiar shape.

"Captain Brodeur," Gustav began, but the smith cut him off, gesturing for the captain to come into the store.

"To what do we owe the honor?" she asked, making it sound like she knew exactly what they owed the honor to, as well as making it clear that the honor was a dubious one at best.

"It's nice to see you, too, Greta," the captain said, stepping aside so that the messenger could pass.

She hesitated at the door, and the sound of people shuffling aside explained her momentary stillness. It didn't last long, however, and she soon darted out of the store and into the street beyond. When she was gone, Brodeur led a small squad of Kerrenin's Ledge Guard into the store, causing Gustav's men to move closer to the emissary and making the space seem small.

"So many," Greta said, her voice full of disapproval, "and all of them too late to be of any use."

Her words made several of them frown in disapproval, but Brodeur's lips only tightened in a smile.

"I'm sorry we didn't listen," he said, his eyes flickering briefly to the sergeant standing with the Guard. "Next time we'll pay more attention."

Greta raised her brows.

"So ye're admitting that there *will* be a next time?"

Brodeur nodded.

"Yes." He reached into a pocket, pulling out a length of painted charcoal and a pad of shroom paper. "Do you have time to make a report?"

"A complaint, you mean?" Greta snapped, and her gaze flicked over those assembled.

She turned to her son.

"Take these gentlemen to the kitchen, Sam, and make sure they stay to drink their kaffee."

"Oh, I…" Brodeur began, but Greta held up a hand.

"I'll not have them cluttering up the store." She glanced at Gustav and Dominique. "This could take a while. Why don't you move your wounded upstairs? There's a spare room at the top of the stairs to the right. Once they're settled, the rest of your men could join the Guard in the kitchen. I'm sure I have enough kaffee to go round."

"Thank you, Master Smith," Gustav said, taking her suggestion as the instruction it was intended to be.

He looked at his men.

"You heard the lady, Roeglin. Time you got off your lazy ass. Marsh, help Piet and Dominique."

They did as he asked, Roeglin not even protesting the insult.

I'll deal with it later, the mage promised, but his voice sounded tired. Marsh doubted he'd be dealing with anything until at least the next day. *You'd be surprised.*

"Yeah, I would," Marsh told him, helping Dominique get Piet to his feet.

By the time they'd been upstairs and back, Greta was well into her report. Marsh let the guards troop into the kitchen, but she positioned herself beside Gustav as the smith finished her tale.

"If it hadn't been for these folks," the woman said, "I'd have lost my son and been forced to go with them. They got here just in time."

Marsh felt her face color and bit her lip to stop herself from protesting that they hadn't done anything important. Captain Brodeur looked from the smith to Gustav and Marsh. Marsh shrugged.

"We promised Dominique we'd make sure Piet was safe."

"We, as in you and the shadow mage?" the captain clarified. "Since the rest of your group were on the wall defending the town."

It was probably not meant to be a criticism, but it felt like it all the same. Fortunately, Gustav intervened.

"I ordered it," he said. "We're a diplomatic mission, but we have other tasks as well, and the tailor and armorer are vital to their success."

He indicated the bodies stacked beside the wall.

"It turned out for the best, and the smith is an asset for more than just us. Tell me, where are her assistants? I'd have thought there'd have been some in training to ensure the Guard's needs were met…"

He let the comment hang, and it was the captain's turn to color. He cleared his throat before replying.

"It is a point I've raised with the council," he admitted. "I'll be raising it again…if the Master Smith is agreeable."

Again, her eyebrows lifted.

"To help you train a dedicated smith and armorer for your force? What about my trade?"

"You won't be able to keep up with a full-strength force. That kind of work takes more than one."

"I could expand my business," Greta pointed out. "Go into partnership. Being invested would be an incentive for quality."

"Are you saying a Guard smith wouldn't be invested?"

"Would he be getting paid the same as you'd pay an outside crafter?"

From the increasing color in Brodeur's face, a Guard smith would not.

"He'd be getting paid for his services," the captain said, "and he'd be limited to working for the Guards, guaranteeing availability when required."

Greta shrugged.

"I can give you that same availability," she pointed out, but Brodeur's reply was just as swift.

"For a fee," he countered, and the smith smiled.

"That's business."

"For a mercenary."

Greta's smile vanished.

"Loyalty in return for loyalty," she snapped back. "I've shown mine."

The captain drew a sharp breath and then closed his mouth, letting the implication that the town lacked loyalty stand.

"Point taken," he said. "I will raise your security with the council."

"Thank you."

The two of them stared at each other for a moment longer, then the captain slid charcoal and notepad back into his pocket. He looked over at Gustav.

"I'll see you tomorrow," he said. "A half-turn before first light."

Gustav nodded.

"We'll be ready."

"I believe your men have finished their kaffee," Greta told the captain, and Brodeur walked to the kitchen door.

From the speed at which his men appeared after he looked through the door, they'd either not drunk any kaffee or they'd finished it long ago—and they'd definitely been listening in. Ignoring this last, the captain nodded toward Greta and led the squad out into the street. Marsh, Greta, and Gustav watched them go, and then Greta turned to the emissary.

"I'm not sayin' you've outstayed ye're welcome," she said, "but 'twould be best if ye got yer men back to the station."

She paused.

"First though, we're going ta need yer measurements."

13

THE KERRENIN'S LEDGE COUNCIL

They were up early the next morning, given that the council meeting had been moved forward from mid- to early morning—and the traders who'd helped defend the town's walls were invited, too. Although the tailor had worked through the evening and late into the night, the new outfits weren't ready, so the Ruins Hall representatives were wearing the altered garments.

Marsh didn't understand why Gustav was disappointed. The new clothes were more than fine, and they outshone what the merchants were wearing by a noticeable degree. She hadn't been at all surprised when Gage had asked for Master Calais' services when next the man was free.

Looking around the room, she noted that several of the gathered councilors were wearing clothes of similar quality, and she wondered how many of them had bought from Dominique. Surveying the seven men and woman seated at the long table at the front of the meeting room, she concentrated on not fidgeting as she waited for them to speak.

Instead of being shown to seats, she and the rest of those summoned to the meeting had been set into groups of petitioners, each of which had to approach the table and explain their presence. As Gustav advanced, the oldest of the council members looked down at him.

"You wished to speak with us?"

"We did." If Gustav was surprised by the abruptness of the greeting, he did not show it. Nor did he make it easy for the councilor to maintain his superiority. After answering the man's question, he waited.

The councilor waited.

Gustav continued to stand there and look expectantly at him.

Marsh had to admire the man. If it had been her standing in front of the dais, she might have given in and started speaking straight away. Instead, Gustav stood silently, waiting for the council members to make the first move. In the end, it was the councilman who gave ground.

"I am Gerard Dupont, head of the Kerrenin's Ledge Council. For whom do you speak?"

"I am Captain Gustav Moldrane, emissary and bodyguard to Monsieur Gravine, Founder of the Ruins Hall communities. I speak on his behalf."

"On what matters would the Ruins Hall Founder wish to speak?"

"He wishes to speak to you regarding an alliance to secure the four settlements and to keep the trade between our towns alive."

The councilor regarded him for a long moment and then nodded.

"We will be glad to speak with you on these matters." He gestured to where a guardsman was waiting to one side. "If you would follow our guard."

Following the direction of his hand, Marsh looked over to where the guard was waiting and was surprised to see Captain Brodeur.

"This way, please."

Gustav followed, and if this was not what he'd meant by having the captain attend the meeting to discuss the security implications of what he had to say, he didn't show it. Behind them, the traders stepped forward. They too wanted to discuss a treaty, only this was between somewhere called Montmartre and Kerrenin's Ledge.

"It is to the northwest, several days' journey on the surface."

And through the Deeps? Marsh wondered. *How long is it, then?*

No one knows, Roeglin answered, keeping his face downturned so no one could see his eyes gleam white. *Although the merchants are wondering.*

Marsh just bet they were. It would be interesting to see just how long it was before they asked for assistance in that regard—especially once they realized her team was responsible for restoring the Ruins Hall route. She listened as the council welcomed the traders and ordered them to be seated. After that, it was down to business, and they wasted no time in coming to the point.

"What do you know of the raiders?" the head councilor asked, looking at Gustav.

He shrugged.

"Very little. They came out of the Deeps, attacking our trade routes and settlements and taking our people for reasons known only to themselves. By the time we realized what was happening, we'd lost the waystation at Leon's Deep, as well as most of the farmers. If it hadn't been for Shadow Mage Leclerc, we'd have had no warning at all."

"Leclerc?" One of the councilors sat up straighter, scanning Gustav and his companions until her gaze came to rest on Marsh's face. "As in Per Cavallon's niece?"

Marsh cleared her throat.

"*Oui*, Madame."

"I thought you were running errands for Kearick at the Emporium?"

Her words caused a stir through the gathering, and the head councilor held up one hand.

"I trust you can explain the association?"

"Yes, Monsieur. I *used* to work as a courier for Kearick, but when the trade route was cut, I agreed to a traineeship with the shadow mages."

"Until the routes were restored, of course," the female councilor prompted, and Marsh shook her head.

"No, Madame. When I accepted the traineeship it was for an indeterminate amount of time—and it was a decision that was made easier when Kearick sent an assassin to retrieve a delivery I had not been able to make."

Her words brought gasps from around the hall, and the councilor's eyes narrowed.

"An assassin? Are you sure?"

"Well, Madame, he tried to kill me and then told me Kearick had sent him, so yes, I am very sure."

Beside her, Roeglin rested his forefinger and thumb against his forehead, further shading his eyes with his hand as murmurs erupted around the room. Marsh took her seat and waited for the next question. With any luck, it would be directed to someone else.

"Master Roeglin," the councilwoman began, "what interest does the monastery have in all this?"

Roeglin's answer was direct and to the point.

"Without Monsieur Gravine's aid, the monastery would fall, and its cavern would fall with it."

"You *are* aware that the raiders send out mages to 'recruit' for their cause?"

"Yes, Madame, we are. We will not be recruiting without an escort from the approved guardians of the caverns we are recruiting in. It is safer for both your people and ours."

He sat back in his seat, but before another councilor could put forward another question, Gustav stood.

"Master Roeglin's statements bring us to the nature of my lord's business with this council. With your permission?"

The members of the council exchanged glances accompanied by subdued murmurs before turning back to the front.

"By all means. Proceed."

Marsh listened as Gustav presented the founder's idea of each city creating its own security force and fortifying its caverns against the raiders. As he reached the end of this suggestion, one of the council members raised his hand.

"As I'm sure you're aware, such a force is expensive to

maintain, and the manning has to come from somewhere. Do you have suggestions as to how we might recoup our costs?"

"I do," Master Gage said, interrupting before Gustav could reply.

He tilted his head and looked at the emissary. Gustav waved for him to continue.

"Since we expect you to source your troops from the caravan guards who are currently unemployed, and since those same guards will be responsible for securing the routes we wish to travel, I suggest you charge for your services."

"Hire our guards for your caravans?" The councilor sounded mildly outraged, but the trader shook his head.

"No, merely to keep the trade routes open, provide secure campsites where we can rest, and perhaps have patrols who will assist if we are attacked."

"How would they know?"

"I heard the bells. Perhaps we could carry horns or whistles in the Deeps. If a patrol was in hearing range, they could come to our aid."

A number of the council members exchanged looks and nods, and the head councilor replied, "We will consider your proposal. Now," he said, returning his attention to Gustav, "about this alliance…"

They went back to it, hammering out expenses and expectations, and then one of the councilors voiced the worry that had been raised with the idea of the cavern protectors.

"Why don't we develop a single force," the woman

asked, "rather than what will amount to four private armies?"

"I'm glad you asked," Gustav told her. "Monsieur Gravine too is more comfortable with the idea of a force that has no alliance to a single cavern or town. However, he does not believe we have the time to establish an independent force until after the threat of the shadow raiders has been dealt with."

"I concur." Captain Brodeur's voice rang across the chamber, and he continued when attention turned his way. "With the routes still being secured, it is better to have four smaller forces each responsible for a particular jurisdiction. It is also better for the division of expenses, at least until trade is restored and the protection force can fund itself from its earnings. I could assure the council that the Kerrenin's Ledge Guard as it stands could expand to fill the role of cavern protectors, *provided* it received assistance from the monastery to staff its ranks." He paused. "That *is* what the founder is doing, is it not? Bolstering his guards with magicians?"

"Yes," Gustav replied, "and the rock mages have agreed to assist us with closing any entrances into our caverns that we do not have the power to guard."

He glanced over at Roeglin.

"I believe Shadow Mage Leger can speak on their behalf."

Marsh figured that if Roeglin couldn't, he was more than able to speak to the Master of Stone.

Oh, you do, do you? What makes you think I have an existing link with her?

Pillock.

The meeting wound on, with the council stopping discussion on the treaty in order to broker an agreement with the traders. Only when Master Gage and his entourage had signed and left did the council return to Gustav's topic. This time they included Per and had Captain Brodeur join them in the discussion.

"How big a force would you need," they asked, "in order to secure the Ledge and patrol the routes between Downslopes and Midpoint?"

"Downslopes?"

It was like they'd hit the captain with a hammer.

"Yes, man. Downslopes. They *are* our citizens—and we'd like them to stay that way, and not be tempted by offers from elsewhere."

His eyes crept to the doors through which Trader Gage and his fellows had exited.

"It would not do to have a rival's interests camped out on our doorstep."

For a moment, Marsh thought Per might protest that his son would never betray his home community, but Gustav waved him to silence and Brodeur gave his somewhat stunned reply.

"I...I do not know if we have that many men to spare."

The councilor's face turned hard.

"Find out."

"*Oui*, Monsieur."

Satisfied the captain would do as he'd asked, the head councilor turned back to Gustav.

"Captain Moldrane, while we have Captain Brodeur to oversee the logistics of the Kerrenin's Ledge Protectors, we need someone to oversee their training. Would you..."

Gustav started shaking his head before the man had finished.

"I'm afraid not. I am under orders to accompany the shadow mages in their search for the source of the raiders. We are pledged to try and return as many of the missing to their homes as we can, and to end the threat the raiders pose." He stopped, then added, "*After*, of course, we restore the trade routes between each of the Four Caverns' settlements."

The councilman sat back in his seat, resting his chin on his fist as he thought about what to do next. It was Captain Brodeur who came up with the answer. While they'd been discussing the matter of manpower, his eyes had strayed to where Per was sitting quietly beside Marsh —not once, but several times. When Gustav had finished speaking, the captain cleared his throat to draw the council's attention.

"The stationmaster has combat experience."

Those five words fell, soft and clear, into their midst, and Per jerked his head around to regard the captain with mild alarm. Before he could reply, however, the captain continued, addressing him directly.

"I can call witnesses from the Surface Wall if you like, but without you directing the defenses, they'd have breached us half a dozen times."

He glanced at Gustav, and the Protector captain nodded. Marsh felt her uncle shift uncomfortably beside her and shot him a sideways glance. To her surprise, his face was red with embarrassment. Brodeur was, however, without mercy.

"I need him."

"But..." Per said, and all eyes turned toward him, "I have a waystation to run."

"You would be compensated," the head councilman offered, and the other councilors nodded in agreement.

"But..."

"The newly founded Protectors would need a leader to report to Captain Brodeur while the first Protector squad is brought up to speed. They would have to be trained and then rotated through the Guard to gain experience, and we need someone with your administrative skill to coordinate that."

"Are you proposing two separate forces?" Gustav asked.

The head councilor shook his head and then shrugged. "In a way," he said. "What I am trying to do is to ensure there is a core body of troops whose sole aim is to protect the Ledge, rather than the cavern. When this is over, and the Protectors become their own force, I want to be able to guarantee the town isn't left without a force to defend it."

Marsh wanted to protest that the man was making no sense, but she clenched her teeth together and managed not to make a sound. Gustav and Brodeur exchanged glances.

"Agreed," they said, their response coming as one.

At the head table, the council members relaxed momentarily, and then the head councilman leaned forward.

"Good," he said. "Also, given that trade is slow to non-existent, Hawks Ledge will act as the headquarters, barracks, and training ground for the new troops."

Per opened his mouth to argue but the councilman kept going, rolling over the stationmaster's open-mouthed protest as though he hadn't noticed it being born.

"We'll renegotiate both your position and the status of Hawks Ledge once trade picks up again. Do you agree?"

Per rolled his head back and then straightened.

"Of course."

From his tone of voice, they were twisting his arm, and he didn't like it. Captain Brodeur smiled, his face tight and hard as he watched Per give in. It made Marsh wondered if the two of them were going to get along. The councilman sighed and made a show of looking down at a sheet of paper on which the day's agenda was written.

"This brings us to records access." He raised his head. "A very interesting point. A number of records went missing from Kearick's Emporium. We trust they can be found, and the information gleaned from them shared. I am sure this could lead us to an equitable *exchange*."

While he didn't say as much, it was clear he believed they had the records, although why he was so sure, Marsh couldn't figure out. Perhaps he wasn't. Perhaps he only suspected they had the papers and expected that if they didn't, they would be able to find and retrieve them. Either way, he was holding any records of the children's family for ransom, and they were going to have to comply.

We'll discuss it when we return to the station, Roeglin reassured her as the councilor moved down his list.

"We have a request to make," he said, and Roeglin tensed.

Uh-oh.

"Continue," Gustav instructed as the councilman did just that.

"Not all of our people live within the city walls. Some of the slightly larger communities have been very insistent that they be allowed to continue their ways of life in the caverns. While the new Protectors train, would you be willing to check on these communities and families and see which ones remain?"

"We would."

The councilman relaxed just a little.

"And…" He hesitated, looking up and down the line of his fellow councilors. He ended by studying Marsh, Roeglin, and the three shadow guards with some apprehension. "It's difficult…"

He took a breath, looking for all the world like he was ordering his thoughts, and then he continued.

"I do not know what it is like in Ruins Hall, or the rest of the Deeps," he said, "but magic is on the rise. People are discovering they have abilities they didn't know they possessed. They'll go to bed normal one night and wake the next day to discover the stone smooths beneath their feet, or the shadows thicken to hide them, or the glows brighten when they pass. And the children…"

Shaking his head, he turned slightly to direct his question to Roeglin.

"Master Leger, I know the monastery is not recruiting at this time, but these people need help. Their abilities come as a surprise, and they're not always easy to control. Would you consider…"

Roeglin started shaking his head before the man could finish the sentence.

"I cannot stay to train. Training takes time and patience, and while I have the second, the first eludes me."

He held up a hand when several of the council rose to protest.

"But I *can* offer you this."

He waited as they settled themselves back in their seats, not continuing until he had their full attention.

"You already know we are reopening the trade route between Ruins Hall and Kerrenin's Ledge, and that Ruins Hall has pledged protectors to staff Mid-Point while it reopens the final half of the route. With the forces clearing the monsters and raiders, there are a large number of mages and shadow guards. There are also several rock mages. If you have somewhere suitable we could use as a school of sorts, we could establish a training center here."

"Within the walls?" One of the councilors looked alarmed at the thought.

"To start with," Roeglin said, keeping his voice mild, "although I'd imagine them wanting their own place *outside* the walls as soon as it could be properly established and staffed. It could also serve as a joint base of operations for the Protectors at that time, and would mean parents wouldn't seek to relocate to the monastery cavern to be close to their children during training. It would also be better for the adults to have a separate training establishment since they learn differently from the youngsters. If that is acceptable, I will speak with Master Envermet and see whether he has mages he can spare for training and if there are any willing to stay behind when he returns."

Monsieur Dupont looked up and down the table, seeking a response from each council member before he nodded.

"This agreement," he asked. "Will it be between us and the monastery, Ruins Hall, or both?"

At this, Gustav stirred in his seat, and Roeglin indicated he should speak.

"The training of magic users is an arrangement solely with the monastery and the rock mages. The one you have just made is similar to the one Monsieur Gravine brokered for his own people, and the matter of newly emerging magicians is one we are also seeing in the Deeps. Master Leger is authorized to make the arrangements. He has Monsieur Gravine's permission to act on the monastery's behalf during this mission, and I have no objections."

He settled back into his seat, leaving the council members to gather their thoughts.

They all rose from their seats and clustered together to discuss their thoughts, and then they returned to the table. Monsieur Dupont, it seemed, spoke for them all. Looking once at each of the members, he turned back to where Gustav and Roeglin were waiting.

"We will draw up the appropriate treaties and alliance documents over the next few days, and reconvene to discuss them when they are ready. If we are all in agreement at that time, we will sign." He paused, casting his gaze up and down the table and then clearing his throat. "There is just one other *small* matter…"

14

ONE 'LITTLE' THING

The other *small* matter wasn't so small, and it was entirely related to the council's need for an answer to the training of emergent mages. It made Marsh want to shout in outrage and maybe burn the entire cavern down around the Kerrenin's Ledge inhabitants' ears.

It took everything she had not to tell the council members to pull their heads out of their asses and stalk out of the meeting. Roeglin's hand on her thigh distracted her enough to keep a leash on her temper—especially because out of any of them, he had the most reason to be offended.

And outraged, Marsh. Don't forget outraged.

She could hear the anger quivering through his thoughts. Marsh swept all emotion from her face and forced herself to listen carefully to what the councilor had to say.

Apparently, news of another youngster with newly emerging abilities had reached the council. Unfortunately, the family was treating the child's magic as though it were an infection, and the child as if she were contagious.

"When you're as isolated as these folks," the councilor said, "anything new can be considered a threat. Their attitude is entirely understandable."

Understandable? Oh, the Deeps, no, it wasn't.

She thought of pointing out that the communities in the Upper Deeps protected those among them who showed skills they could use.

That's the point, isn't it? Roeglin interrupted. Useful *skills.*

He followed that private comment by asking his next question out loud.

"What *talent* did she show?"

The councilor glanced at his colleagues and they met his gaze, some with raised eyebrows and others with blank faces. His voice was hesitant when he turned back to reply.

"We don't know. They didn't say."

"Yet the community says it feels threatened…"

He shifted his feet.

"I…yes, they do."

"Strange they didn't tell you what exactly they found threatening."

The councilor sighed, looking at Roeglin in exasperation.

"Will you look into it or not?"

Roeglin stared at him, letting the silence stretch until the council members shifted uncomfortably, and then he spoke.

"I will look into this, but I need your permission to act in the best interests of the child if the situation requires it."

The councilor was aghast.

"You mean to take her!"

Roeglin shook his head.

"No, I mean to make sure she is safe where she is, *but* if she is not, then I ask your permission to find her a place where she can develop her talents safely, either with the shadow mages or with a family in the Ledge…or do I need to describe what happens when a mage decides to use their powers against those who would do them harm?"

Shock rippled through the councilors on the stage.

"She wouldn't!"

"Not Ninetta! She is such a sweet child!"

"I don't believe it."

Roeglin watched them, his lips curling into a small, satisfied smile. When their protests died down, he cut in.

"I have your permission then?"

The councilor turned to answer his question, his face a little paler than before. His reply was reluctant at best.

"Do what you must, but also act in the best interests of the community."

"We will."

Roeglin glanced at Per and Brodeur.

"Perhaps we should take representatives from the Kerrenin's Ledge Protectors," he suggested, but the councilman shook his head.

"The captains will be meeting with us to discuss what they need to get the Protectors operational. This task you must do alone."

"But in your name," Roeglin pressed, "and with your authority."

"Yes."

Roeglin rose, wincing as his injury reminded him of its presence. Marsh quickly slid a hand under his elbow, while Gustav moved to support him from the other side.

"Weakling," the emissary muttered, but softly, so the council members couldn't hear.

"Go pleasure the shades," Roeglin muttered back just as quietly. To the council, he said, "By your leave?"

The councilman nodded and turned to his colleagues.

"I believe that's all," he said, "unless—"

"I'd like to see the shadow mages on their return."

The familiar voice caught Marsh's attention, and she looked up to recognize the councilor Brodeur had brought to see them. The woman's tunic was fancier than it had been the night before and it was colored a soft russet-red, but her hair was still in a French plait, and her eyes were just as dark as she took them in.

"Is there a time?" Roeglin asked, addressing her directly.

"Any day around midday," she replied, but did not elaborate on why coming earlier or later might not work as well.

Nor did Roeglin question her.

"We will meet you at midday the day after we return," he said, and Marsh felt the weight on her arm increase even though he showed no sign of pain.

Gustav must have felt it as well because he said, "With your permission, Councilors," and then he waited for neither permission nor reply but started for the door.

The head councilman's reply had more than a hint of irony and chagrin coloring its depths.

"Granted."

Gustav did not slow down or turn back. Marsh focused on keeping Roeglin upright and moving toward the door, and Roeglin didn't say a word. He was silent in her head too, and that worried her. Marsh wondered what Greta would say, and was glad the smith couldn't see them.

It was well after midday when they stepped out of the council chambers and into the street. Marsh could tell from the way the cavern was lit by more than just glows and shrooms. She knew the light-levels, having lived in the Ledge for most of her life. It was strange how everything came back.

Gustav didn't stop when they hit the street, but he did shift his hold on the shadow mage, pulling Roeglin's arm over his shoulder.

"I don't suppose you'd let me carry you," he said, and Roeglin's response was swift.

"No."

Even in that one syllable, Marsh heard pain, but she couldn't think of anything to say. There really wasn't anything that would fix it. They needed Aisha or Ilias or Lennie, and none of them were available.

You could try. Roeglin's mind voice was thready. *Dan could help.*

Marsh resisted the temptation to stop but shifted her arm from under his elbow to around his waist. There she found what he'd been hiding from the rest of them, and she did stop.

"You're bleeding," she whispered, and Gustav cursed the Deep.

"Sit your ass down," the emissary ordered, taking Roeglin to the edge of the boardwalk and lowering him so that he could sit on the edge.

The shadow mage resisted but couldn't fight them both.

"We shouldn't be doing this in the open," he protested, but his voice was soft.

"No choice, boy," Gustav told him, lifting his tunic to one side. "There's another set of clothes you've completely ruined."

Roeglin managed a weak chuckle.

"And I thought it was me you were worried about."

"You wish," Gustav muttered, inspecting the wound and swearing all over again.

"By the Deep's dick and fundamentals, you've done a good job of it. Greta's going to have your innards for a waistband."

"Marsh," Roeglin said, "I need—"

"Fine!" she snapped. "But I don't know if I can."

"Try."

Marsh sighed.

No doubts, right? Well, she'd pretty much ruined that. What had Tamlin said? The rock mages had shown Aisha how to draw the energy from the creatures and plants around her, and that was what she used to heal. She glanced around. No shrooms. No plants at all in the middle of town.

No kat, either.

That just left...

Oh, Deeps, no, Roeglin protested, but Marsh didn't reply.

He tried again.

Don't you da—

Marsh shoved him out of her head, smirking as she thought about how much energy she had to spare. Given she already had her hand around his waist, it was a simple matter of wriggling her arm a little lower until she found bare skin before sending the energy into him.

"What in all the Deeps was *that*?"

Marsh remembered that she hadn't warned Gustav what she was about to do.

She also realized she might have misjudged the amount of energy she had to spare.

His *"Yuh think?"* was not helpful, but at least Roeglin sounded stronger.

The world spun, and Marsh was glad she was sitting down.

It left her so much less distance to fall.

"Well shag me stupid and sing me a chorus," Gustav said as she collapsed to the sidewalk. "I can't carry the two of you."

Beside her, Roeglin stirred.

"Won't need to," he told the emissary, and then added, "I've got enough energy for the pair of us."

He didn't have to sound so sarcastic, Marsh thought. This whole healing thing was new.

Sure, whatever you say, girl.

Roeglin slid his arms beneath her and swung her off the sidewalk with a grunt of effort.

"Hey!" Gustav protested. "You're supposed to be taking it easy."

Roeglin turned, and Marsh assumed he was facing the warrior. She wished she could open her eyes.

Couldn't. Too...tired.

Too stupid! Roeglin snapped, and Marsh wished she had the energy to flip him off.

It almost made her regret healing him.

Really?

No, Marsh thought. Not really, but she wished he'd shut up because all she wanted to do was sleep.

She'd have laughed at Gustav's next question if she wasn't already drifting off.

"What did you do to her?"

She wasn't even sure she heard Roeglin's reply correctly.

"It's what I'm going to do to her when she wakes up, the irresponsible *merde*-for-brains, dunder-headed shroom beetle."

15

LITTLE MISS POPULAR

"I'm going to kick her ass." Those were not the words Marsh wanted to hear when she resurfaced, nor was the reply.

"You'll have to get in line."

"You and whose army?" the first voice challenged, and Marsh recognized her cousin's angry tones.

"Hey," she managed, knowing she had to say something.

It was a battle to open her eyes, but she managed it... and then wished she hadn't, or that Roeglin and Daniel would just back the Deeps up a few dozen feet. Roeglin gave her a feral grin.

"Not likely."

Daniel shot him a frustrated look.

"What's not likely."

"Dung for brains here wants us to back the Deeps up."

Daniel raised his eyebrows, but Marsh had to give him credit for being a quick learner because those brows just as quickly furrowed and he shifted focus to glare at her.

"Huh. She does, does she?" He loomed nearer, with Roeglin mirroring his movement.

That was it for Marsh. She reached out from under her blankets intending to bang their heads together…or she tried. Problem was, they'd tucked her in tight, trapping her arms under the sheets—which they were leaning on. The attempt had them grinning like a pair of clowns or a pair of hunting cats that had just caught their prey.

"Oh, yeah. Very funny, *boys!*"

"What have they done this time?"

Gustav's voice was both a welcome and worrying distraction, and Marsh's reply was lost when both Roeglin and Daniel answered.

"She's awake."

Honestly, it was like listening to an unholy chorus.

Hey!

Hey, yourself, numbnuts, Marsh thought, scowling at him and trying to get her arms free. It was a relief when Gustav's face appeared above their heads and he looked down at her, even if Roeglin's eyes had flared white like he was still reading her mind.

"You're supposed to be resting," Gustav said. "Ilias's orders."

Ilias was here?

"No," Roeglin answered. "I talked to him and one of the rock mages helping Aisha and Lennie get a handle on their healing. They both say you need to rest and that you're an… Let me see, how did they put it? Oh, yeah. An irresponsible, foolhardy, dung-for-brains, Deeps-forsaken idiot who's lucky to be alive."

They had? The idea that the healers thought she was an

idiot gave Marsh a moment of dizziness, but she closed her eyes and pushed it away.

"Thanks for that."

When she opened her eyes again, both Daniel and Roeglin were moving for the door, and Marsh wondered what she'd missed. Gustav motioned for them to keep going and came over to sit on the chair beside her bed. Marsh watched him, wondering why he looked so serious.

"How do you feel?" he asked, and Marsh felt the first twinge of misgiving.

"Okaaay," she told him and waited for him to get to what he'd really come to say.

He stared at her a moment longer, then sighed.

"How do you *really* feel?" he asked, and Marsh thought about it.

She'd woken up feeling a bit run-down, but now that she thought about it, she felt fine.

"Not too bad," she said, pushing back the covers. "Not bad enough to stay in bed, anyway."

Gustav studied her as she propped herself up and swung her legs over the side of the bed. The intensity of his gaze made her glad that whoever had put her to bed had just dumped her in new clothes and all, although she was glad they'd taken off her boots.

She wiggled her toes against the cool stone floor.

"See? Fine."

Gustav gave her a speculative stare.

"Are you telling me the healers got it wrong?"

That gave her pause, but she couldn't think of a good explanation for why she didn't feel as wrung out as she usually did after pulling so much magic. What made it stranger was that she'd pulled the energy out of herself to help Roeglin, and she still felt fine.

"Nooo," she said, "but I don't have any answers for you, either."

Gustav held her gaze for a moment longer and then stood.

"Right," he said. "In that case, I'll see you downstairs dressed for the road in a half-turn."

He took two steps toward the door and then stopped.

"On second thought, I'll see you downstairs ready for a fitting inside the next quarter turn, and then back and dressed for the road a quarter turn after that."

He didn't wait for her to reply but walked out the door, closing it behind him.

Marsh looked at the hourglass sitting on the dresser and flipped it. A quarter turn! By the Deep's dark trousers!

And she stank like a mule!

Rummaging in her closet to find a change of clothes that might be suitable for both road and fitting, Marsh lifted the towel from the back of her chair and raced to the bathroom. It didn't take her long to get clean and dressed, and she threw her dirty clothes into a waiting basket before hurrying out to the dining room proper.

The look on Roeglin's face when she appeared was comical, but Marsh didn't have any time to enjoy it. The minute she arrived, Dominique looked up from what he was doing and turned in her direction. Gustav was waiting as well.

"Ah. About time, young lady," he said, but Dominique didn't let him get any further.

"Marchant! Over here. Now, stand still...still..." He

turned to the tailors who'd come to stand beside him. "What do you think?"

Marsh listened as they debated the functionality of pleats and a sword belt, the lines of the tunic, the cut of the trousers. She opened her mouth to say they didn't need her any longer and heard Gustav clear his throat.

The Protector captain caught her eye and shook his head, and Marsh sighed.

The fitting continued, with Marsh changing several times before the tailors were through. She watched the light through the dining room's windows turn from an early morning silver to something brighter and stifled another sigh. It seemed to take forever before the tailors were done with their measuring and pinning, but at last Dominique let her go.

"Right. Be back in two days for the final fitting," he ordered and turned back to the table he'd been working at when she'd arrived.

This time, Marsh caught the motion as Gustav opened his mouth to argue and then closed it again. For some reason, the emissary didn't want to upset the tailor, which was as entertaining as the Deeps even if Marsh couldn't work out why.

He was going to leave before Dominique was ready, Roeglin told her. *It was spectacular, and Dom told him how much more expensive it would be if he tried.*

Marsh shot another glance toward the tailor and couldn't imagine him behaving anywhere near as scarily as Roeglin suggested.

Next time, try moving when he wants to adjust a seam.

Marsh thought about it, remembered the tailor's reaction when she'd shuffled her feet to maintain her balance, and decided against it.

I'm not suicidal, she thought.

Exactly.

He broke contact as Gustav spoke.

"A quarter turn, Leclerc."

"*Merde.*"

Marsh headed for the stairs at a jog, breaking into a run the minute she was out of sight. She didn't care that the echo of her footsteps would give her away; she just didn't want to be late. Behind her, she heard Roeglin's voice raised in puzzlement.

"Is she well enough to do that?"

And Gustav's dry response.

"Clearly."

Followed by the kitchen door banging open and Daniel's very clear threat. "She hurts herself again, and the pair of you will know about it."

Who would have guessed her youngest cousin could sound *that* fierce?

Marsh didn't let the exchange slow her down, though. All she'd been planning on doing was grabbing her gloves and pack, but the sight of a small pile of clothes laid out on the end of her bed brought her to an abrupt halt.

They were new, the colors of the cloth too bright and the fabric too clean for them to be otherwise. She was clearly meant to be wearing them when she returned.

"Well, *merde* in the Dark," she muttered, shutting the door behind her and hurrying across the room. "Does the man want me ready in a quarter turn or not?"

It was almost like Roeglin had been waiting for her to think it.

How much do you want to annoy Master Calais?

"So much for a bit of privacy…"

Ooh, touchy…

Marsh grabbed hold of her temper and started to change. She was halfway through when she wondered where Mordan was. The big kat hadn't been there to greet her when she'd woken, and she hadn't been waiting downstairs. In fact, Dan had been startlingly absent. Marsh made a note to find the kat as soon as she was dressed.

She glanced at the hourglass and hurried. The kat probably hadn't gone that far. She didn't when they were in town.

Stepping into the corridor, Marsh looked up and down it. The open door halfway along looked like the most likely place, but she couldn't work out whose room it was. She didn't remember anyone being in there.

Dan? she thought, reaching for her link to the kat as she reached the door. *You in there?*

A soft mew confirmed the kat's presence and Marsh slipped inside.

"What are you doing here?" Piet's voice stopped her in her tracks.

Marsh gestured toward Mordan, who was lying alongside the bed, Piet's hand resting on her head.

"Looking for the kat."

"Oh. She's been keeping me company. Pa says I set one foot outside this room and he'll stitch me to the sheets."

The thought of the tailor doing exactly that made Marsh smile.

"How are you feeling?"

"Like someone hit me on the head with a very big fist?"

Marsh looked out into the hall, then pulled the door closed behind her, and Piet eyed her warily. Mordan lifted her head, nuzzled Piet's hand, and slowly sat up.

"Easy, girl," Marsh told her, remembering what Tamlin had said about Aisha drawing the energy from the creatures around her.

Oh, the Deeps, no!

Roeglin wasn't impressed, and Marsh had the fleeting impression of panic.

Don't you dare!

Like he could stop her trying.

As she crossed the room to crouch beside the kat, Marsh caught Mordan's eyes, trying to convey her need to borrow just a little bit of her strength so she could mend Piet. The kat rubbed her head along Marsh's arm, nudging her hand.

"Yuh think?"

The kat bunted her hand again, and Marsh took a deep breath.

Turning to Piet, she asked, "Do you trust me?"

Worry clouded the young man's face, but he gave her a single jerky nod.

"Sure."

He didn't sound very sure, but it was enough for Marsh.

"Okay, let me see your head."

She didn't ask for any more permission than that, but leaned in closer to inspect the wound, drawing just a little bit of nature magic so that she could see the way his life colored the area around the injury. It was there, a little darker than it should be but not touched by poison.

Marsh entwined her fingers in the fur on Mordan's neck and concentrated on drawing just a little bit of the kat's energy. It took a moment, but then she felt the big beast's power touch her skin. She stopped, wary of drawing too much. When she was sure she could control how much she drew, she focused on directing the borrowed power into the wound on Piet's head.

At the same time, she tried to feel what effect she was having on the wound. It took her a moment to realize she could gauge that better if she was watching the wound as she worked, and she opened her eyes. It healed much faster than she'd anticipated, and Marsh wondered what to do with the excess power she had taken.

"Try sending it back into the kat." Roeglin's suggestion startled her when he spoke quietly behind her.

For a heartbeat, Marsh thought she was going to lose control of the energy, but she forced herself to maintain her connection with the sensation of Mordan's warmth and power and lifted her hand from Piet's head. Holding the feeling of the kat's energy in focus, Marsh thought about returning it, sending the excess back into the kat, and then took her hand off the kat too.

"Thank you," she said, although her thanks blended with Piet's gratitude as he sat up.

"I ought to wring your neck," Gustav muttered from just inside the doorway, and his anger was followed by the tramp of his boots receding down the hall.

Marsh stayed where she was and then pushed slowly up off the floor, dusting her knees to delay the moment when she had to face Roeglin. The Deeps knew why the mage was still standing in the doorway. It wasn't like there was anything left to see.

He snorted at that but didn't comment on it.

"Gustav says it's past time we left."

He didn't add anything more, even though Marsh was braced for another tirade on just how stupid she'd been. She glanced down at Mordan, sending thoughts of concern for the kat's welfare.

The kat yawned, stretched, and padded toward the door.

Hungry.

"I'll see what Per has in the storeroom," Marsh told her, and Roeglin snorted, again.

"You're set on making everyone happy today, are you?"

Marsh resisted the urge to tell him where in the Deeps he could go, turning instead to Piet.

"How do you feel now?"

The youngster swung his legs over the side of the bed.

"Like I could take on a wall-full of raiders on my own."

"Good. I'll let your pa know so he doesn't get mad at you when he sees you, okay?"

"Thanks, Marsh."

Marsh didn't wait for him to say anything more but followed Mordan. She was surprised to see that Roeglin hadn't waited.

I'm feeding the kat.

Oh, he was, was he?

Gustav wants to see you.

Uh-oh.

Gustav was waiting at the bottom of the stairs.

"You—" he began, only to be interrupted by the dining-room door opening.

The look on his face when he saw who had arrived almost made Marsh laugh, but she didn't dare. For one thing, the man had probably been pushed far enough, and for another, the councilor had asked them to see her on their return. For her to be visiting now meant something was afoot.

Marsh wondered what it was.

"Councilor," Gustav began. "Forgive me, but we don't know your name."

The councilor's dark eyes swept the dining room, but her footsteps didn't slow.

"I take it you have somewhere we can speak in private?"

It was less a question than a demand, but Gustav took it in his stride, offering his arm as she drew near.

"Of course, if you would come with me." He glanced over at Per. "Could you ask Daniel to send something up?"

He paused.

"Preferably something edible."

There was an oath from the kitchen that suggested Gustav's parentage was in doubt and Marsh stifled a laugh. Served her cousin right for listening in.

I wouldn't go into the kitchen right now if I were you, Roeglin said, and he offered Marsh his arm as he turned to follow Gustav and the councilor up the stairs.

"I'll feed the kat," Per said when Marsh looked in his direction. "She'll be fine."

Mordan gave Marsh a look of disdain and flicked her tail before walking over to the counter.

See? You're just flavor of the month today. Roeglin teased, and Marsh felt her heart sink.

How she was ever going to make it up to the kat, she didn't know.

Just the kat?

"She's all that matters."

"Thanks, Marsh. Thanks a lot."

16

MERCY MISSION

Gustav was waiting when Roeglin and Marchant arrived at the meeting room upstairs. He indicated the woman perusing the files they'd stacked in a neat pile on the table.

"This is Councilor Ines Asselin-Labat."

At his introduction, the woman paused in her inspection of the papers and looked up. Roeglin closed the door behind them, his eyes gleaming white. The councilor caught it and frowned.

"I'd appreciate it if you stayed out of my head, shadow mage."

Roeglin returned her gaze, his mouth quirking up in the tiniest of smiles.

"Most people would, but we don't know you."

Marsh watched as the councilor shot Gustav a glance and received a shrug in reply. She sighed.

"Very well." She turned away from Roeglin to take a seat at the end of the table.

Gustav gestured for Marsh and Roeglin to join them and then went to sit at the other side of the table.

"You wanted to see us?" he began and then waited for the woman to reply.

After a moment's hesitation and another wary glance at Roeglin's attentive but still-white eyes, she started.

"I know it's earlier than expected, but I feel we can't wait any longer. The raiders are threatening Brodeur."

As an opening, Marsh thought, there wasn't much better. She snuck a look at Roeglin and caught the mage's slight nod. So that much was true, then. The councilor continued as though she hadn't noticed.

"He has a sister who lives on a farmlet a half-day's ride from the city wall."

Gustav sighed, and the councilor paused. When the emissary didn't say anything, she continued.

"I need you to go and see if she and her family are safe…and I need you to convince them to come within the city walls if you can."

She paused and then spoke again.

"I was going to ask you to go after you returned from the council's mission, but when I heard you were still in town, I thought this would provide us with an opportunity to keep my mission secret a little longer. I fear that if the raiders knew I was sending someone to safeguard the captain's family, they would move on them. This way, given everyone knows you are leaving late and won't reach Mika's Outlet tonight, we have a window for secrecy."

"What happens when we arrive late at the Outlet?" Gustav wasn't convinced.

"You won't," the councilor replied. "Well, you won't

arrive *much* later, and hopefully you'll have the family with you, so the secret won't need to be kept much longer. You *will* do this for me, won't you?"

"What's in it for you?" Gustav asked.

Marsh wanted to know why he'd felt the need to be so blunt.

Ines blushed.

"The fewer distractions the captain has, the more he will be focused on keeping the Ledge safe—"

Roeglin cleared his throat, and the lady's blush grew deeper. The mage opened his eyes and raised his eyebrows at her.

"It would be better they heard it from you than me," he told her, and she scowled at him.

He held her gaze until she broke eye contact and looked down at the table.

"Fine," she said. "I love him, and he's been distant since he's had to worry for his sister, and that's even though I argued for him to be allowed to go and see to her safety."

"How does he feel about you?" Gustav wanted to know, although Marsh didn't know why that would matter.

It matters, Roeglin told her, and the councilor's next words proved him correct.

"I thought he returned my feelings," Ines admitted, watching as Roeglin's eyes sheeted white once more and frowning. "If he doesn't, I don't know…"

"The city needs you," Gustav said, and her face hardened.

"It's not enough."

The emissary made a broad-armed gesture that took in more than the room around them.

"Where would you go?"

"Away. Somewhere Brodeur wasn't."

Roeglin's intervention was unexpected.

"He would miss you."

That brought her to sudden stillness, followed by just a little hope.

"He would?"

"Oh, yes. He would. He misses you now."

"He does?" Her eyes narrowed with suspicion. "How do you know?"

Roeglin looked at her, his eyes returning to their usual shade of green.

"How do you think?"

Ines looked mortified.

"You didn't…"

Roeglin smirked.

"What else was I going to do? The city needs you. You needed to know. He needs his family to be safe."

He looked at Gustav, clearly leaving the decision in the emissary's hands although it was obvious what they needed to do. The Protector captain sighed.

"Very well. We'll take your detour and see what we can do."

The councilor breathed a sigh of relief, taking Gustav's hand as she rose from her seat.

"Thank you," she said, shaking it. "Thank you very much."

As Gustav rose with her, there was a knock at the door —and Marsh remembered Gustav's request to Per.

"You'd best sit down again," she told them. "Daniel's in a foul enough mood already."

Her words brought sudden realization to Gustav's face and he froze, keeping the councilor's hand captive. The knock came again and he turned to her, the pleading look on his face almost comical.

"Councilor…"

"Ines," she corrected and resumed her seat with a smile, "and yes, I would be honored to join you for lunch."

Gustav gave a sigh of relief and followed her example.

"Come in!" he called, and Daniel arrived with the food he'd requested.

The look he gave them said he was glad to find them still present, and Marsh breathed a silent thanks to the Depths for the councilor's understanding. Exactly how her unpredictable cousin would have reacted if he'd found them all on the brink of leaving, she hated to think. Lunch was eaten with swift efficiency and no speech, but it *was* eaten. Daniel would have no complaints.

When they were done, Ines cast an anxious glance at the door.

"Do you think it's safe to go now?" she asked, and Marsh knew the woman wasn't trying to rush them.

Gustav followed her look, and then he pushed back his chair and stood, offering the councilor his arm.

"I think so. Let me accompany you downstairs."

Ines smiled and rose to accept his offer.

"Thank you," she said, and Marsh watched them leave.

Once they were gone, she and Roeglin gathered the dishes and took them down to the kitchen. Daniel looked up as they entered.

"How was it?"

"Very good, thank you," Marsh told him, and Roeglin nodded a hasty agreement before he left.

Daniel caught Marsh's hesitancy and frowned.

"What is it?"

"I'm heading out shortly. Just wanted to say goodbye."

His frown deepened.

"How long will you be gone?" he asked, and Marsh caught a hint of anxiety in his tone.

In reality, he wasn't asking her how long she'd be gone. He was really asking her if she'd be coming back, and they both knew it. Marsh's mind raced, calculating the journey to Brodeur's sister's place and then to Mika's Outlet and back. She tried to guess at how long it would take to sort the difficulties between the emerging mage and their family and decided four days was likely.

At least, she hoped four days was all it was going to take. Anything longer meant trouble they hadn't expected, and she didn't want to think of what form *that* might take.

"Seven days," she said, factoring in the travel time before clarifying. "Seven days, six nights from now, okay?"

From the look on his face, it really wasn't okay, but they both knew it couldn't be helped.

"Anything you want me to get you while I'm out there?" she asked, knowing there were a lot of ingredients that could only be gathered in the cavern outside the Ledge's walls.

When Daniel turned away from her, she thought she'd upset him more than she'd meant to, but he merely crossed to a bench and reached out for a notepad hanging on the wall above it.

"These," he said, tearing off the top page and handing it

to her. "Don't lose the list. I'll need to copy what's missing when you get back."

Marsh was about to ask him if he wanted to copy it while she was still there, but Gustav's bellow reached them before she could speak.

"Shadow Mage Leclerc!"

She rolled her eyes, tucking the list into her pocket.

"Sorry, Dan. Got to run." She hurried over to embrace him in an awkwardly-returned hug. "Be safe until I get back, okay?"

She didn't wait for him to reply but rushed back to the door leading into the dining hall. His answer reached her just as she stepped through it to the room beyond.

"You too."

The tears hidden in those two words brought a lump to Marsh's throat, and it was all she could do not to turn back. Some of what she was feeling must have shown on her face, though, because her uncle hurried over to engulf her in a swift hug.

"I'll take care of him," he told her. "You take care of yourself."

The lump grew larger, blocking her voice, so Marsh nodded and hugged him back. When she could clear her throat, she said, "You too, Per. I'll see you in a week."

His eyebrows rose.

"A week?" He glanced toward the kitchen. "Is that what you told him?"

"Seven days, six nights," Marsh confirmed, and heard Roeglin groan while Gustav slapped a palm to his forehead.

"Great. Now we have a deadline."

Marsh wanted to know why that should bother

them and Roeglin replied, "Because, if we take any longer, that stubborn, over-dramatic son-of-the-Deep is going to come looking, and none of us want him doing *that*."

"I heard that," echoed out of the kitchen, and Roeglin made a sound of exasperation.

He didn't get to say anything else before Henri, Jakob, and the three shadow guards arrived.

"Mules are prepped," Henri reported.

"We even snagged a couple as pack beasts," Izmay added, shooting a look at Per. "I hope you don't mind."

The stationmaster had reached the kitchen door. He shrugged.

"They all need the run," he said. "Take what you need, but leave at least three in case I need them."

"Will do," Izmay replied, and Marsh caught the faint sense of relief beneath her words. She was curious about what the woman might consider to be "a couple."

Half a dozen.

Marsh surveyed the mules tethered to the hitching rail in the courtyard and wondered exactly how much of a fight the woman had expected from Per. Gustav looked from mules to the guard and back again.

"How many did you leave?" he asked.

"Six."

That was enough to settle it. Gustav stepped off the porch and walked over to the mule Izmay indicated was the lead. She'd also said the creature was a troublemaker, something it lost no time in proving by laying back its overly long ears and turning its head to watch Gustav approach.

"This should be interesting," Roeglin muttered, trying to watch the emissary as he made his way to his own mule.

Marsh had to agree. She might not have known the mule, but she knew the signs. The big beast was looking for trouble and wouldn't be satisfied until it had determined if Gustav was worthy of getting on its back.

She watched as Gustav reached to unloop the reins and saw the sudden snap as the mule tried to take a piece of him. When the captain slapped his hand over the creature's muzzle, pushing its head down and back while he retrieved the reins and flipped them over its neck, she wasn't sure who got the bigger shock, her or the mule.

"Yours is over there," Izmay said, tugging on her sleeve, and indicating another mule. "He's a real sweetheart."

Something in the shadow guard's tone was off, and Marsh shifted her attention from Gustav and his continuing "negotiations" with his mount to her own ride.

A real sweetheart, was he?

She studied the brown-coated beast tethered next to Roeglin's and saw it grow suddenly alert at her approach.

Uh huh.

Judging from the equally alert way the three shadow guards, and Henri and Jakob were watching her, there was something not-so-sweet about this one. Mordanlenoowar stalked along the porch, paralleling her progress but not getting near the mounts. Marsh thanked the Deeps for small blessings and focused on the mule.

He tilted his head to observe her, and Marsh wondered what he was thinking. It became clear enough when he lashed out with a hind hoof and then danced away. Marsh stopped, and the mule repositioned his hindquarters.

Okaaay, then.

"Get a move on, Leclerc."

Gustav had managed to get into the saddle and was keeping a tight hand on his reins.

"Be right with you," Marsh told him, coming round to the front of her own beast.

She figured if Aisha could do it, then so could she.

She stood within reach of the reins but didn't make a move toward them. The mule eyed her uncertainly, and Marsh looked into its liquid brown eyes. What was its problem? Hadn't it had enough of its stall? Didn't it want to walk new trails? Discover new pastures? What did mules think of when they met a new rider, anyway?

For a long moment, she was aware of the mule returning her stare and all too aware of looking into its eyes, and then she was falling, coming to stand before it mind to mind, so to speak.

"I need a favor," she told it, impressing her need to be carried, impressing the urgency of their mission into its mind.

It sidled back and forth, the tether acting as a pivot point, clearly nervous. Marsh tried to reassure it, projecting comfort and a promise to protect it. Uncertainty answered her, and clear apprehension about the hoshkat accompanied it.

"Friends," Marsh told the beast. "We will *both* protect you."

The mule stilled, considering her promise, and then it relaxed.

Marsh let it go, descending back to her own mind before approaching the creature one more time. This time it let her mount without any resistance. Gustav remained unimpressed.

"Well, now that *that's* over, let's move out."

Marsh didn't really have an answer for that, so she just mounted and went to move her mule in behind Roeglin's. Again, Gustav had something to say.

"You're riding behind me, Leclerc. I want you scanning ahead once we're outside the gates."

Oh, he did, did he?

Looks like, Roeglin said, *unless* you *want to tell him otherwise...*

Marsh didn't dignify his teasing with more than a covert flip of her fingers as she nudged the mule into its position in the caravan. It looked like it was going to be a long ride.

17

DINNER GUESTS

The approach to the farmlet was overgrown by a combination of shrooms and shrubs, but Marsh's scan of both shadows and life didn't reveal anything out of the ordinary. She picked up a couple of big centipedes prowling the edges of the cavern, and a number of smaller life signs that bounded and scurried through the vegetation.

Not joffra or shroom walkers, and no beetles either. These life forms reminded her more of rabbits or rats, or something similar. It was hard to know; she hadn't been to the surface since discovering she had magic. Maybe when this was over…

Gustav's voice interrupted her thoughts.

"Anything?"

It almost jolted the magic loose from her grasp, and Marsh scowled as she kept hold of it.

"Two big pedes and a bunch of small and furries," she told him. "Nothing outside of that."

"Nothing? Are you sure?"

The questioning tone made her let go of the nature magic allowing her to detect the life forms around them, and she looked at him.

"No. Why?"

He gestured at the small stone house standing in the clearing in front of them.

"Because we're here, and I was hoping someone would be home."

Marsh cocked her head to one side. "You ever tried knocking?"

He mimicked the movement, then swept his arm toward the door.

"No. Why don't you show me how it's done?"

Marsh stared at him, momentarily shocked by the smartassery, and then she dismounted and headed for the door.

"Sure, boss. Whatever you say."

She lifted the reins over the mule's head and dropped them to the ground, hoping this one had been trained the same way Per usually trained them and that it would stay in one place as though tethered by the reins at its feet.

No one answered the door when Marsh knocked. She glanced back at Gustav, Roeglin, and the guards, and saw they'd arrayed themselves so as to keep the surrounding hollow under observation. Marsh did her own scan of the cavern, tugging on the shadows to see if they were connected to anything hidden and searching for any sign of human life.

When she came up with nothing, she knocked again, flinching when the sound of it echoed through the cavern as well as the house beyond. Again there was no answer, and Marsh sighed. Her shoulders slumped as she laid her fingers on the door handle.

Poor Brodeur, she thought, pushing the handle down and shoving the door inwards.

She was pretty sure of what she'd find, but there was no use acting on assumptions. If she was lucky, there was some other reason no one had answered the door.

Like what? she scolded herself, letting the door swing wide as she peered into the dimly-lit corridor beyond.

There was a door set into the wall on either side and another at the end of the corridor. Marsh decided to start with the door on the left and scanned the corridor once more to make sure nothing was waiting in the shadows.

What's the matter, Marsh? Afraid of the dark? Roeglin taunted.

Marsh wanted to give him the finger, but she was already pulling a blade and buckler from the shadows. She stepped inside without responding, sliding along the wall to the door. A quick flick of the wrist and a slight push had it open. Marsh tweaked the shadows linked to the inside, and when none of them had anything to show, she side-stepped through the door and scanned the room.

Nothing.

No signs of life—and no sign of disturbance.

All the toys were in a perfect array, and the bed was made.

It's not looking good, she thought, aware of the cautious steps following her inside.

No, Roeglin agreed as she turned back. *Let's see what's next.*

It was no surprise to find Gerry and Izmay waiting in

the hall. Neither warrior moved, though, as Marsh and Roeglin opened the other door. This room was the same, except it wasn't a child's room. Marsh tried to remember if Ines had mentioned the sister having a husband to go with the child and thought she might have.

That doesn't matter now, Roeglin told her, surveying the room from beside her.

Marsh sighed. Of course, he was right. That didn't mean she had to like it. Together they went through the room, opening closets and checking under the bed, and then they returned to the child's room and did the same, Marsh kicking herself for forgetting it before.

"Do you think they'll come out once they know we're here?"

Roeglin shook his head.

"No. They're gonna think we're raiders."

"Not funny, Ro."

"Not meant to be. Let's just hope they work out we're not *before* they try to take one our heads off."

"I can't see them, and the shadows don't show anyone…" Marsh began, but Roeglin had turned toward the door at the end of the hall.

"The shadows don't do so well when there are obstacles in the way, remember?"

Marsh did. She also did not want to see the state of the kitchen-come-dining room beyond the door. She'd had enough of half-eaten dinners, and half-cooked meals to last her a lifetime. The fact the next ones would belong to folk important to someone she knew only made it harder. She took a deep breath and reached for the door.

"Let's get it done," she said, and turned the handle.

Roeglin was beside her when they entered the room beyond.

To their surprise, it was well lit, and a fire crackled in the hearth. Glows shone brightly from sconces on the wall. The table was set for two, but one of the forks was askew, as though someone had left in a hurry. A large pot had been set on the bench beside the stove as though someone was worried the food would burn.

The kitchen was as empty as the rest of the house.

Marsh and Roeglin spun in a careful circle.

"Do you think they're still here?"

"I don't think they've gone far."

"Do you think they'll come out if we call?"

"Would you?"

Marsh felt her heart sink.

"We can't give up," she said. "They have to know we're not here to hurt them, that they weren't forgotten and help was sent."

"We're going to need proof."

"What sort of proof?"

Roeglin looked stunned.

"You're asking *me*? I'm probably part of the reason they're not coming out." He caught Marsh's look of disbelief and gestured at his clothes. "Look at me. How much difference is there really between the raiders' uniforms and what I'm dressed in?"

"You could always strip down naked." Izmay's snide suggestion was followed by the equally unhelpful, "Hasn't been a single report of any shadow raider doing *that.*"

"Yeah, thanks, Iz. Thanks a lot."

Marsh left them to it and tried scanning the room once

more. First, she asked the shadows, looking for any that might be connected to someone hiding in the dark. When that failed, she looked for any lives to which they were connected, hoping her nature magic would reveal something beyond themselves.

Nothing.

Both methods came up empty and she wracked her brains, trying to think of some other way to sense those around her. If shadow magic wouldn't work and nature magic failed, what did that leave her? She glanced at Roeglin, realizing the shadow mage had been suspiciously silent while she'd been trying different alternatives. Then it came to her.

"You," she said, releasing her sword to the shadows so she could smack Roeglin on the shoulder. "Why don't *you* try?"

He gave her a funny look.

"If the shadows aren't working for you, what makes you think they'll work for me?" he asked, and Marsh smacked him again.

"Not the shadows," she said. "Mental magic. You *can* sense the minds around you, right? Well, *can* you?"

He stared at her, and Marsh began to think she'd made a mistake—right up until he answered.

"I should have thought of that."

"Yeah," Izmay snarked, "you really should."

"Not helping, Iz," Gerry commented, fielding the female shadow guard's glare with a sort of whatchagonnadoaboutit-oohbringiton look until she turned away.

Roeglin closed his eyes.

"Right. Keep watch for me."

Marsh wanted to ask him what else he thought she was going to do, but she was more interested in seeing if he could find what she could not, so she kept quiet. It seemed to take him an eternity, during which time heavy steps signaled Gustav and the other guards arriving through the front door.

"Mules are in the barn. Thought we heard joffra or one of the pedes moving in. Figured it was best we didn't volunteer to be supper."

Henri sniffed appreciatively at the smell of the meal that had been set aside.

"Speaking of supper…"

"Don't even think of it," Marsh scolded. "We haven't found them yet."

"They're just outside the door," Roeglin told her. "Wait one!"

His second call stopped Marsh and Gustav as they made for the back door. He continued when the turned to look at him.

"Give me a moment to convince them we're not here to hurt them. Starting with the fact," he added, glaring at Henri, "that we're not going to eat their supper."

Henri sighed.

"Well, can you at least ask them if we can borrow the hearth. Rations taste better if you can heat them."

Marsh had to admit the big guard had a point, but she wished he could have waited a little longer. She was about to say as much when the door to the kitchen cracked open and they all turned. The door froze, but it was open far enough for them to see two curious faces peering around it.

Two sets of dark blue eyes framed by honey-colored

skin looked in at them from under bangs as black as pitch. There was wariness in those twin gazes, but lively curiosity, too…and Marsh would have sworn that she saw mischief mingled with the rest.

After a few heartbeats' silence, the door was swung wide enough for the two women outside to come through. The taller of the pair slipped an arm around the other and stopped her from going too far into the room. A closer look showed that she was much older than her companion. The sister and her child? Marsh wondered. Brodeur hadn't said the girl was in her teens.

"Wait, Claudie."

Claudie?

Marsh hoped she hadn't missed the details, but she couldn't recall either councilor or captain mentioning the names of Brodeur's sister or her child. The girl had caught sight of Mordan, but she stopped, although she shot her mother a reproachful look. Her mother followed the direction of the child's gaze and smiled.

"Oh. Wait a moment, because even if not eating our supper is a good start, and asking for permission to use the hearth a step in the right direction, I still have one question to ask."

Marsh felt the guards still. Even Roeglin froze as though trying hard not to startle the pair.

"Which of you can speak with minds?" the mother demanded.

The mage cleared his throat, moving one hand slightly to draw her attention. "Me," he said. "Roeglin Leger of the Cavern's Deep Monastery."

The mother quirked an eyebrow at him.

"You said you rode with an emissary?" Gustav raised his hand. The woman glanced at him and then continued, her eyes traveling over the gathered company as though assessing where and what each and every one of them was. "And a newly minted shadow mage who speaks to the beasts." Marsh raised her hand and the woman continued, ticking them off her fingers. "Two ex-caravan guards." Here Henri and Jakob signaled who they were. "And three shadow guards."

She caught sight of Gerry, Izmay, and Zeb standing in the hall.

"Ah, yes, I see."

Her gaze returned to Henri.

"Now, what was this about borrowing my hearth?"

The ex-caravan guard reddened, but the woman gave him no time to recover.

"I won't hear of it. Fetch me that pot."

He followed the direction of her pointing finger and cast Gustav a troubled look.

"I'd do what she says, lad, or you won't be getting *any* supper."

There was a smile in the Protector captain's voice, but it vanished pretty quickly when Brodeur's sister turned to him.

"I'll thank you to go sit at the table. You and all the rest."

Her daughter tugged at her hand, and she glanced down.

"What is it, Claudie?"

"The kat, mama," the girl whispered. "Can I…"

The woman lifted her eyes from her daughter's face and looked at Marsh.

"Can she?"

Marsh looked at Mordan, who had taken shelter under the table.

"I have someone who wants to meet you," she told the kat and used the link between them to draw Mordan's attention to the girl.

Mordan yawned and stretched, but she didn't get up. Instead, she eyed the young woman, who was staring at her in fascination. The girl cast Marsh an anxious glance.

"Can I? Is it okay?"

Mordan huffed out a sigh and laid her head on her paws, sending a deep feeling of resignation as well as her consent over the link. Marsh laughed.

"It's okay, but she's had a long day, so be gentle."

She hadn't finished speaking before the girl had hurried over to the table and slipped beneath it to kneel beside the kat.

"Oh, aren't you the prettiest girl?" she cooed, and Roeglin rolled his eyes.

Marsh looked at the woman.

"She's always liked animals," the woman said and pointed to a door at one side of the kitchen. "Could you find me some vegetables for a stew?"

Marsh nodded, and the woman turned to Roeglin.

"There's also some meat." Roeglin followed Marsh, pausing as the woman added, "Bring some for the kat, too."

Opening the door and discovering the pantry, Marsh tried to think what vegetables Daniel or Per would choose. The Deeps knew she'd worked in the kitchens often enough when she'd been growing up, although her recent forays into cooking had consisted of heating her rations or hitting a caf or dining hall. Not much cooking at all.

Roeglin followed her in and opened the stone meat-safe set in the back wall. He grunted at the weight of the lid and hauled out two small haunches.

"Think this will be enough for Dan?" he asked, holding one up.

Marsh nodded, staring at the unfamiliar array of vegetables, and Roeglin came to stand beside her.

"That one, that one, that one…and…ooh, that one," he suggested, and she wondered how he had any idea.

"Rock mages," he replied as he carried the meat into the kitchen. "They like their food."

Thinking of the Beast Master, Marsh could see how. She grabbed the vegetables Roeglin had indicated and carried them out. Henri and Roeglin were standing by the pot, which now hung over the fire, but the rest of the team were seated at the table and looking very uncomfortable at not having anything to do.

Fortunately, their hostess had a solution for that too. She smiled when she saw Marsh's selection and pointed to the table.

"Set them there," she ordered and took cutting boards, bowls, and knives from a nearby shelf, distributing them to those at the table. She settled herself into a spare seat and divided up the vegetables. "We can talk while we work."

It was as if she'd given a signal. Gustav breathed a sigh of relief and waited for the first lot of vegetables to land on his cutting board. The woman ignored him and introduced herself.

"I am Felicity Bisset, and the young *lady* under the table is my daughter Claudette. And you are?"

She waited for them to introduce themselves and then asked, "Why are you here, and clearly looking for my daughter and me?"

"Ines—"

At the mention of the councilor's name, Felicity gave a short bark of laughter and then finished the surname in chorus with Gustav.

"Asselin-Labat. Of course."

That last was said with a twist of bitterness and Gustav looked puzzled.

"Is she not a friend?"

Felicity blushed and looked down at her lap.

"She is. I was just hoping Louis…"

Marsh got it.

"He tried," she said. "The council wouldn't let him."

"Then how did Ines come to ask you? She's on the council too. *Wedded* to it, I thought."

Marsh looked at Gustav, and the emissary picked up the story.

"Perhaps, but more concerned for your brother. She's afraid the raiders are trying to pressure him by using threats against you."

Felicity's eyes widened.

"Oh, but he wouldn't let them. He…" Her voice faltered. "That must be killing him."

Gustav's voice was gentle as he replied, and he didn't stop working through the vegetables as he spoke.

"The councilor thinks so, and she cares enough for him that she doesn't want him to have to live with that choice."

"Why? She could always pick up the pieces afterward." Felicity's voice was bitter once more.

Marsh wondered what the councilor had done to earn the woman's anger, but Gustav was already answering.

"I think she loves him," he said.

Felicity started to debate it, then stopped. After a moment's silence, she sighed, then lifted the cut vegetables from in front of the Protector captain and carried them to the pot.

"I suppose she must, then," she said. "I just thought she found him useful, another tool to keep her in power. It would be nice if that's not the case."

She dropped the vegetables in and gave Henri a stern glare.

"Stir, and don't let them burn."

She went and collected the meat from where Gerry had been cutting one of the haunches into small cubes, and she added that too.

"How about some kaffee while we wait?" she asked, lifting a large kettle from a cupboard beside the stove.

"Thank you," Gustav said, and let the silence stretch a little before continuing, "Do you and your daughter live here on your own?"

His question caused a brief storm of emotion to play across Felicity's face, but she set the pot on the stove, checked the stew, and started to set the table. As she worked and the kaffee brewed, Felicity began. "No, but my husband drew the raiders' attention long enough for Claudette and me to get away. We haven't seen him since."

"And the raiders?"

"Oh, them. We've seen them plenty, but we avoid them every time."

"How?"

Felicity gave a small, small smile, casting a proud look at where her daughter sat beneath the table, her hand tangled in Mordan's fur.

"Magic."

18

PARTY CRASHERS

Felicity explained how Claudette could call the shadows to hide them and how the girl could draw them both into the very stones of the cavern, which was what they did every time the raiders arrived.

"How do you know they are coming in time to hide?" Gustav asked, and Felicity grew sober as she served the kaffee and added herbs to the stew.

"It's hard to explain," she said. "After that first attack, I thought about going to the Ledge for help, but I always hoped…" Her breath caught, and she momentarily closed her eyes before gathering herself to continue. "I hoped… that Claude would come back, and then the longer I left it, the more I realized we were trapped out here. That the raiders were everywhere and we had no hope of reaching town."

"I found myself listening all the time, trying to pick up the slightest sound of movement, the barest whisper. I used to imagine I could hear them thinking…and then, one day, I wasn't imagining it. I *could* hear them thinking, and I knew they were coming and hoped to catch Claudie and me as we came in from the fields. Well, I panicked.

"I'd left Claudie alone at home to tidy the house and pickle some of the shrooms before they spoiled. Who knew how long it would be before her father came back, and we didn't want to run out. And she never did like it when we hunted, so I started to run for the house, thinking if I only ran fast enough I would get there in time, and knowing there was no way."

"It was like she was shouting." Claudie's voice interrupted, making them all start with fright. "Only I couldn't hear a thing. Just inside my head. The raiders were coming. They were almost here. I took the pickles off the fire and went to find her. Someone knocked as I left, and I'm sure I heard voices in the yard outside, but I didn't stop. If Mama hadn't warned me, I might have. Instead, I ran as fast as I could to get away from them."

She paused, and Felicity took up the tale.

"I met her above the house, and she towed me off the path to Stroker's Stack. It's a big pile of boulders that looks like it's trying to be a chimney or the corner of a building or something. Who knows what it used to be, but it stands where part of the cavern has fallen in and is perfect for hiding in. We could hear them coming up the trail behind us, so Claudie just pulled me into the rock. I was so cross!"

Claudette giggled.

"She was. It made it very hard to keep her inside the rock until the raiders arrived, and then it was all 'how are you doing this, Claudie?' 'Claudie, we've got to run,' 'Claudie, stay still,' 'Claudie!'"

That last was said with such exasperation that Felicity laughed.

"You're lucky you're under that table, young lady."

"Yeah, or you'd what?" the girl teased, but she didn't move from Mordan's side.

Felicity sighed.

"She's learned to give her skin the consistency of stone," she said. "Giving her a good smack has absolutely no effect."

Another giggle sounded from under the table.

"Except on your hand."

Felicity glared.

"I'm still your mother."

Silence greeted that remark, and then Claudette sighed.

"I'm sorry, Mama. I shouldn't tease you." She was quiet for a moment, and then she asked, "Are we going with them to see Uncle Louis?"

The plea in her voice said she really wanted to leave but she wasn't going to beg, and Felicity's expression softened.

"Yes, *petit chou*, we're going to go live with Uncle Louis for a while. He needs us."

"To protect him from the Hellkat?"

Felicity blushed and rolled her eyes, and Marsh guessed they'd never been meant to learn that particular phrase for Councilor Ines.

"No, *chou*, to help him win the Hellkat's heart."

An inarticulate squeal of delight met this and Mordan rumbled a protest, drawing a string of apologies from the girl. Felicity turned to her guests.

"When do we leave?" she asked, testing the stew and serving it into bowls that she set Henri to deliver.

"In the morning," Gustav told her, "as early as you're able."

He was about to continue, but Felicity smiled and handed Henri the last bowl.

"Thank you," she told him, cutting across Gustav. "Now, go sit with the rest. I appreciate your help."

The big man was blushing as he joined the other guards at the table, but he didn't argue. He blushed even harder when Felicity placed a large shroom roll in front of his plate before setting a stack of bread-and-butter plates and a loaf of bread in the center of the table for everyone else.

"Welcome to my house," she said before seating herself on a stool by the fire. "Come out and eat, Claudette. Our guests deserve your company, and the company deserves some peace."

With a reluctant sigh, the girl did as her mother ordered, washing her hands at the basin by the door without having to be told and then moving to sit by her mother. They both looked surprised when Gustav and the other guards moved their chairs to sit near them, but not too surprised for Felicity to remember that she'd broken across what Gustav had wanted to say next.

She accepted the bread he offered her and dipped it into her stew, taking a bite before turning back to him.

"What were you going to say about the journey?"

She watched as he swallowed his mouthful and washed it down with a gulp of water.

"We won't be returning directly to Kerrenin's Ledge," he told her and kept going as she took another mouthful of stew. "We have an errand to run for the council over in Mika's Outlet."

"Oh, that poor girl!" Felicity exclaimed. "I'm glad you're going to help. Don't you believe a word of the wickedness those folks are saying. Netti is the sweetest child you could ever meet."

Gustav's mouth had dropped open in surprise and he closed it as she finished, hastily gathering his thoughts.

"You know her?" he asked, taking another spoonful of stew.

"Yes, of course, I know her. We *are* neighbors, after all."

Marsh watched as the emissary almost choked on his food and saw him focus on the necessary information as he finished what he was chewing.

"Neighbors?"

Felicity ate some more stew before answering.

"Oh, yes. They're a half-day out of the Outlet and a half-day from here if you know the shortcut. She and Claudie used to play together all the time. The little scamps would meet halfway, as if their mamas didn't know."

This last was said with a sly dig in Claudia's ribs and the girl blushed, clearly surprised by her mama's knowledge. Still, she had to go one better.

"I bet you didn't know it was Netti who taught me to play in the shadows though, did you, Mama?"

From the way the guards opposite almost choked on their stew, the look on Felicity's face said it all. Claudette continued on, oblivious.

"And I taught her to play with the rock. It wasn't fair when the others threw stones at her."

"They *what?*" Marsh watched Gustav's knuckles turn white around his spoon and the others paused, their eyes turned to him as though they expected orders to leave immediately.

Felicity laid a hand on his arm.

"That was weeks ago," she said. "I was going to have Claudie ask the girl to come and stay with us, but then the raiders came."

She stopped, her expression troubled, and she hastily dug into her stew.

"She'll be okay for another night."

Marsh thought she was trying to convince herself more than anyone else, but none of the guards argued otherwise. Not even Gustav, and he seemed just as unconvinced. She was about to suggest they go anyway when Mordan growled softly and lifted her head.

"Marsh?" Gustav asked as Claudie looked at Felicity.

"Mum?"

Felicity's spoon stopped halfway to her mouth and then she rose hastily from her stool, setting her bowl on a sideboard and taking her daughter's hand.

"We have to..." she began and froze. "They're already here."

Her terrified whisper echoed through the kitchen and the guards set themselves around the pair, with Marsh reaching the back door just as the handle turned. She threw herself against it, but she was too slow and too light and was thrown back as the door burst open.

Roeglin acted swiftly, pulling a dart from the shadow and hurling it at the large surface-worlder pushing his way into the room. The man swayed to one side, and the dart flew harmlessly past. He straightened, sidestepping to keep the wall at his back as he took in the number of people in the room.

"They've got—"

His shout of warning died in a blood-soaked gurgle as a second dart flew from between the tightly-grouped guards. Picking herself up off the floor, Marsh saw Claudie pull a second one from the shadows.

The girl was a quick study!

Lucky for us, Roeglin commented. *I can sense another ten out back, and fifteen out front.*

"Lightning?" Marsh asked, trying to divide her gaze between him and Gustav.

"Lightning." The captain's voice was quiet and sure. "Close the door, shadow mage."

Roeglin moved to do as he was ordered, but Marsh laid a hand on his shoulder.

"Wait," she said. "It's easier if I can touch the shadow outside."

"They'll come in," Gustav said as Gerry and Izmay moved forward to stand with Roeglin.

Zeb moved to face the corridor.

"Not if she's fast," he said and Marsh closed her eyes, thinking of the shadows cloaking the cavern's ceiling. She touched them, felt them at peace, and tried to remember how she'd called them before. At the prospector's, she'd wanted to destroy every single shadow monster trying to get into the cabin, and outside Madame Monetti's, she'd been angry at being ambushed by shadow raiders, and then there had been the dining hall at Mid-Point.

Yeah. She wanted that.

She wanted to rain destruction on every single asshole

outside this cottage. She wanted the shadows to protect her, sure, but she wanted them to protect Felicity and Claudette more. She channeled her anger at them being attacked and her outrage at Netti's treatment by her own— By. Her. Own!— into lightning and spears. Sound roared outside the cottage, as though a fierce wind blew through the cavern. Marsh didn't care; she wanted craters. She wanted...

"I think the shadows heard you, Marsh," Roeglin said, "and I'm pretty sure you can tell them to stop now. I don't think there's anyone left alive out there."

Marsh blinked, and the roaring that had filled her ears stopped. Purple static crackled, its savage gleam drawing her eye to the open back door. There were bodies piled up high enough to almost block it. The raiders had died in terror, trying to reach the safety of the kitchen, and not a one of them would move again. Marsh felt herself grow calm.

"They're all dead." Claudette had come to stand beside her and was staring at the flickering darkness outside, her voice soft with amazement. "How did you *do* that?"

"I'll show you later," Marsh muttered, her eyes drawn once more to the bodies outside. "First I have to calm the storm, thank the shadows for their protection, and ask them to return to their homes."

"Yeah, but *how?*" Claudette was nothing if not persistent.

Marsh felt herself smile even as she focused on the roiling dark.

"Like this," she said, thinking of safety and demanding calm, focusing on soothing the shadows' agitation and returning them to the way they'd been. Only when the shadows had become still and calm did she turn to the child.

"How old are you, Claudette?"

The girl regarded her with a solemn azure gaze.

"Twelve," she said, and her mother nodded behind her.

"Twelve," Felicity confirmed, her face pale, "and far too young for killing like this."

"I stopped him, though, didn't I?" Claudette demanded, jabbing a finger toward the first raider through the door. Marsh remembered the second dart, the one that had pierced the man's throat.

Roeglin turned to her.

"That was you?"

Claudette lifted her chin, looking unrepentant and proud, but Roeglin wasn't finished.

"And who taught *you* that trick?"

The smile that flitted across the girl's face was pure mischief.

"*You* did."

Marsh watched Roeglin's jaw drop and was glad he'd taken the child's attention. The magic had left her feeling weak at the knees and slightly light-headed. Given that the last time she'd conjured up a storm like that, she'd been told she'd slept for close to two days, it really wasn't surprising. Marsh really hoped that wasn't going to happen now.

She sagged, reaching out behind her to find the wall and then leaning quietly against it. From the look on his face, Gustav remembered the last time she'd expended that much energy, and he wasn't pleased. He didn't argue though, just picked up a chair and set it down beside her.

"You going to be okay?" he asked, and of course, Claudette overheard and was as curious as the Deeps.

"What do you mean, is she all right?"

Felicity came to stand alongside her daughter, the same questions riding through her expression. Gustav gestured toward Roeglin.

"The mage will explain."

Marsh listened as Roeglin told them how expending a lot of energy took its toll on a magic user and was surprised when Izmay pressed a cup of sweet kaffee into her hand.

"No chocolate," she said. "Sorry."

"Chocolate?" Felicity wanted to know.

"It's sweet. Restores energy faster. If we're lucky, she's not about to sleep for a few days."

Marsh wanted to reassure them that she wasn't going to sleep for days. She was pretty sure just the one night would do it. Gustav patted her on the shoulder.

"Stay right there," he said. "We'll clean up your mess."

"Hey." Marsh wanted to protest that she could clean up her own damn mess, but she knew she couldn't. She was already having trouble keeping her eyes open.

Felicity must have noticed because she brushed Gustav aside and tucked her hand under Marsh's arm.

"I've got somewhere she can sleep," she said, guiding Marsh back out into the hall and into the child's bedroom. "Claudie and I can share tonight, and you need to rest."

Marsh wanted to argue but couldn't figure out how to string two words together. Staying upright was hard enough. It was a relief when Claudette turned back the sheets and Felicity tucked her in. An embarrassment, sure, but a relief nonetheless.

She wondered how many raiders she'd killed and hoped she hadn't left too big a mess for the others to clear. Maybe there was some way she could make it up to them...tomorrow...when opening her eyes was within reach...

19

SNOT DUST

To her relief, Marsh woke without trouble the next morning, and there was no lurking fatigue like there had been before. She yawned and stretched and slid out from under the covers, wondering at the long, hot line of warmth stretched out beside her. Glancing back at the bed, she saw Mordanlenoowar lying against the wall and was amazed the kat hadn't woken her when it had hopped up beside her.

You were pretty out of it.

"Good morning, Roeglin. Get out of my head. I'll be out in a minute."

"You'll get out here now, Leclerc." Oh my, wasn't Gustav just in the finest of forms today?

Marsh hustled. There was no point in making the Protector captain and Ruins Hall emissary any grouchier than he already was. She wondered if Felicity and Claudette were ready to leave, but before she could ask, Izmay saw her.

"Here. Eat."

As a morning greeting, there wasn't much better, Marsh thought, taking the hot bread roll and overly sweet kaffee the shadow guard thrust into her hands. Following the example of those around her, Marsh ate quickly, not bothering with words. She figured Gustav would raise anything important, and she didn't have anything to say.

When he'd finished his own roll, Gustav turned to Felicity.

"Do you think the girl will still be at her parents' farm?"

Felicity gave him a bewildered look.

"Where else would she be?" she asked. "There's nowhere else she could go."

"Except here," hung unspoken between them, but no one called the words into being, and they loaded the mules with the things Felicity wanted to take with them, as well as enough supplies for several days. They left behind quite a bit, and Felicity insisted on penning a letter to leave on the kitchen table in case Claude returned.

"He deserves to know we're all right," she said, "and where we've gone. The raiders would work it out easily enough anyway."

Marsh couldn't argue with that, and it wasn't as though Felicity had been very explicit. She had merely written that she'd be "over at Louis's" until it was safe and that he could find her there. If the raiders read it, they could only guess at Kerrenin's Ledge. There was no way of learning of the journey taking place in between.

They were mounted and preparing to head out when Izmay looked at Gustav.

"Who's to say there will be anyone at the farm?" she asked. "The raiders are pretty thick in this part of the cavern."

She had a point, and Marsh wondered why she hadn't thought of it. Gustav regarded the shadow guard with a contemplative gaze and then turned his mule toward the trail.

"That's the question, isn't it, shadow guard? Why would there be anyone left outside the Ledge's walls right now?"

Put that way, it made Marsh think about why there might be any communities outside the Kerrenin's Ledge walls when the raiders had worked so studiously to clear as many as they could from the communities below. What did they need more than the people she'd overheard them claim were the main reason for their invasion?

It's an interesting question, but we need you.

Roeglin's interruption was an unwelcome jolt back to reality, but Marsh was grateful.

Gustav was glaring at her, and he'd halted his mule so he could turn in the saddle while he waited for her response. Marsh gave him her brightest smile and hoped he wouldn't realize she'd been a very long ways away. It was too late.

"I said, when you've finished collecting shroom spores, I'd like you to take point. Roeglin tells me you've worked with the scouts. Is that true?"

It had been just one scout, and Marsh really wished Clarinay had been assigned to travel with them rather than Master Envermet's forces, especially now.

"Yes," she managed, wishing it didn't feel like she was

blushing bright enough to be a beacon for the entire cavern.

"Good. I need you to scout. Roeglin says you can shadow step faster than a mule can travel. Is that also true?"

Marsh wished Roeglin had just shut the Deeps up but she didn't deny it.

"Yes. That's true," she said and then moved the subject forward. "How far ahead do you want me to scout, and will you be advancing while I do it?"

"To the farm and back, and yes."

Marsh slid from her mule's back, handing its reins to Roeglin as she altered her body to blend with the shadows. She felt the energy shift inside her, and the first edges of tiredness. That would never do.

Remembering when she'd drawn the energy from Mordan to heal Piet, she looked around. This time she might not need the kat; there were plenty of shrooms growing on either side of the trail. If she asked all of them to give her a piece of energy, drawing a little from everything, rather than all from one, she might have enough to recharge herself so she wasn't completely useless when they reached the farm.

How had Tamlin said it worked? The rock mages said they could feel the energy of the life around them and pull a little of it to themselves. She thought about it, working to stay within the shadows as she drew on the life around her. It was like...like a river, a green warmth that soothed away the tiredness creeping into her bones.

As soon as the tiredness was gone, Marsh let go of the

connection, gradually becoming aware of the awed whispers behind her.

"What did she do?"

"*How* did she do *that*?"

"I don't know. I'll ask her when she gets back."

If that wasn't a cue to leave, Marsh didn't know what was. She stepped into the darkness clustered around the base of a stalagmite, tugging on the shadows around her to see what or who else shared her surroundings. Once she had that and it was stable, she drew on the natural magic within to sense the lives nearby.

There were no raiders, just a small group of shroom walkers streaking away, and more of the small furry creatures she hadn't yet had time to identify. She circled back to the trail, picking up the faint life signs of Gustav and the others riding along it, and then she sped ahead, scanning for any danger that might be lying in wait.

When she arrived at the farmhouse, she was relieved to see it was occupied, and not by raiders; the children playing in the yard proved that. Marsh crept closer, looking ahead to select the next patch of shadows she needed. As she did so, she scanned the house, taking in the details of those she could see or sense working inside and around it.

It was fairly large as farms went, and well-staffed.

Given how many times Felicity had said she'd been attacked and how close her farm was to this one, it seemed very strange that the people she could see should be going about their daily routines as though nothing threatened. The sheer calm of their demeanors made Marsh think they knew nothing of the raiders plaguing their cavern—or that they did, and it somehow didn't matter.

It was very strange.

She circled the farm, searching for a child around Claudette's age but not finding one. Where could the girl have gone? Once she was sure she had learned as much as she could, she stepped away from the farm proper and made a meandering circuit back to the trail, taking in the number of outbuildings, some of which housed animals and others which sheltered farm equipment or provided storage for feed and crops.

There was still no sign of Ninetta.

Once she was sure, Marsh started back. It was better to have nothing to report than to be kept wondering. She stepped to the shadows between the glows lighting the edges of the house, and then moved into the shelter of a cluster of calla shroom growing at the edge of the path. The sudden sickening stench of rotten brown noses came as an unpleasant shock, and nausea rippled through her.

She fell out of shadow form coughing and retching as she put her hand out to one of the callas for support. The solid thunk of a wooden pole across her back knocked her to her knees, and a hard kick lifted her and tossed her a couple of feet while she was still trying to grasp the fact she'd been seen and ambushed.

That spoke of some kind of magic all by itself. She contemplated it as she tried to move, but another kick rolled her onto her back, and a boot stomped down in the middle of her chest. The sharp tines of a pitchfork settled just above her throat and she froze, trying to focus on the form above her.

We're coming.

Oh, good. Roeglin had managed to catch all that. Marsh tried to get her eyes to work and to find her breath.

"Gotcha!"

Yeah, you got me, *merde-pour-cerv*, she thought. It had been meant to come out as words, but her mouth wasn't working. The face that swam into view had the long chiseled look of a Kerrenin's Ledge local, even if he was built slightly taller and a little bit more solid.

He didn't seem a bit bothered by her silence, but stabbed the pitchfork into the ground not far from her head and leaned the handle against a calla trunk. Crouching beside it, he watched her as she struggled to make the world stand still. He didn't even stop her from rolling to her knees and throwing up.

When she was done, Marsh turned her head and stared at him.

"What…" she managed, and he smiled.

"Snot dust," he said. "Toxic when inhaled, and *very* effective against those who walk the shadows. It's a family recipe."

Marsh closed her eyes, trying to keep her balance as she shuffled slightly to one side. Her first attempt to stand saw her land heavily on her side, but this time she was hauled to her feet. At least he hadn't called the snot dust a family secret. It might mean she got to live after all.

"So," he began, collecting his pitchfork, "where are your friends, then?"

Or not, she thought. He might *not* let her live. She could be in the very deep-and-dark right now. She decided to answer honestly anyway.

"Coming."

He didn't ask her anything more after that but started dragging her toward the farmhouse, shouting as he went.

"Ring the bell! Bernard! Ring the Deeps-damned bell!"

Marsh did her best to keep up, losing her footing twice as the world twisted and blurred around her and her stomach rolled. They hit the back door of the farmhouse, and she was towed unceremoniously through a kitchen and then down a set of stairs, where she really *did* lose her footing. Fortunately, he didn't let her tumble the rest of the way but settled for dragging her as she fought to get her legs to work.

A sturdy wooden seat waited in a small stone room on the other side of a storage cellar and Marsh was slammed into it, her arms dragged back and lashed down tight.

"You're not going anywhere," her captor snarled, jerking on the ropes.

The chair rocked beneath her, but he steadied it and then lashed her ankles to the two front chair legs.

"Not. Anywhere," he emphasized, which was fine with Marsh.

What was not so fine were the three other men who came to join him in the cell. At least, she thought there were three. The way their shapes were wavering in front of her eyes, there might have two or twenty.

Nah. Not twenty, she thought. That would be too many for the cell.

Her captor crouched in front of the chair, and she looked into his eyes.

"Shadow mage," he said, and Marsh waited.

His point was?

"How many are coming?"

She rolled her eyes. How in all the Deeps was she supposed to remember that? She felt like something she'd scraped off her boot and maybe like she should be throwing up on *his* boots. After all, if it was his fault she was sick, and turn-about was fair play, wasn't it?

Tell him Felicity and Claudette have an escort of seven.

Roeglin's voice was a welcome distraction.

"Felicity and Claudette..." she began, and the look on his face grew tense.

Marsh tried to find the rest of the words, but she took too long and he shook her.

"Felicity and Claudette *what*?" he demanded.

"Deeps, please don't..." she managed, but that wasn't the answer he wanted.

He pulled a knife from his belt and laid the edge of the blade at the top of her cheekbone, pressing hard enough to split skin.

Well, there was only one reply to that.

Marsh threw up on him, feeling the blade tear deeper as he recoiled. She counted herself lucky when the wiggly shapes resolved themselves into two men who dragged him out of the room before he could do more than shout in outrage and disgust. She wondered what was happening when a third shape wandered into view, casually kicking the door closed and locking it behind them.

Marsh lifted her head and hoped she was done because something told her things had just gone from bad to worse. It was a relief when the newcomer dragged the chair to a clear patch of floor, and not so much when he stood over her and bent to put his forehead against hers.

"Now, *I* know you're not one of us," he said, keeping his voice soft enough not to carry to the door, "but they don't. So, tell me, just how many of your friends are escorting the very elusive Felicity and Claudette?"

Well, shag the shadows and screw the shrooms, Roeglin said. *That changes things.*

"Yeah. You go on. I'll be fine."

You'll be dead if we're both not careful. Hang in there while I talk to Gustav. He was back in her head a few heartbeats later. *What did they hit you with?*

"Snot dust?"

Roeglin's reply was knocked from her head by the gloved backhand that struck her hard enough to send the chair spinning. Marsh felt gums split and teeth shift and wished she could shadow herself out of her bindings, but it was just too hard to concentrate that deeply when she felt this sick. She hoped she could manage it soon because she was going to need more than the shadows to protect her if she couldn't.

The shadows.

She remembered how they'd answered when she hadn't even been aware she needed them, swarming in a sticky mass down the café's walls and boiling overhead in the Mid-Point dining room. Well, if ever she needed them, it was now. Tied as she was, she couldn't even curl into a ball as the raider crossed over to stand in front of her.

"How many?" he asked and nudged her with the toe of his boot.

Behind him, the door rattled.

"Just a minute!"

"I swear, Idris, you kill another one, and I *will* end you."

The fury in the farmer's voice made Marsh want to laugh. It wasn't as if he could actually stop Idris from doing anything from out there. Sure, he could kill the man once the deed was done, but that didn't leave her anywhere good.

Idris nudged her again.

"What do you say, shadow mage? Are you going to promise not to tell him our secret, or am I gonna see how much a man of his word he might be?"

"Safe," Marsh managed.

She'd wanted to tell him that his secret was safe, but her mouth wouldn't cooperate. He seemed to get it anyway, or maybe he just thought she'd had so much snot dust she wasn't going to be a threat to anyone. Blood trickled down one side of her face from where the farmer's blade had sliced her cheek, and she tasted iron where the raider had struck.

He settled the chair back on all four of its legs and the world danced before her eyes.

"By the Deep's Mandibles, what did you do to her?" the farmer asked when Idris let him back into the room.

The raider shrugged.

"She has a smart mouth. I slapped some manners into it. She was just about to tell me how many men were accompanying your neighbors."

He glanced at Marsh, and she got the message.

"Shev'n," she managed.

"Sheven," she repeated when they looked at her in puzzlement, and then she closed her eyes.

The world was doing wild gyrations, and she didn't

want to see them. She heard footsteps, and then someone shook her.

"What?" came out tired, and someone peeled her eyelid up—the other one. The one that hadn't spoken yet.

"By the Deep and Dark, how much snot did you hit her with?"

"She walked right into it. Got the full dose and went down like a sack."

"And you never thought she might need the antidote?"

"What do I care? She's just another shadow mage."

"Yeah, but she's not a raider, and we might need—"

The farmer was on him in a shot, knocking him to one side and sending Marsh's chair over onto its side. She managed to keep her head from hitting the floor, but by the *Deeps* that hurt.

Not as much, she decided, as the beating the farmer was giving his worker.

"That's. Not. How. We. See. It," he said, landing a punch with every word. "We. Don't. Need. The. Likes. Of. Her. Breathing. Our. Air. Gottit?"

Marsh watched him as he stood, letting the other man drop, flinching as he came and stood beside the chair. She flinched again when he took hold of it and set it back on its feet, and his mouth twitched into a humorless smile.

"The only reason you're breathing now is that your friends have saved my neighbor, and they might be upset if I kill you before they get here." He reached into a pouch at his belt, pulling a small flask from inside it. "That's *also* the only reason you're getting this."

Marsh turned her face, trying to avoid the flask, but he took her jaw in a firm grip and worked the mouth of the flask between her lips, tilting her head back so she couldn't avoid the bitter liquid that followed. He pinched her nose shut until she swallowed, then he released her before turning for the door.

"Nikolas will bring you to the kitchen. The Bissets' place isn't far from here, so I expect your friends will arrive soon. Do what you're told and I might let you live. Come on, Idris."

Yes, go on, Idris, Marsh thought, and breathed a sigh of relief when Idris left on the farmer's heels.

Her sigh was echoed by the farm-hand, and Marsh wondered what the man was going to do. After the beating he'd just received for trying to defend a mage, she didn't think he'd be staying. It took a moment before he rolled slowly to his feet, and Marsh tensed at the grace of it. He must have noticed because he gave her a mirthless smile as he limped over to her chair.

"Hold still," he said, but she flinched as a blade was drawn in front of her for the second time that day. "Easy. See?"

Marsh did see, but she didn't relax until he'd cut her bonds and was rubbing the feeling back into her hands. Farmhand or not, he moved like a warrior, and he knew how to get the circulation back when they'd been bound. Those weren't traits she usually associated with farmhands.

"I'll have to leave," he said. "I can't stay here. Not after what happened to the children. Not after you."

She wanted to ask what about the children, but the sound of knocking thundered through the house above and he looked up.

"We're out of time," he said, half-helping, half-hauling her to her feet. "Come on. You can lean on me."

She wanted to know what the hurry was, but it became clear when he steered her through the back door and around the side of the house instead of taking her through the kitchen and down the hall leading to the front door.

"I won't let him use you as a ransom," he said even as the farmer shouted his name from the front door.

"Nikolas! Bring her!"

"Not likely," he muttered, taking her out through the kitchen door and along the back of the house before turning the corner leading to the front, where her friends were waiting.

It was a good plan, but they were only halfway along the house when Marsh heard the back door slam open.

Fortunately, Roeglin hadn't given up his habit of peering into her head and was trotting toward them by the time Idris turned the corner behind them. The shadow mage didn't hesitate; he pulled a dart from the dark and flung it through the man's chest, following it with a second through his throat and a third that penetrated his head as he fell.

By then, he'd reached where Nikolas had stopped and was trying to keep Marsh from falling over.

"You're coming with us," he said, eyeing the farmhand, and there was no compromise in his tones.

Nikolas looked back at Idris's body and then up at the shadow mage.

"Help me get her on the mule," he said. "I can't."

Roeglin pulled the memory of his beating by Idris from Marsh's head and slid from his mount.

"Stay here," he told her, propping her against a wall, and he turned to Nikolas. "Let's get you into the saddle."

By the time he'd gotten the man into the saddle of the mule he'd been leading, Gerry and Izmay had arrived to guard them. Zeb followed, leading Marsh's mount, and he helped Roeglin get her onto it while Gustav and Felicity asked the farmer where Ninetta had gone.

20

COMPETITION

"I tell you, I don't know where the little brats have gone, and what's more, I don't care either!"

The farmer was shouting now, his disapproval of his vanished daughter and another of the children rolling through the cavern and bouncing back in sharp echoes. When she replied, Felicity sounded like she was the verge of tears.

"Davide! How could you say that?"

"How can *you* stand to be near them? They're an abomination, a crime against nature. They're not fit to walk this world."

"Davide…" Felicity began, but Gustav cut her off.

"Don't," he told her. "There's no reasoning with folk this far gone, and our priority is the children."

He turned to the farmer.

"How long have they been gone?"

"And why should I tell—" Davide's words cut off in a surprised gurgle. Marsh was surprised to see shadows gripping his throat in the form of a hand.

255

Gerry shook the hand he'd extended, his fingers curving as though he felt Davide's flesh beneath them. His normally dark blue eyes were as black as coal. In the doorway, Davide was shaken by the shadows at his throat.

"Tell me," Gustav thundered, and Marsh swore she felt his voice go right through her.

It made her want to tell him exactly where the children were, except she didn't know. Maybe she should go find that out. She tapped her heels against the side of her mule, only to feel Roeglin's hand close over her wrist and pull back so that the reins drew tight.

The mule bounced forward a step and then stopped, its ears flicking back and forth in confusion. Marsh shook her head, clearing it of Gustav's voice as she heard Davide's choked reply.

"Two…no, three days."

His eyes darted to where Marsh and Nikolas sat their mules, a shadow guard on either side. Gerry shook him again and lowered him to the ground.

"What happened?"

Again Davide's eyes went to Marsh, and then his gaze swept Nikolas, Felicity, and Claudette.

"Answer me."

Gustav's soft growl was just as bad as his shout, and Marsh felt her insides curl. Davide choked against the shadow hand, and Marsh saw Gerry relax his arm.

It was just a fraction, but it was enough. The farmer started talking. "They were playing out in the yards. You know, as children do. They were supposed to be milking, and they'd almost done that, but one of the other girls said something and Ninetta said there was nothing wrong with what Pierre could do. I'd come to check on them, but I wanted to hear what was wrong with the boy, so I stayed out of sight. The other girl sounded really upset, and the moutons grew restless as if to prove the point, and she said…" He gulped. "She said that Ninetta couldn't possibly call *that* natural.

"Well, I had to see, so I crept up to the corner and looked inside, and there was Pierre building a castle out of stones, only he wasn't touching a damned one of them! He was just looking at them, and they were moving in the air in front of him. I must have made a sound then because the other girl looked around, demanding I look, and Ninetta just grabbed the boy and ran. She'd tipped over her stool and the bucket, wasting…" He gulped. "All that milk, and she ran away, taking Pierre with her."

Davide looked upset, but whether he was upset about the spilt milk or the children running away, Marsh couldn't tell—and Gustav didn't care.

"Which way did they go?"

Davide shrugged, grabbing the shadow hand and trying to wedge his fingers between the darkness and his throat.

"Where?" Again, Gustav's voice rumbled through her skin and caused Marsh's stomach to churn.

Davide stopped struggling.

"I don't know," he whined. "I figured they'd be back come supper and we could tan their hides then. They both knew that sort of thing was forbidden."

As if using a natural gift was some kind of crime. Marsh felt disgusted with the man, but Gustav had one question more.

"Where would they go?"

Davide didn't know.

"How would I know that?" he asked. "They're kids. Unless they didn't finish their chores on time, we didn't care where they played."

"Do the other children know?"

He shook his head.

"No. We asked. The boy's mother was beside herself. She's been out there every day. She'd be out there all day if she didn't want to get paid."

"Can we speak to her?"

"No. Last time, she didn't come back. The Deeps know where she's vanished to."

Remembering Idris, Marsh had a fair idea, just like she had a fair idea that they'd need to hurry if they were to find the children before the raiders. Kids with magical abilities? That sounded like something those bastards would be chasing in a heartbeat.

Gerry shook the man again.

"You know there are raiders in this cavern, don't you?"

Davide sneered.

"So? They don't bother us, and we don't bother them. I don't know why everyone's so worried."

Felicity made a small sound of distress but both men ignored her.

"What about the empty farms and the people who have been taken?" Gustav pressed, and Davide's face took on an expression of semi-superiority.

"Those folks must have done something to draw their attention. They probably deserved everything they got. They came here asking after children with magical ability.

I told them they were welcome to take any they could find."

Felicity gasped but Davide continued, oblivious.

"The little abominations need to have somewhere to go, and I don't care where, as long as it's nowhere near me."

There was a second gasp, and then a dart flew past Gustav and buried itself in Davide's chest.

"What in the Deeps!" Gustav shouted, turning in the saddle.

The fist curled around Davide's throat dissipated, and Marsh caught sight of Claudette pulling a second dart from the shadows.

The girl paused when she caught sight of Gustav's anger.

"What?" she asked. "He hurt Ninetta. He was going to hurt Pierre. They're *children, and* he was working with the raiders."

She shrugged.

"He deserved to die."

She looked over at where Davide's body lay in the doorway of the farmhouse.

"He's not going to hurt anyone else now, is he?" She gave Gustav a defiant stare. "And we have more important things to be doing."

In the face of the Protector captain's shock, she turned to her mother.

"Don't we, Mama?"

Felicity was horrified. She looked at her daughter in disbelief and then at Gustav, as though he could fix anything that had just occurred.

*This is bad…*Roeglin mumbled, and Marsh kicked her mule forward.

"Come on, Claudette. I'll show you how to ask the shadows for their help."

"Come on!" she repeated, wishing she knew how Gustav could make his voice vibrate through a person's skin or that she had Roeglin's ability to use his mind to compel people to do what he wanted.

Yeah, either of those things would be good right now.

In the end, she reached out to grab Claudie's reins and towed the girl away from the farmhouse and the rest of the group, leaving Gustav and Felicity to absorb what they'd just seen and heard. When she was a safe distance away from the group, Marsh stopped. From the look on Claudette's face, the girl was expecting a scolding, so Marsh decided not to say anything about the dart or Davide. Instead, she got on with what she'd promised to teach the girl.

"You can ask the shadows to help you find things in the dark," she began, and Claudie frowned.

"But the shadows don't speak, and they're not smart enough to think."

Marsh smiled.

"All true, but look around you." She waited until the girl had done so. "What do you see?"

"Shadows and darkness."

"Can you see in the dark?"

Claudie shrugged.

"Sure. I just make my eyes see differently, and everything is pretty clear."

"Heat?"

Again the girl shrugged.

"Probably. The shrooms are darker than the insects and the cave bunnies."

Cave bunnies. Marsh wasn't sure what they were, but she figured they might be the small furry shapes she'd been unable to identify earlier.

"Good. Well, what lies in between the things in the cavern?"

"Shadows?"

"And what do they do?"

Claudie pouted.

"I don't know. They kind of just hang all around us. They're everywhere, touching everything."

"That's why we can use them to show us what we can't see. They touch everything, connecting everything together. We just think about what we need to find, and if the shadows are touching it, we can find it."

"Like the air?"

It was Marsh's turn to be a little puzzled.

"Sure, kid. Like the air. Why?"

"Because the air touches everything, and sometimes when I lose something, I think about the air it touches and I know where I have to look to find it."

Marsh struggled to hide her surprise.

"There you go, then," she said, trying to work out what to say next. "Well, Ninetta is surrounded by both air and shadows, and so are Pierre, and Pierre's mum. Why don't we see if we can work out where they are?"

"I'll have to close my eyes," Claudie answered, "and I won't be able to see if any raiders come."

They both started when Izmay's voice came from a few feet away.

"That's okay. We'll hold the mules."

Claudette and Marsh gasped, and Marsh kicked herself for focusing so much on the girl that she'd forgotten to keep an eye on the cavern around them. Izmay laughed.

"Chicken."

"*You're* a chicken," Claudie retorted.

"Uh huh."

Izmay sounded unconvinced.

"You wanna look for your friend or should I do that for you?"

"You can't."

"Marsh just showed me how. I reckon I'd be faster than you."

"Would not."

"Wanta see?"

Before Marsh could stop her, Izmay had closed her eyes.

"*Merde,*" Claudie muttered and copied the guard.

Marsh rolled her eyes and slipped off her mule, reaching out to gather their reins. Her legs felt wobbly as she moved, but she realized she could fix that...just as soon as someone came to hold the mules.

"I got it," Roeglin said, and Marsh wondered when he'd arrived.

"Followed you over," he told her, then added. "You're lucky I'm not a raider."

"Smartass."

"That the best you got?"

Marsh thought about it, but she was tired from the snot dust and its antidote and she hurt where Idris and Davide had used fist and knife. She decided that it really *was* the best she could do.

"Yeah," she muttered and handed him the reins, kneeling on the ground at the mules' feet.

This time it didn't take very long to pull the energy from the earth and plants around her to make the pain and fatigue from the morning drop away. As soon as she felt all right, she straightened up, moving carefully so as not to startle the mules.

One of them snorted and stamped its feet, but it didn't back away. Marsh reached out and laid a hand on its muzzle, letting it take in her scent and sending it thoughts of peace and calm.

"You done?" Roeglin asked, and Marsh nodded. "Good. Why don't you see if you can do the same for Nikolas? He's not doing so well."

"I'm fine," the farmhand protested, but Marsh wasn't convinced.

"And don't pull the energy from yourself this time."

As if she needed reminding. Marsh glared at Roeglin, and he raised his eyebrows in challenge.

"You didn't?"

Since she'd been about to do exactly that, Marsh didn't dignify his challenge with an answer. The fact she could hear him laughing inside her head was not helpful.

"Give me your hand," she said, reaching out to Nikolas, relieved when he did.

This time, instead of kneeling back on the ground, she

leaned on the mule and thought about drawing on the energy from the world around her to heal Nikolas's bruises. The flow came slightly faster than before and she slowed it, turning her head so she could direct the energy to the parts of Nikolas's body where his life force glowed less brightly.

The man gasped, his hand jerking in hers as though he'd nearly pulled it out of her grasp but then thought better of it. When she'd pushed in as much energy as she thought he needed, Marsh released what remained back into her surroundings.

"Ha! Got it!" Claudette exclaimed and looked at Roeglin. "Give me my reins."

Roeglin stared at her, and the girl tried again.

"I said, give me my reins!"

"To borrow a saying from a five-year-old I know, '*Ruuude!*'" the shadow mage retorted.

"But..." Claudette was stumped. "But..."

Marsh glanced at the girl.

"Won't you need to focus to keep following the trail?"

Claudette rolled her eyes.

"No. I can do *that* with my eyes open. It's like following a thread..." She looked at Roeglin. "...as long as *someone* doesn't make me lose it."

She bit her lip and tried again.

"Okay, *pleease* give me the reins."

"And me, please," Izmay asked from beside her.

"What *lovely* manners," Roeglin told them, using the same tone he would have used on Aisha when she'd done something well.

He was met by twin glares as he handed back the reins, and both girl and shadow guard kicked their mules into a trot and headed slightly off the trail.

"No sense of humor," Roeglin muttered, following them.

Glancing around, Marsh saw that Gustav and the rest of the guards had joined them, a pale-faced Felicity among them. She wanted to ask the woman if she was all right, but any idiot with half an eye could see she wasn't.

"Best follow them," Gustav said with a glance at Marsh that told her the situation was all her fault. "Leclerc, you're riding with Felicity."

If the look hadn't told her whose fault it was, him using her surname did. Marsh waited beside the trail until Felicity came alongside her, and then she rode beside the woman until she decided to speak.

"Will she be okay?" Felicity asked.

"Claudette?"

"Yes."

"She should be. Why?"

"It's just...the killing...I didn't think she...I mean, she shouldn't, should she?"

Well, that was a hard one to answer.

"It's not exactly the way *we* were going to handle the situation," Marsh told her.

"But?"

Marsh sighed and almost regretted just how much the world had changed in the short time since the monsters had first attacked her caravan.

"He was helping the raiders," Marsh said and hurried on

when Felicity drew a breath to argue that Davide would do no such thing. "You heard him. He refused to believe that anyone they took hadn't deserved it, and he totally agreed with those able to use magic being handed over to them."

"But they must be looking for magic-users for a reason," Felicity added. "Surely they wouldn't hurt them if they need them so badly."

Marsh favored her with a stern look.

"If you believed that, why didn't you give them Claudette? Why did you hide every time they came? Why did your husband risk his life to draw them away if they're not so bad?"

She stopped, letting the silence grow between them while Felicity put all the pieces together for herself. In the end, the woman sighed.

"I know," she finally said, "but it's the killing. I don't want her to…"

"To kill so easily?"

"Yes…or at all."

Marsh decided to let that one go. There really wasn't anything she could say to make Felicity feel any better. The truth was, Claudette had killed a man who thoroughly needed it, but saying so wasn't going to make her mother feel any better about it. The pair would just have to sort it out for themselves.

She settled down to ride beside Felicity and stretched her senses out into the dark, feeling her way through the shadow threads to see what lay in the cavern. Mordan paced alongside them, separated from the mules by shrooms and rocks but content to follow. Marsh looked farther, trying to sense what shared this part of the cavern with them.

The mules picked their way across the rough floor, avoiding tussocks of grass and the odd straggly bush as well as working their way through the knee-high brown noses and crushing clusters of blue buttons beneath their hooves. Marsh slowly became aware of the bright warmth sneaking into the cavern and turned in her saddle to find the source.

"We're coming close to the opening," Felicity said, catching the look of puzzlement on her face. "It's why the town's called Mika's Outlet. Mika discovered the opening into the surface world and thought he'd build a farm near it. The stories say he liked to watch the stars."

"The man must have had stones for eyes if he could stand a glare like this," Gerry muttered, and Marsh turned back to look at him.

The shadow guard was holding his hand up to shade his face and squinting against the light. Beside him, Zeb looked like he was in pain. He caught her looking at him.

"Don't tell me this isn't painful for you."

Marsh shook her head.

"No, never has been."

Beside her, Felicity tutted and pulled out two cloths made of dark gauze.

"Here, tie these across your eyes. They'll cut the glare, but you'll still be able to see." She caught Marsh staring at her. "My Claude used to complain something fierce, but these seemed to help."

She held one out to Marsh.

"You sure you don't need one?"

Marsh smiled at her, pushing it back toward her.

"I'm sure. I used to think I was the only one."

"Not by a long shot, girl," Gustav told her. "Just one of a few, like Roeglin here."

Marsh looked and saw that what he was saying was true. Roeglin was staring around them as though he'd always seen the world this way. Ahead of them, Izmay had slowed her mule to a walk and was looking like she was in pain.

To Marsh's surprise, Claudette hadn't ridden off and left her behind. Instead, the girl had turned her mule and come alongside the guard. She was holding out another of the gauzy black cloths.

"Here. You'll need one of these. Tie it around your eyes."

The girl waited while Izmay did as she was told and then she frowned.

"You ready to go again?"

"Sure" Izmay answered. "Just give me a minute to get it all back."

Claudette tutted and rolled her eyes.

"This means I win," she said. "*I* don't need to find the path. They're this way."

She didn't wait, she just turned her mule around and guided it to where the light grew brighter.

"Cheater!" Izmay protested.

"I didn't have to stop to help you," the girl reminded her. "You're just a sore loser."

"I...*hey!*"

Claudette had kicked her mount into a faster walk and left the shadow guard behind.

"Excuse me," Marsh said to Felicity, "but I'd better..."

"I'll come with you," Felicity answered. "She *is* my daughter, after all."

The words made Marsh feel just a little bit better. If Felicity was still claiming Claudette as her own, the two of them should be all right. They kicked their mules forward, getting them to go a little faster even if they still had to be careful as they traveled over the rough ground.

THE WOLF PACK

Even hurrying, Felicity and Marsh didn't catch up with Claudette before a low growl rumbled through the cavern.

"Mordan!" Marsh exclaimed and the kat growled again, sending Marsh a warning through the link that lay between them. "What is it, girl?"

Images of half a dozen large gray dogs facing off against the kat reached her. They looked for all the Deeps like krypthunds, save that they were larger and rangier, with long gray fur and vivid amber or green eyes. Their lips were curled to reveal long yellow fangs, and their answering growls rolled through the cavern.

Marsh kicked her mule into a trot, ignoring the rocky ground as she hurried to reach the kat. It was almost a relief when Izmay got there first, sliding from her nervous mount to kneel beside Mordan, crossbow at the ready. Marsh followed Izmay's example by dismounting from the mule before she reached the wolves.

The mule snorted and backed up, stopping when

Gustav reached out and snagged its reins. Marsh hesitated long enough to see it secured and then turned back to the six creatures ranged before them.

Mordan growled again, and Marsh reached out and laid a hand on the big kat's neck.

"Easy, girl," she said. "Let's see what they want."

"They want to eat us, is what," Claudette snapped. "It's not like it's hard to work out."

"I say we ask them first," Marsh told the girl, and didn't give her time to argue.

She also didn't give Gustav or Roeglin time to stop her from walking out to stand right in front of the most central wolf of the pack.

"We need to talk," she told it, staring into its eyes and seeing the green flare of her own in their depths as she sought to make a connection.

The first impression she had when the connection went through was that she had just done something incredibly stupid. The wolf's presence was huge, towering over her like the tallest of shrooms, its eyes blazing with hunger and resentment. She had disturbed the pack's hunt.

Now they would go hungry for another day unless they found something else.

Marsh wondered why they couldn't hunt in the surface world and got the impression of something large and vaguely humanoid striding through the trees and twisted ruins.

"What *is* that?" she murmured, pushing against the wolf's memory to get a closer look.

For a moment, the wolf resisted. It was as though it was

trying not to remember what it had seen, trying to hide from the terror of it. Marsh pushed again.

"I can't help you if I can't see what it is," she told it. "Please let me see…"

The wolf hesitated, and Marsh tried to reassure it by promising to help the pack.

"Show me. We can keep you safe."

For some reason, it found that funny, but it agreed to let her see what had forced them from their usual hunting grounds. As the image became clearer, Marsh recoiled. The thing was a wolf and not a wolf, a man and not a man, and it was beyond reason.

The eyes it turned toward her were red-rimmed and full of hate. Its pelt, wolf-like in texture and color, was unkempt and matted with brambles and blood. It took her in in one scornful glance, and snarled, bounding toward her with unseemly speed, one of its claws reaching out to slash at her until her world went black.

Marsh yelped and rolled away, clawing her way out of the wolf's mind to find herself scrambling away from it. Finding herself back in the daylit cavern, Marsh stopped. She was breathing fast as the wolf bounded forward to close the distance between them.

This time the wolf was the one to demand she come back to its mind.

She heard people moving uneasily behind her and held up her hand.

"Wait!" she told them, pulling the wolf's name from its head. Blizzard. "Wait. They're… He's bonded!"

Sadness washed across her, and she knew it wasn't hers.

She caught a glimpse of the body the beast had left behind, and knew it would run with the pack no more.

"Was," Marsh corrected herself. "*Was* bonded. Some kind of wolf-man shadow monster killed the rock mage it was with."

Druid. Lycanthrope.

The words dropped into her mind unbidden, and Marsh raised her eyes to meet those of the pack leader.

"More than one" was not a phrase she wanted to hear in reference to the thing it had called a lycanthrope.

"How many?" she asked and raised her gaze to meet the wolf's.

There were four, and they had hounded the pack mercilessly, coming out of the buildings at the foot of the hill. They had not found the waystation, even though the wolves knew of its existence. If the humans inside that cavern were lucky, they would not be discovered. Blizzard did not think the human cave would stand against them.

What he feared most, though, was that the beasts were tracking the pack and they were not safe.

They needed food.

They had hoped the abandoned young were permissible.

"No!" Marsh snapped, and the wolf recoiled.

Mordan's snarl echoed around them, and the wolf whimpered an apology, even as it prepared to defend its pack. It unceremoniously dropped Marsh into her own head as it backed away, and she reached out and laid her hand on the kat's head.

"Friends, Dan. They're friends."

She reached for the wolf, but it avoided the connection

even as it watched her warily from two body-lengths away. Stretching her hand toward it, she patted the kat on the head, willing her to stay where she was. The kat continued to hold her place, but Marsh felt her tension and knew her tail was twitching even without looking.

"The children are not permissible," she told it, "but we will find you meat. Will you help us?"

The wolf gave a sharp yap and looked along the line of its pack, its amber eyes meeting each one's gaze. One by one, they lowered their heads in reply, and then they sat, waiting.

"Thank you," Marsh said, and the wolf yapped again.

The pack rose as one, fanning out and circling back in the direction Claudette had been traveling. The girl was mortified. She turned to Marsh.

"What have you done?" she demanded.

Marsh met her angry gaze and indicated the wolves.

"Got them to help us find your friend."

"But they'll eat her."

"Nope. They'll help us find them, and then we'll help them find food. I made a deal; they're hungry." She turned to Roeglin. "What's a lycanthrope?"

Her question drew sharp breaths from the guards and they all cast wary glances around the cavern.

"Why? Is there one nearby?"

"There are four on the surface. Their leader killed the wiz...*druid* traveling with the wolves. The wolves are hiding here and hoping the lycanthropes don't find them."

Gustav snorted.

"Some hope." He looked at the other guards. "They'll be coming."

Marsh watched him, not sure what to do, but he hadn't finished.

"They'll hunt until they've killed every living thing in the area, but they'll hunt the wolves and humans first. It's like they take our existence as some sort of insult. They'll be tracking the pack whether the wolves are aware of it or not, and once they make it into the cavern, they'll kill every human they can find. If it was just the raiders, I'd leave them to it, but I doubt the people of Mika's Outlet deserve to be slaughtered."

Thinking of the attitudes on the farm, Marsh had her doubts. After all, the Outlet had so far survived the raiders. What if its people had already sided with the outsiders and were betraying the cavern to ensure their own survival?

You are such a trusting soul, Roeglin said, interrupting her thoughts and bringing her back to the present, *but I think you need to hurry in order to catch up with our new friends...and the girl.*

The girl?

"What's she done now?"

Roeglin just pointed, and Marsh was in time to see Claudette running after the wolves. The child wasn't saying anything, but she wasn't waiting for anybody either. Marsh was torn. On the one hand, they needed to find the children, and, on the other, they had four lycanthropes to worry about and a wolf pack to feed.

"We'll take care of it," Roeglin said. "You just catch up with Claudie and the pack. We'll be along."

Marsh wanted to ask him how he thought he was going to take care of it, but she didn't have time. She'd already lost sight of the wolf leader, and Mordan was trotting along behind Claudette, and they were almost out of sight.

"*Merde*," she grumbled and took out after them.

Honestly! What was it with her and children? She always seemed to get stuck with them.

You shouldn't be such a motherly type, Roeglin teased, and she flipped him a mental finger as she raced after the kat and the child.

"Where are they going?" she heard Felicity ask.

Yeah, Marsh thought. Where in all the fornicating Deeps are they going?

Couldn't Ninetta have chosen somewhere *safer* as a refuge?

As she thought it, she heard a howl echo through the cavern, but not from the wolves ahead. This howl came from the direction of the brighter light and the surface. Marsh froze in her tracks and then raced forward. She had to catch up with Mordan and Claudette!

"Marsh!"

She heard Gustav's voice ring out behind her, but didn't stop. If the children were going to be facing lycanthropes, they weren't going to face them alone. A small voice tried to remind her that the wolf pack would be with them, but she couldn't be sure the wolves would stay. After all, they'd run from the lycanthropes before. Why would they stay this time?

Because they made you a promise?

That might be almost true, but Marsh thought it had been her who had made the wolves a promise and not the other way around.

Doesn't matter; they had a bargain to fulfill if they wanted to eat. They're hungry, Marsh, and used to working with a druid. They'll stay.

Marsh wished she had his confidence, but she didn't. She scrambled after Mordan, knowing that the kat would be doing her best to keep all the kits safe. Knowing also that the kat expected her to be there to fight alongside her by the time the lycanthrope arrived.

"A la putain!"

And didn't Roeglin sound like he was only just starting to understand what she intended to do?

She caught sight of Mordan's tail disappearing behind a clump of rocks just as a flash of movement caught her attention. Not stopping for a closer look, Marsh followed the kat and discovered a narrow crevice leading deeper into the hillside. She'd have missed it if she hadn't been behind them.

The space beyond it was crowded and very noisy.

A slender blonde girl was standing with her back to the wall of a squared-off cavern, her eyes as black as pitch. She had extended one hand in front of herself and was using her other hand to push a small brown-haired boy behind her.

The wolves had arrayed themselves around the cave, ignoring the children as they faced toward the door. Their lips raised in six identical snarls as Marsh appeared and were just as quickly lowered.

"I am here," she told them, sending them feelings of reassurance that help was coming; her pack was coming. She surveyed them, willing them to have the courage to stand their ground, promising them refuge and food at the end of the fight.

Claudette dodged around her, racing across the room to where Ninetta and the boy were waiting.

"You came!"

"I promised! I'm sorry it took so long." There was a moment's quiet before Claudette continued. "That's Marsh, and the big kat is her friend…and ours. The wolves are new, but they seem to be on our side."

"And that?" Ninetta asked as another howl tore through the cavern.

Claudette shook her head.

"That's not so good," she said. "I think that's the thing the wolves are afraid of, and I *think* Marsh said she was going to help them with it."

A second howl ripped the air outside their hiding place, and the children gasped.

"There's more than one of them?"

Marsh turned away from the entrance long enough to take in their three young faces.

"There are four," she told them, "but Gustav and the others will help us."

She looked around the cavern.

"We can't fight in here," she said. "There's not enough room."

"We're going to have to fight to protect the door. You kids stay here. We've got this."

She glanced around at the wolves, catching the leader's eye and showing it what she wanted them to do.

He flattened his ears against his skull and then looked right and left, selecting three others from its pack. Marsh gave the children one more stern look before going back through the crevice.

"Stay here!" she said and led the wolves out.

She wasn't entirely surprised when the leader and only three of the pack emerged, Mordan following them.

"Where are the rest of you?" she asked, sending a question to the leader. He answered by sending an image of pups and the need to protect the mother and the coming cubs, as well as the children.

Well, that explained a lot.

"We can do this," Marsh reassured him. "See? My pack stands ready to help you."

Your pack is going to kick your ass, Roeglin told her. *Get your tail back in the cave.*

You and what army? Marsh wanted to know.

Roeglin rolled his eyes.

"We have incoming." Zeb's voice was soft but firm. "They're trying a pincer."

"They're not smart enough for that...surely..." Felicity murmured, and Gustav and Zeb shot her an incredulous look.

As if in answer, the unearthly howls split the air again, coming from either side and sending tremors of fear running through them. Marsh started when rocks rattled quietly behind them, and she tilted her head so she could see. It was exactly as she had expected and feared.

Claudette was slowly emerging, one hand helping steady her as she came out of the crack, the other hand in Ninetta's.

"Get back in the cave," she ordered.

THE HUNTERS HUNTED

Claudette heard Marsh's order. She cocked her head, folded her arms, and then took a step forward, her arms swinging down to her sides and back up again to reveal a ball of shadow spinning between her hands.

"Not likely." she snapped, giving Marsh a look that said the shadow mage could try what she liked but Claudette was joining the fight.

"What in all the Deeps is *that*?" Marsh asked, staring at the spinning ball of shadow, and the child flashed her a grin.

"You can call the lightning from the shadows," she said. "You work it out."

Marsh took another look at the ball, this time seeing the faint purple streaks glittering inside it.

"*How* did you do that?" she asked, but Gerry's voice cut across them before Claudette could reply.

"Here they come!"

"Don't get bitten!" Gustav ordered. "And keep those wolves back. Tell them we'll deal with this. The kat, too."

Marsh sought the faint connection she'd made with the lead wolf and found it, willing them to hang back behind the line of shadow mages and protect the children if the lycanthropes broke through. She didn't dare look to see if they obeyed. She'd just caught her first glimpse of a lycanthrope.

The wolf's memory hadn't shown her the half of it.

The monster was more than seven feet tall and built heavier than the biggest surface worlder she'd ever seen. It surveyed them with hunger and disdain, and then its eyes caught on hers and it roared. As if its outrage was a signal, the other three came bursting through the shrooms and scraggly bushes, hitting the line of shadow mages as one.

Marsh saw Zeb stagger back under the weight of the first one's attack, saw Gerry barely raise his shield in time to stop it reaching around and clawing his fellow guard. Marsh watched as Roeglin took shelter behind his shield from a second beast's attack. The shadow mage pulled a blade of pure shadow from the dark, as Gustav came in beside him, drawing his sword and raising his shield to hold off its attack. The third beast went for Izmay, and the lycanthrope facing Marsh, leapt away.

"Lightning, Marsh!" the captain ordered, effort wheezing through his words. "Lightning. Now!"

Claws reached around the shield, only to abruptly release it when Gustav lunged forward with the sword. There was an agonized yip followed by a howl of pain, but the lycanthrope continued its attack. As she surveyed the battle scene, Marsh realized what the Protectors were doing.

They'd created a perimeter—an edge for her to aim for.

She glanced at the ceiling, calling the shadows, willing them to gather, asking them for lightning and destruction; asking them for protection. Even with the sun's interference, there were shadows to find. Daylight might edge the cavern, but the cavern was still the shadows' home. Time they defended it.

She focused. Now that she could see it, she realized that calling the lightning was just like calling a dart or spear from the darkness and throwing it. She should even be able to hit the lycanthropes without cratering the entire perimeter.

A sphere of glittering darkness flew past her, catching Gerry's beast full in the face as it tried to yank the shield from his hands. It roared in pain and anger and stumbled back, the smell of burnt fur and flesh tainting the air.

"Move your ass, shadow mage!"

Gustav was having problems of his own. The lycanthrope was leaning on his shield and trying to reach around it. Every time the captain lifted his head to see where it was, it took a snap at him, its jaws perilously close to his skin.

A dart of shadow lightning it was, Marsh decided and pulled her hand abruptly down in front of her, noting how a shaft of darkness lanced out of the ceiling and skewered the lycanthrope through the back. She sent three more after it, then looked for the next target.

A second sphere flew past her, and the lycanthrope menacing Izmay's shield pulled its head back in time for the ball to skim its face. It snarled and raised its head, its eyes searching out the source of the ball. When it saw Claudette, it snarled again, the sound almost forming words.

"You!"

The child was unfazed.

"Me, pooh-breath!" She hurled a second ball made of shadow and light.

This one caught it on the shoulder and throat, and it howled with rage as lightning scalded fur and flesh. Izmay took advantage of its distraction to stab it with the shortened blade she'd drawn from the shadows. Marsh finished it off with a glimmering spike of shadow, saw Zeb put a shadow spear through the third, and then turned, looking for the fourth.

The mages fell back, tightening the circle and looking nervously around. Mordan found the danger before them. Marsh got the impression of a monster climbing around the pile of rock inside which the children had hidden, and then the kat was gone.

"Dan!" she shrieked, directing the shadows to protect the big beast.

It was like pulling a blanket of storm-lit dark from the ceiling and dragging it between the kat and the lycanthrope's first strike. Claudette followed that with another ball of lightning and then collapsed to the ground. Felicity cried out in alarm and Gustav swore, but Marsh kept her eyes on the lycanthrope her kat had challenged.

She willed the shadows to coat Mordan in darkness, willed the lightning to flow around the outside of them so that anything touching her would regret it, and then she called another bolt from the ceiling onto the lycanthrope. The crackle as lightning arced above it caused the beast to look up, and it leapt to one side, landing at the base of the rock-pile.

The lightning followed, lancing down in a series of jagged strikes, each one missing the beast by a hair's breadth. The lycanthrope was so busy trying to avoid it that it didn't see Izmay leap forward, calling on the shadows to lengthen the blade in her hand until it became a spear. Running until she was behind the beast, she set the spear haft against the rocky floor and leveled the blade at the lycanthrope's back.

It caught sight of her just as the lightning flared again, and this time it could not twist out of the way of either. It died with a pained yelp, Izmay barely leaping clear of its flailing limbs and snapping jaws. As silence descended over the cavern, Felicity could be heard sobbing by her daughter's side. Marsh hurried to see what could be done, aware of the wolves slinking cautiously back into the crevice of rock.

She was aware too of Mordan picking her way down the rock pile and of the little boy moving to stand in front of Ninetta. It was hard to focus on Claudette.

I've got him, Roeglin said, moving past her. Marsh relaxed, crouching beside Felicity.

The woman turned a tear-stained face toward Marsh.

"Will she be all right?"

Marsh caught the faint rise and fall of the girl's chest and nodded.

"Yes, but she'll need to sleep. Let me see what I can do."

Felicity shuffled to one side, giving Marsh room to work. As she expected, there wasn't a mark on the girl.

"She's just used too much of her magic," she explained. "Her body needs to replenish its energy."

She let her words sink in while she lifted Claudette's hand and held it in her own. Again the energy came at her request and she had to steady it, aware of the way it flowed from her and into the child. Claudette murmured in her sleep, took a deeper breath, and turned onto her side, pulling her hand from Marsh's grasp.

"She's fine," Marsh reassured Felicity. "Just needs to sleep."

"That's damned inconvenient."

Trust Gustav not to be impressed. Marsh looked up at the Protector captain.

"It's the best I can do."

He stared at her and then gave a heavy sigh.

"Of course, it is," he said, "and we don't need to get to the Outlet after all. Just back to the farm."

Marsh looked at him in alarm, Felicity doing the same beside her.

"But...but why?"

"Because we have to see if these two have a home to go to, and" he continued, holding up his hand in the face of their protests, "*and* we have to make sure there are no more raiders."

He gave another heavy sigh.

"We also have to confirm that they all shared Davide's view, and then we have to report back to Kerrenin's Ledge to see what the verdict is regarding their alliance." He looked at Felicity. "I'm sorry, but we have to get the council to clear your daughter of any charges."

He held up his hand as the woman started to protest.

"I will speak for her."

"We all will," Izmay said from behind him.

She'd returned from where the lycanthrope had died. She looked at the captain.

"It's getting late. We could camp here tonight."

She glanced over to where Roeglin had convinced the boy to say hello to Mordanlenoowar, and then she looked at the lycanthrope bodies.

"We need to clean up here, and I believe *someone*," she gave Marsh an accusing glare, "promised some wolves some meat."

Marsh sighed and pushed to her feet.

"You're right." She frowned. "Wanna help me hunt?"

"Oh, no you don't," Izmay told her. "You caused that problem knowing you didn't have a clue how to solve it. She walked back to one of the mules and unhooked a shovel from her pack. "You can dig the latrines while the boys and I do the hunting, and then you can help us bury these critters."

Marsh looked from the shadow guard to the captain and met Gustav's look of amusement. He raised his eyebrows and nodded toward the shovel.

"Better get to work, shadow mage. We'll bring back kindling for a fire." He glanced at the crevice. "It should be safe enough in there."

Marsh wanted to argue but Roeglin laughed, rising to his feet and dusting off his trousers. He came over and patted her on the shoulder.

"Remember what Clarinay said?"

Marsh frowned. Master Clarinay had said a lot, so what…and then she had it. Scouts got to the campsite first, and their first responsibility was usually to make sure the latrines were dug.

"Really?" she complained. "You're in this too?"

Roeglin merely laughed and followed Izmay to the edge of the camp. To her surprise, Gustav didn't join the hunters. He merely crossed to the mules and led them into the space in front of the crevice, unsaddling them while Marsh found a suitable site for latrines. She was well into digging them when he joined her, shovel in hand.

"Mules are done," he said, "and the wolves have set up house in the cave."

He could only mean one cave, but Marsh knew she'd have to negotiate a sleeping place with the wolves once she was done.

"Has Roeglin said how the hunt is going?"

"They've struck it lucky. There were goats and deer grazing on the slopes above the cavern."

"They went *outside*?"

Gustav shrugged.

"Sure. It wasn't that far off. No wonder the wolves came in here. They probably thought it was just a cave they could hide in. They're lucky it was more."

They finished the latrines, and Marsh went to negotiate space inside the small cave for the humans.

"The pack is hunting for you," she told the leader, giving them the impression of the shadow guards returning with a goat and hoping they'd had that much luck.

The wolf leader gave her the impression the pack was

welcome to join them if it brought meat and then tilted its head to where Mordan had settled herself in a corner with Pierre resting between her paws. Marsh frowned.

"You can't keep him, you know…" she began, and the big kat opened her mouth in a mock yawn, showing all her fangs as she curled a paw around Pierre. Marsh sighed and hoped this didn't mean more trouble ahead.

Gustav followed her gaze and smiled.

"Someone's got a new pet," he said, and Marsh glared at him.

"Oh, really?"

He turned to her.

"Well, do *you* want to be the one to tell her she'll have to give that cub up?"

In all truth, Marsh did not, even though she couldn't see how she was going to avoid it. Gustav nudged her.

"It'll be all right," he said and indicated the wolves. "Now, if these guys agree, I'd like to bring the girls inside so they can sleep…and I'd like to start a fire so we can cook the meat."

One of the wolves growled.

"*Our* portion of the meat," Gustav amended, and the wolf laid its head on its paws.

It was up and moving minutes later, and Marsh followed it to the crevice and out into the cavern proper. The daylight was fading to a more tolerable grey, and none of the returning guards were wearing the gauzy eye-bands Felicity had given them. The wolf pricked its ears and gave two excited yips that drew the others from the cave to join it.

If the hunters were surprised to be greeted by a small

but very happy wolf pack, they didn't show it. Instead, they called Marsh over so the wolves could let them know which of the two goat carcasses they preferred. It was an easy choice, and they put it down so the wolves could feast uninterrupted.

It didn't take them long to dress the second carcass, leaving the discarded innards for the pack to enjoy. The mules watched the whole proceedings with unease, not letting any of the humans near them until they had washed the blood from their hands and arms. Everyone ate well that night, the wolves surprising the humans by returning to the cave to take their places by the fire.

Marsh caught the eye of their leader, and it reminded her of the druid they had lost, allowing her the image of a young man with dark-brown curls and laughing brown eyes. Pointed ears and a lithe build caught her eye and then the image was gone, the wolf resting its chin on its paws with a huff of sadness.

"Would you like another to run with you?" Marsh asked it, and the wolf raised its head.

Another?

"There are more druids coming from the Deeps," she told it. "There should be at least one among them who would like to walk the upper caverns."

This one? the wolf seemed to ask, giving her the impression that the pack liked the cavern they had found. They particularly liked the small cave inside the cavern, although it would seem lonely without a human to keep them company.

"I can ask," Marsh told them. "Would you like to come and meet them or should I bring them to you?"

She pictured the options and let the wolf think about what it wanted. In the end, it decided it would accompany Marsh back to Kerrenin's Ledge, and that its pack would come with it. There were many hunting grounds, after all, and who was to say that this one was the best?

"The wolves are coming with us," she said, and Gustav froze mid-bite.

He met her gaze and then took his bite, chewed, and swallowed, his eyes roving over the gathered pack. It took him a few moments, but finally, he spoke.

"What, all of them?"

Marsh nodded.

"They want to find another druid."

He glared at her.

"I suppose you told them there would be druids coming to the Ledge and they could take their pick?"

He sounded so unamused that Marsh wondered if she'd done the wrong thing. Roeglin snorted with laughter but said nothing, focusing on his dinner when she looked his way.

Uh-uh. You're on your own with this one, he told her, but his face was alight with amusement. *You Deeps-ridden troublemaker, you.*

"I..." Marsh stopped as Felicity put her hand on her knee.

"He's teasing you."

Roeglin took a sharp breath and Marsh scowled at him, then saw the funny side of it.

"You forgot, didn't you?"

The look on his face said it all and Marsh started laughing.

"You forgot. How does it feel when someone does it to you?"

"Does what?" Gustav wanted to know.

"Reads his mind," Marsh replied and glanced at the shadow mage. "Not nice, is it?"

"I… It's been awhile," Roeglin admitted, and Felicity smiled quietly and went back to her meal.

BRATS CONTAINED

Marsh woke to the sound of voices speaking softly in the dark. It took her a moment to realize she was hearing children, and that they very much didn't want to be heard.

"We could hide on the surface," the boy was saying, "or down at the waystation. Pretend we were lost and just needed shelter. They wouldn't turn us away."

"Do you think they'd take us?"

"It couldn't hurt to try, and we could join a caravan if they didn't want us around. It's a waystation, after all."

"It couldn't be any worse than the farm," Ninetta added, and Marsh had to admit that the child had a point.

There was silence as they all contemplated that idea, and then Claudette spoke.

"Okay," she said. "Let's do that. Mum will be okay."

There was enough doubt in her voice, though, that Marsh decided to intervene. She waited for the three of them to make their very quiet way out of the cave and into the cavern proper and then she followed them, Mordanlenoowar padding softly in her wake. She let them get to the edge of the campsite before she spoke.

"And just where do the three of you think you're going?"

She'd forgotten about Claudette's propensity for attacking first and asking questions after, but the flare of purple light was just warning enough for her to pull a shield from the shadows, and catch the ball of caged lightning against it.

"Hey!" she shouted. "That's enough of that."

As if to emphasize her determination, Mordan's growl rumbled out around them and Marsh stalked forward.

"Claudette Bisset, you get your tail over here right now. And you, Ninetta. And you, Pierre. Do not make me come out there and get you."

She jumped as Gustav's voice bellowed out after hers.

"Do not make *any* of us come out there to get you. We've had to come far enough as it is."

They waited, listening to the cavern's silence while the mules snorted and moved restlessly at their tethers.

Mordan's growl was all the notice they had that the big kat had moved.

"No," Claudette said. "No, I won't."

Pierre gave a frightened shriek, and Mordan bounded back to Marsh and dropped the child at her feet before leaping back out into the cavern.

Moments later, they heard Claudette again.

"But…"

Mordan snarled, and Marsh kept a grip on the boy in front of her. Part of his shirt was damp from where the big kat had picked him up, but the rest of him was fine. He didn't move, just stared out into the cavern. It didn't take long for Mordan to guide the girls back to them.

The big kat stalked into sight, with the troublesome pair taking one step back for every step the feline took forward. They stopped and turned when Mordan looked past them to where Gustav was waiting, his hands on his hips.

"I don't suppose you two young ladies would care to tell me what you were doing over a cup of kaffee?" he asked.

The two girls hung their heads, their hands joining as they looked up at him.

"We were just…"

"We needed…"

"Uh-uh. You can speak to me when we're back inside. You've scared the mules quite enough. The Deeps know just how long it's going to take to calm the beasts down again. I swear trouble is a female!"

"Hey!" Marsh protested.

She didn't need to hear Zeb's response.

"If the boot fits, shadow mage. If. The boot. Fits."

Marsh resisted the urge to tell him what to do with his boot and led Pierre back into the cave after them instead. Felicity was waiting, and so were the wolves. Once everyone was inside, they filled the space between the fire and the crevice and sat down.

Marsh saw Claudette eye the big creatures with dismay and then take her place by the fire. She also felt Pierre's small hand tighten around hers and wondered what it was that kids seemed to see in her, because she was the *last* person she'd have thought was any good with them.

Don't bet on it, Roeglin told her, and Marsh felt the warmth of Felicity's agreement.

Realizing there were now two mind mages inside her head didn't make her any happier than she had been moments before, but she said nothing. She supposed she couldn't blame Felicity for wanting to take a peek.

"Now," Gustav said, turning to the children when everyone was settled, "exactly where did the three of you think you were going?"

Three sets of eyes returned his look with silent reproach but the Protector captain was silent, letting the quiet increase the pressure until one of them cracked. In the end, Claudette gave a loud sigh and rolled her eyes.

"We don't want to go back to the farm," she said. "It's not safe for Netti or Pierre. They'll only be hurt."

Gustav pretended puzzlement even though Mordan gave a grumbling sound of worry and the nearest wolf sat up, ears pricked with concern. Marsh had to wonder if Claudette had some form of nature magic, the way the animals were responding to her voice.

If she does, she doesn't know it yet, Roeglin muttered. *Let's keep it that way for a bit, shall we?*

Marsh had to agree. The thought of an animal-speaking Claudette was a bit of a worry, given the stunt she'd just tried to pull. Later, perhaps, when she'd calmed down a bit, or maybe discovered it for herself, but certainly not now.

"But they're your parents," Gustav continued. "Why would they hurt you?"

Claudette tossed an apologetic look toward Felicity and answered, "*Mine* won't hurt me, but *theirs* don't like magic, do they?" She looked at the other two, and Pierre gave a wide-eyed shake of his head. Ninetta just stared, her brown eyes dark with distress and her face pale in the light of the fire.

Gustav turned to her, his face gentle.

"I've met your father," he said. "Is what Claudie says true?"

It took Ninetta a moment to answer, and when she did, her voice was quiet.

"He did this the first time." She turned and lifted the back of her tunic.

Felicity gasped and Marsh drew a sharp breath, her eyes stinging with the threat of tears. Ninetta lowered her tunic and sat back down.

"Don't take me back," she begged, and then looked at the boy, "and don't take Pierre back, either. His dad is just as bad."

Marsh saw Gustav swallow as though moistening his throat. When he spoke next, his voice rasped with suppressed emotion.

"What about your mothers?"

Yes, Marsh thought. What *about* your mothers?

It was a good question, and she waited, feeling Felicity tense beside her.

Across the fire, Ninetta bit her lip and twisted her hands in her lap. Her reply was almost impossible to hear, but it was there.

"She helped."

There was a world of betrayal in those two words, and Felicity was around the fire's edge and pulling the girl into her arms before any of the rest of them had worked out how to respond. She looked across at Marsh, her chin tucked over Ninetta's head as the child cried against her, and her eyes pleaded for Marsh to do something.

Marsh lifted Pierre from the ground and walked around to sit next to Felicity. She nestled the boy in her lap and laid a hand on Ninetta's arm, her heart aching when the child flinched at her touch. Not saying a word, she reached into the ground beneath her, seeking for the energy that ran through the soil and the stone, drawing on the slow flow of it and guiding it into the girl.

She pictured the crisscross of welts on Ninetta's back and sent the energy over them, imagining the skin whole and smooth again before letting the excess subside back into the ground. When she was done, she lifted her hand away and looked into the girl's eyes.

"How's that feel?"

Ninetta wriggled carefully, lifting first one shoulder and then the other before twisting slowly from side to side. When she was done, she settled back into Felicity's arms, staring at Marsh in wide-eyed amazement.

"I didn't know the shadows could do that!"

Marsh shook her head.

"That was different."

"Show me how?"

"Later, when we've worked out what we're going to do next, okay?"

"Okay." The girl sounded happy enough that Marsh figured she might stick around a bit longer.

Claudette didn't look pleased, but she didn't say anything. Gustav studied them through the flames and then he spoke.

"We need to go back to the farm and see if they are

willing to have you return," he began and raised his hand when they drew breath to protest. "I promise, we will not leave you with them—and they will not want us to, given that we will be leaving you on the condition that we can leave a shadow mage with each of you to teach you how to control your abilities *and* to teach anyone else who has magical ability. Agreed?"

"Agreed," Ninetta said, and Marsh heard the smile in the girl's voice.

As plans went, it was solid. If Davide's attitude had been anything to go by, the surviving farm hands would never agree to a shadow mage staying to tutor any budding magicians. All she could hope was that the mothers could be convinced to leave the farm, instead.

When Gustav asked Pierre if he was okay with that idea, the boy just gave him a wide-eyed stare and nodded. They broke camp shortly after, loading up the mules and riding back to the farm. This time Gustav didn't ask Marsh to scout ahead; he had Mordan and the wolves scout instead.

When they returned with the news that the farm was deserted, the moutons still in their barn and no humans in sight, a feeling of déjà vu settled over Marsh. Gustav gave her a worried look and they rode carefully forward, stopping just out of sight of the main house before the captain looked at her and Roeglin.

"Go in," he said. "Tell me what you find."

They weren't gone long. The farm was like all the other deserted properties they'd ever visited. Food on the table—the evening meal, from what Marsh could tell—with dessert long burned on a stove left to go out on its own.

Valuables had been left in their drawers, and supplies left in crates and boxes.

"We need to bring the moutons back," Marsh said, and Ninetta nodded.

"All the animals," the girl added. "They won't survive without someone to look after them."

Gustav gave them both a look that said they were trying his patience, and in the end, they compromised agreeing to take the moutons the donkeys and the mules and release the rest. Nikolas's help was invaluable, as was Felicity's and the children's, as they went to work getting the animals together. By the end of the morning, they were ready to move out again.

This time, the wolves kept the moutons together until they reached the Kerrenin's Ledge's gates. The woolly troublemakers stayed crammed tightly on the path, running between the mules without complaint and showing no interest in straying. It was past dusk and the gates firmly were closed, but that didn't stop Gustav, Roeglin, and Marsh.

They marched up to the gates, Gustav drawing his sword so he could hammer on them with its pommel.

"Halt!"

The cry came from the top of the wall as they approached and they stopped, Gustav sheathing his sword as they did so. This time the gates creaked inward, and the waiting guards were arrayed to form a corridor into the city proper. Captain Brodeur came to join them, mounted and riding beside Councilor Ines.

"I saw you coming from the walls," she told Gustav, "and ordered him into the saddle."

She looked over at where the captain had ridden so that he could reach across and embrace his sister and smiled.

"*That* is a sight worth waiting for. Tell me, how did you find the Outlet?"

"We didn't reach the Outlet," Gustav told her, and Marsh let their words flow around her as they discussed the path of their journey and what they'd found at both the Bisset farmlet and the larger steading farther on.

"And you say it's now abandoned?" Ines sounded disappointed.

"We did not reach it in time to stop it from happening," Gustav said, and Marsh noticed he didn't say they'd had no way of knowing the raiders would strike so fast.

The councilor turned to Marsh.

"This Idris…did you know him?"

"No," Marsh said. "He was new to me."

"Would you know him again if you saw him?"

Marsh frowned, wondering if the councilor was truly listening to anything she said.

"He's dead, but if I saw him again, I would kill him just the same."

Ines smiled.

"Good."

Marsh's frown deepened.

"May I ask why?"

"I may know the family," Ines replied. "They run to multiples."

Now, *that* was something Marsh hadn't wanted to know, although she was glad she did.

"How do you know of them?" Gustav asked, but the councilor didn't answer straight away.

Marsh was thinking she might need a nudge when Ines sighed.

"Let's just say I've run into them before," she said, and there was a finality in her tone that made it clear that the subject was closed.

"Uh huh," Gustav replied, making it equally clear he wasn't done but he'd let it lie for a little longer as he pursued another subject. "How are Master Greta and her son?"

Ines gave a short bark of laughter.

"Took you long enough."

REDEFINING PACK

Marsh slept late the next day, but she slept in her own bed and managed to banish Mordan to the rug on the floor…or so she thought. She awoke with the big kat stretched out alongside her. Not knowing what had woken her, she struggled to untangle herself from Mordan's paws, becoming aware of the figure in the doorway as she did so.

"That's going to get awkward when you want to share your bed," Roeglin told her as she slipped free.

"You try telling *her* that," Marsh grumbled as the kat yawned, stretched, and settled herself in the center of the bed.

"So it's a good thing the tailor wants to see you," Roeglin said, eyeing Mordan.

Marsh followed his gaze.

"Well, it's not like I could go back to bed."

"Gustav says you've got—"

"Leclerc! Get your ass down here!"

Marsh cocked an eyebrow at the shadow mage.

"You were saying?"

"Leclerc!"

Marsh looked down at her tunic.

"Do you think he'd give me enough time to—"

"Marchant! Marie! Lec—"

"Oh, crap."

Marsh hit the stairs at a run, reaching the bottom to find Gustav glaring at the stairwell and her uncle standing at his shoulder looking both anxious and amused. The captain's expression relaxed the moment she appeared.

"Oh, good, you're here." His brows beetled downward, and he added in a roar, "Now, go and explain to your wolves that the moutons were not brought for their convenience!"

Marsh went, painfully aware of her bare feet and state of undress as she headed for the door. She saw what the problem was the minute she stepped out onto the porch.

The wolves had arrayed themselves across the front of the two entrances into the courtyard, their growls echoing through the enclosed space as they faced off with Daniel and two of the kitchen hands on the kitchen side and the tailor on the other.

Cries of "Marsh!" and "Miss Leclerc!" greeted her the second she stepped into view, and neither Daniel nor Dominique sounded happy.

The wolves, for their part, didn't let her arrival distract them, and Marsh winced at the thought of taking her unarmored feet down into the yard with its horde of milling hooves, but she did, avoiding the moutons by heading straight for the wolves. She moved without doubt or hesitation and knelt before the pack leader.

At first, it ignored her, even when her action drew sounds of alarm from both Daniel and the tailor. Marsh knew exactly how to deal with her cousin—she flipped him the finger—but the tailor she ignored. Looking into the pack leader's eyes, she demanded its attention.

The leader snarled, but it let her make the connection.

The moutons were its to protect. That one—and it meant her cousin, in uncomplimentary terms—had come to prey on the herd. Marsh glanced back at where Daniel was watching her with a mixture of alarm and admiration. The man was holding a rope, the knife he used for slaughter dangling from his belt.

"He means to feed the pack," Marsh explained. "He is the…"

She stumbled over what term to use. Wolves did not cook. In the end, she tried, "He prepares meat for all."

The wolf cocked its ears, and a sense of hunger crossed the bridge between them.

Us too?

"Yes, of course, you," she said.

Daniel made a sound that might have been denial, but Marsh turned her head and glared at him.

"*All* the pack," she repeated. "Understood?"

She didn't look away until he nodded.

The lead wolf relaxed, then looked over at the gates—and Marsh sighed.

"They are guests of the pack. Please let them in."

It was hard to find the right pictures and impressions to send, but she must have succeeded. The wolf gave a yip and lunged at her face, dabbing her cheeks and nose with its tongue and nipping the side of her neck before bounding into the herd of moutons. As if on some unspoken signal, the pack joined it, separating one of the woolly creatures from the herd and driving it to Daniel's feet before tearing out its throat. Marsh watched as they backed away to give Daniel and the kitchen hands room before sitting in a semi-circle, their backs to the restless herd. Across the courtyard, Dominique and his people moved to stand just inside the doorway.

"Is it safe to come across now?"

Marsh waved him over, staring at the herd until her eyes were caught by movement at the far end of the yard.

"We need them in the barn, Leclerc," Gustav said from the safety of the verandah behind her.

Marsh rolled her eyes.

Of course, he needed the damn moutons in the Deeps-damned barn. She'd told him as much the night before and had him tell her the task could wait for morning. She watched as the barn doors slid open, and the moutons crowded between them and Dominique, trying to avoid the tailor and his party while staying as far as they could from the gaping cavern that had appeared in their prison.

"To the Deeps with this!"

Marsh stood, wiping her hands on her tunic as she stared at the restless herd. She could think of only one way to get them moving in the direction she needed; she just needed to catch one's eyes. There were enough of them that it didn't take long, and the woolly beast paused long enough for Marsh to send it an impression of safety and food and water lying beyond the open doors.

It bleated at her and she repeated the promise, then noticed that the creature's query had drawn the attention of the others. She moved fast, sweeping her gaze across the herd and emphasizing the idea of safety and food beyond the barn doors. It was like touching a hundred minds at once and trying to impose her will on all of them…and it seemed to take forever.

She nearly melted with relief when the herd turned and trotted to the barn. The lead moutons hesitated briefly when they reached the doors and Marsh sent another broadcast of safety. It might not have been enough if one of the wolves hadn't lifted its voice in a sorrowful howl. Marsh didn't know what the sound meant, but it sent a shiver through her and raised gooseflesh on her arms.

The moutons responded as one, racing into the shelter of the barn and not coming out as two of Per's stablehands closed the doors behind them. As soon as the herd was out of sight, the connection between them ended and Marsh became aware that she was the center of attention.

Again.

Right when she didn't want to be.

Right when she felt like she was going to fall over…in nothing but a tunic…with mouton droppings and damp encrusted on her knees. Because, why not?

She gritted her teeth, fighting the urge to collapse as she looked back to where Gustav was standing on the verandah.

"I'm going to need another mouton," Daniel said, and Marsh turned slowly to glare at him.

"This time," she told him, trying to stay upright despite the swooping dizziness threatening to take her down, "you can get your own damned mouton."

"No lunch for you."

"Matches breakfast, shit for brains."

She might have said more, except hurried boot steps signaled Roeglin's arrival. He wrapped an arm around her back and pulled her close to his chest before turning her toward the stairs.

"It's not smart to piss off the cook, remember?" he whispered, giving Daniel a smile and a wave.

"I'll send someone," Gustav told Daniel, but Nikolas had appeared at the door.

"I'll do it," he said. "How many d'you need?"

Marsh left them to it and let Roeglin guide her across the dining room toward the stairs.

Gustav took one look at her as she passed and his lip curled in disgust.

"Get cleaned up."

Marsh wanted to remind him that it had been his idea, but Roeglin hurried her past before she could say anything.

"I can't kick the kat off your bed, you know."

"No bed," Marsh managed. "Dirty."

"Uh huh, and you stink like a mullock heap."

"Thanks."

"I'll take it from here."

Marsh looked up in time to move the two steps she needed for Izmay to grab hold of her.

"By the Deeps, girl. You know better than to use your magic when you're running on empty." She looked at Roeglin. "What did she do this time?"

The shadow mage shrugged, but the look on his face said it all.

"Uh, you know, the usual. Charmed a herd of moutons into going into the barn after beast-speaking the pack leader of the wolves and getting it to let the tailor into the yard and make a kill for Daniel. Nothing particularly strenuous." The tone of his voice said she'd pushed it *way* too far.

Izmay was nowhere near as subtle. She slapped Marsh on the shoulder.

"Idiot!"

Marsh ignored them. There was no way known she wanted a piece of this conversation.

"Bath," she managed and tried to ease her way out of Izmay's hands to get to one on her own.

The floor came up pretty fast, but Izmay caught her before they connected.

"Why don't you use me to pull a little energy," the shadow guard suggested. "We've got a long day ahead, and it's better you don't miss it."

Marsh's initial reaction was to resist the idea, but Izmay stopped her three feet from the tub.

"How badly do you want to get clean?"

Marsh looked at her, trying to figure out two things: how likely Izmay was to carry through her threat...and if she could make it to the tub on her own and get clean without drowning. The truth was she couldn't.

"You," she said, hearing the words slur, "are a Deeps-damned bitch."

Izmay smiled.

"Aw, Marsh. You say the sweetest things." The smile vanished, and the guard's expression hardened. "Now get it done."

Marsh laid a hand on Izmay's cheek and concentrated on the energy she felt moving beneath the shadow guard's skin, then she drew the smallest amount of that to herself—just enough that a good meal would take her the rest of the way.

It was hard to stop, but she managed, and then looked at Izmay's face.

"Are you okay?" she asked, and the guard managed a jerky nod.

"Remind me never to volunteer like that again," she said.

Marsh sighed. "I'm sorry."

"You stink," Izmay told her. "Now get in the Deeps-damned bath."

She turned abruptly and left Marsh in the cubicle on her own.

With a sigh, Marsh stripped off her soiled tunic and climbed into the tub scrubbing the stink of mouton, wolf, and kat from her skin and worrying about Izmay. The sound of someone coming quietly into the cubicle had her on her feet and pulling a sword from the air as she opened her eyes.

Roeglin froze, his jaw dropping as he saw her—and then his face turned scarlet, and he dumped the armful of clothes he'd been carrying onto the small bench in the corner.

"Izmay! She needs to know you're okay," he called as he backpedaled out of the room as fast as Marsh had ever seen him move.

The shadow guard appeared shortly afterward, carrying two cups of chocolate and looking completely perplexed.

"What did you do to..." She stopped, taking in Marsh, the sword, and the tub, and then she started to laugh. "Oh, my. Ohmyohmyohmy. Girl, you sure know how to make an impression on a man."

"I..." Marsh began, but Izmay thrust a hot chocolate into her hand and didn't let her get any further.

"I'm fine, by the way. No hard feelings and all that—and Gustav's getting restless, just so you know. You should get dressed before he starts shouting your name again. Pretty sure the rest of the cavern's sick of hearing it."

She left, not giving Marsh an opportunity to respond.

Marsh took the hint and was soon trying on the outfit Master Calais had created in their absence.

"There," he said when he'd finished placing the final pin. "We'll have everything ready in the next couple of days."

He turned to Gustav.

"You said something about wanting a uniform designed for a mage school?"

Marsh left them to it, glad to be able to get into the new tunic and breeches he'd somehow managed to conjure up in her absence. When she returned, Daniel was waiting with her breakfast, and looking a lot happier than he had been earlier.

He wasn't alone, though. Felicity and the three children had arrived, and Daniel steered her over to the table to join them.

"Captain Brodeur should be with us soon," he told them. "He needs to speak with Per. Breakfast?"

When Felicity nodded, he left, leaving Marsh alone at the table with them. She didn't feel comfortable eating while they had nothing, so she laid her knife and fork by the side of her plate and looked at them.

"So," she said, "what are you going to do now?"

"Gustav says there's a magic school the children can go to?"

"There's one near Ruins Deep," Marsh told her, and saw her face fall, "but I hear the shadow mages will be setting one up in the Ledge as well. We're just waiting for the rest of them to arrive."

"The rest of them?"

"The ones clearing the cavern of raiders," Marsh told her. She indicated Gustav and Roeglin and the guards breakfasting at another table. "We're just the advance party. We had a message to deliver."

"Oh, I see. And have you delivered it?"

Marsh thought about it.

"Yes," she said, "but *I* still have something I need to do."

She looked up as Daniel returned and received a stern glare for her trouble.

"Eat your breakfast," he ordered as he delivered the others their meals, and he turned abruptly and left. Felicity watched him go.

"Older brother?" she asked, her voice full of sympathy, but Marsh shook her head.

"Younger cousin," she replied, "Something he forgets all the time."

She ate her breakfast all the same, ignoring Felicity's knowing smile. She'd been more than truthful when she'd said she had some errands to run, and, now that she remembered it, she had a lot to get done before Master Envermet arrived with the rest of Monsieur Gravine's promised assistance.

THE PECKING ORDER

It didn't take Marsh long to find an opportunity to slip away. When Captain Brodeur arrived and came straight over to see his sister and niece, taking time to make the other two children feel welcome as well, Marsh slipped away, taking her plate to the kitchen.

"Took you long enough," Daniel muttered, but Marsh ignored his grouchiness and hugged him just as soon as she'd dropped her dishes in the sink.

"It was late," she said by way of explaining why she hadn't let him know as soon as she'd gotten back, "and you're even grouchier if you're woken than when you are in the kitchen."

"Get out," he said, but he hugged her back and was smiling as she left.

"Daniel okay?" her uncle asked when she emerged, and Marsh got the impression he'd been standing by in case she needed rescuing.

"He's fine," Marsh told him, and raised her voice so it

could be clearly heard in the kitchen, "Nothing a good girl-friend wouldn't fix."

"Hey!"

Marsh ducked as a ladle came flying through the kitchen door, and Per grabbed it before it could hit anything that mattered, like Gustav. The Protector captain stopped short of the flying utensil and stared at Per and Marsh, then focused on Marsh.

"Stay out of the kitchen."

"*Oui.*"

Marsh took a step away from the kitchen door and, satisfied his order had been heard and would be obeyed, Gustav looked at Per.

"Ines will be here shortly to help you and Brodeur draw up the submission for the Kerrenin's Ledge Protectors."

"Thank you," Per said, and Gustav pushed his way into the kitchen.

"Daniel," he said, "I need to ask you about lunch…"

Marsh looked at Per.

"I'll go find something useful to do," she told him, and her uncle nodded.

"It's good to have you back, Marsh," he said and hugged her. "I've missed you."

"I've missed you too, Papa," Marsh told him, surprised to find it true. She cleared the tears threatening to clog her throat and hurried toward the dining room door.

She half-expected to have Roeglin or Brodeur or even Gustav call her back and was surprised to reach the court-yard with no such summons. Not wanting to push her luck, she half-jogged, half-sprinted to the waystation's entrance and let herself out into the street beyond. She was still surprised to discover that she hadn't been followed when she reached the corner leading to Kearick's Emporium.

It was no surprise, however, to find the place still closed and boarded up, although Marsh would have sworn that the shelves looked emptier than the last time she'd been here. She peered through the clearrock windows, looking for any sign of movement, and jumped when someone cleared their throat behind her.

"You looking for Kearick?"

Startled, Marsh spun to face the speaker and then relaxed. The man lived across the street and was probably just curious as to who was peering through his neighbor's windows. She nodded, aware that his eyes searched her face for answers.

"Went seeking," she said as though that explained it all, and the man relaxed.

Part of Marsh relaxed too. So far he hadn't called her on being away too long or the fact her last mission had been to Ruins Hall. If she was very, very lucky, he might not even recognize her.

"Thought so," he said. "Well, you're out of luck. Kearick left weeks ago, heading for Downslopes and then maybe Dimanche. Said he'd be back but wasn't sure when."

"Oh." Marsh did her best to look crestfallen. "I was hoping… I found something."

She stopped, watching the play of expression on the man's face. In the end, he just shrugged.

"Well, it's the same as I told that other feller. He's been gone a couple of weeks, but you might catch him. He never said how long he was stopping at Downslopes." He leaned in closer, lowering his voice as he did so. "I got the impression he was hoping to meet someone, and might even wait a bit to give them a chance to arrive. No one's saying that someone can't be you, are they?"

"Got a point," Marsh told him and forced a smile. "Downslopes, you said?"

The man nodded.

"Just like I told that other seeker, and he headed for the surface the same day. I don't think he even bothered stopping at the Hawks."

He looked Marsh over.

"Although he had a lot more to offer than you seem to; his mule was loaded down like I've never seen."

Marsh laid her finger alongside her nose and gave him a conspiratorial smile.

"Never judge the value of a load by its size," she murmured and pulled one of the Founder's gemstones from her pouch.

Taking the man's hand, she pressed the stone into his palm and curled his fingers around it.

"I was never here."

She didn't give him time to respond to that but released his hand and sauntered back down the street to the alley that ran parallel to the Emporium, turning into it as though she had every right to be there. The glance she cast his way showed him still standing on the boardwalk, his gaze alternating between the gem in his palm and her departing figure.

So there's a surface route to Dimanche, she thought, and wished she could risk breaking into the Emporium one more time. She could really do with seeing the maps if

Kearick had left them. Figuring that was probably a bad idea, she turned the corner at the end of the alley and headed back to the waystation. If Ines was still there, maybe she could convince the councilor to let her see the council's records.

She still had two children she was supposed to be finding relatives for. Fortunately, Brodeur, Gustav, and Ines had decided it was time to hand Kearick's records to the council.

"It should keep them busy for a while," Ines said, "and what they choose to hide will reveal more than they would hope for. I'll let Gustav send word that he's found the records and then remind folk they said you could have access to the population records so that you could find the children's family. It shouldn't take them too long to get back to you after that."

It took them another week, but when Marsh thought about it, that really wasn't very long for a council. Unfortunately, it took her only two days to work out that there really *were* no relatives for Aisha and Tamlin in the Kerrenin's Ledge cavern. In fact, it looked like the records supported the boy's anecdotal report that there was a brother in Dimanche.

"But Tamlin said his father and uncle didn't get along," she reported to Gustav and Roeglin, "and I don't want to deliver the children somewhere where they're not wanted."

"We couldn't let that happen," Gustav told her, his voice gruff. "Not to those two. They're too valuable to the Founder's plans."

"And the mages," Roeglin added with a sharp look at

the emissary and the Protector captain. "Let's not forget where their apprenticeships are held."

Gustav gave him a crooked smile.

"We could never forget that," he said. "Your Shadow Master is charging too much for their services for that little detail to be lost in the paperwork."

Marsh sighed, and their good-natured bureaucratic bickering stopped as they both turned their heads to look at her.

"What?" she asked, noting the curiosity in their gazes.

"You know they arrive today, right?" Roeglin said, and Marsh froze.

"They do?"

Gustav started to grin as he looked over at Roeglin and held out his hand.

"Told you she'd lost track of the time."

Roeglin rolled his eyes and handed over two of the gems that had made up his pay. He glared at Marsh.

"And I said that was a detail you'd *never* forget," he grumbled. "Just goes to show that you think you know a person..."

Marsh wanted to argue that he did know her but the sound of footsteps echoed up from the floor below, accompanied by the sounds of mules snorting and men and women coming from the courtyard outside. Marsh grabbed Gustav by the arm as the captain turned for the door.

"We need to go to Dimanche," she said. "The raiders—"

"*Oui*," he replied, cutting her off. "The raiders and the relatives, and don't tell the children or the little monsters will want to come along."

He glowered at her.

"And who, Shadow Mage Leclerc, is the one giving the orders around here?"

"You, sir," Marsh managed, and he shook his arm free as he headed out the door.

"By the Deep's dark ass it is…"

Thank you, once again, for joining me in another story. I trust you are enjoying Marsh's journey as much as I am. Every time I take a break, I look forward to finding out exactly what she does next. That's the thing about stories: it doesn't matter how carefully you outline, there's still space in between what you plan, for the characters to surprise you.

I live for those surprises, even when they make my life... interesting.

As I write these notes, I'm planning for a house inspection, which means I have to pay attention to those small spaces I don't get to very often. So, in addition to researching things made from mushrooms, I've also been looking up how to clean the oven using bicarb and vinegar – since it does a better job than anything else I've tried, and smells a whole lot better than any of the chemical cleaners I've come across so far.

I mean, vinegar, right? When you use the oven for the first time after cleaning it down, the whole house smells like fish and chips. It's not a bad deal, plus the oven actually shines, which makes the agent happy, so it's kind of a win-win situation.

On top of that, I'm also coming to the end of Book 4 in this series, which makes me kind of sad, because I'll have to leave these characters for a while, and I don't think I'm ready to. I also think they're a bit like some of the pets I've had; they can sense something is up, and they're being downright crotchety. It's like they don't want this series to end, either.

I keep telling them they're lives will go on, just without me peering over their shoulders all the time, to which Marsh's response usually involves shrooms and shadows, and other interesting things, while Roeglin just gives me a look that says he's seen inside my head and, damn, it needs a spring clean. The kat, on the other hand, just yawns, stretches and flicks her tail in a derogatory way, leaving me to wonder if any of them will complain if I open a shadow door right underneath them.

Still, recalcitrant characters aside, it's been a bit of a wild ride, and I might be glad to write something restful for a while... if only I can work out what that is. In the meantime, Book 4 will be here soon, and the adventure continues.

I hope to see more of you on the way.

AUTHOR NOTES - MICHAEL ANDERLE

MARCH 28, 2019

THANK YOU for not only reading this story but these *Author Notes* as well.

(I think I've been good with always opening with "thank you." If not, I need to edit the other *Author Notes*!)

RANDOM (*sometimes*) THOUGHTS?

I was walking through a pulp-fiction con last Sunday (where they sold a bunch of old paperbacks from the '50s to the '80s) and I ran across a Tarzan table.

I was first thinking, 'Oh cool, Tarzan!' (Yes, I speak like that in my mind. I'm over 50, I get a pass.)

The next thought was 'Wow... that is a LOT of Tarzan.'

Finally, as I turned to keep walking (I have very little space in our Vegas Cave in the Sky (™) I can't really purchase anything) I wonder...

Is Post Apocalyptic fiction a present-day version of Tarzan?

Think about it a moment...

Tarzan was anti-technology (for the most part) in the story.

Tarzan was man (or woman) against the environment.

Tarzan had a different environment than the readers.

Tarzan had mystical events layered over the story (meaning, they would bring in 'weird' stuff.) I am suggesting that changes to the World Post-Apocalypse would be similar.

You never knew what was going to happen, but there were going to be fights involved...

I'm suggesting that those who love to Read Tarzan, would enjoy a good Post-Apocalyptic book or series as well...

So, would YOU enjoy a Tarzan, or did you in the past?

AROUND THE WORLD IN 80 DAYS

One of the interesting (at least to me) aspects of my life is the ability to work from anywhere and at any time. In the future, I hope to re-read my own *Author Notes* and remember my life as a diary entry.

The Cave in the Sky(™), Las Vegas, USA

It's early morning, I've been awake about twenty-five (25) minutes and my glass doors are both covered in black scribbles.

I've learned that I can use black erase markers on the doors, and then just wipe it off. This (#Probably) means that my glass will never all be clean again until we sell this condo in the future.

My wife came walking into my office last night after a particularly lengthy *conceptioning* period working on a book and told me it looked like 'A Beautiful Mind' happened.

I haven't seen the movie, but I'm taking that as a compliment.

FAN PRICING

$0.99 Saturdays (new LMBPN stuff) and $0.99 Wednesday (both LMBPN books and friends of LMBPN books.) Get great stuff from us and others at tantalizing prices.

Go ahead, I bet you can't read just one.

Sign up here: http://lmbpn.com/email/.

HOW TO MARKET FOR BOOKS YOU LOVE

Review them so others have your thoughts, tell friends and the dogs of your enemies (because who wants to talk with enemies?)... *Enough said ;-)*

Ad Aeternitatem,

Michael Anderle

C.M.'s Collections

#1 *365 Days of Flash Fiction*

#2 *365 Days of Poetry*

#3 *A Collection of Dragons*

#4 *366 Days of Flash Fiction*

#5 *366 Days of Poetry*

#6 *Another 365 Days of Poetry*

#7 *Pixie-Dust Dreaming*

#8 *Tales of Mack 'n' Me*

#9 *Tales of Odyssey and Miss Delight*

Lunar Wolves

#1 *Lunar Wolves: The Unwilling*

#2 *Lunar Wolves: The Unwanted*

#3 *Lunar Wolves: The Undiscovered*

The Ransomeers

#1 *A Planet's Ransom*

Chronicles of a Dark God

#1 *Dark God Emergent*

I also have work in the following publications:

The Expanding Universe: Volume 4

I also write fantasy, urban fantasy and short stories across the genres, all of which can be found <u>on my Amazon author page</u>.

CONNECT WITH THE AUTHORS

Colleen Simpson Social Media Sites

Amazon author page: https://www.amazon.com/C.M.-Simpson/e/B0086QFGFO

Blogspot: http://cmsimpson.blogspot.com.au/

Facebook: https://www.facebook.com/CMSimpsonWriter/

Pinterest: https://www.pinterest.com.au/cmsimpsonauthor/

Twitter: https://twitter.com/simpsoncolleen1

Youtube (Writing): https://www.youtube.com/channel/UCFUNN9PxeSu6DjNPFjoLRjQ

Youtube (Gaming): https://youtube.com/channel/UCjOK2SvOHoT_ru9rlnlVS-g

Linked In: https://au.linkedin.com/public-profile/in/c-m-simpson-8279344a

Patreon: https://patreon.com/cmsimpsonwritergamer

BOOKS BY MICHAEL ANDERLE

Sign up for the LMBPN email list to be notified of new releases
and special deals!

https://lmbpn.com/email/

For a complete list of books by Michael Anderle, please visit:

www.lmbpn.com/ma-books/